MW01229371

Fall of Avalon

Verse One of the Chronicles of Nodd

J. R. Froemling

This is a work of fiction.
Names, characters, places, and incidents are used fictitiously.
Any resemblance to actual events, locales, or persons, living
or dead, is entirely coincidental.

This book is for all the dreamers and storytellers.
Without your magic the world would be a darker place.
Never stop believing.
Forever chase your dreams.

Fair Verona

Garden
of
Nimh

Silver
City

Neverland
Sea

Aesop
Nation

Wonderland

Ozrail

The Labyrinth

N
W E
S

The Beginning of the End

The distant rumble of thunder, like the beating drums of a far-off army, rolls over the shimmering city. His gaze turns upward with a censoring look. "Hmph," he snorts forcefully through his nose. It gives the distinct imitation of a mule about to refuse to comply with any task any person dares to require of it. He is reminded of a time when he was considered nothing more than a mule. His masters all believed themselves to be clever.

A smirk lingers across his face before he shifts the large sack. It is bulging at the seams with books, scrolls, and other randomly assorted baubles. It is not the normal fare for a man of his stature. With a cautious look over his shoulder, he picks up his pace. As he approaches the city's gilded gates, he frowns. The thunder bellows again in the distance, a promise of violence coming, and the clouds look as though an artist has daubed them with black watercolor for effect.

With a firm hand, he rests his fingers on the lock of the gate, his other hand clutches the sack tightly. "Open says me," he murmurs. It is dangerous to use magic for such a trivial thing, but he has no time to march the three-mile trek around this newly minted cage. The main gates of Silver City would be guarded and to be caught with this sack of things would be most unlucky. He carefully pulls the gate closed behind him to verify it locks again. Then he takes one last look to the South with a heavy sigh. He hoists the sack higher, turns, and migrates towards the buildings glittering in the late afternoon sunlight.

He bobs and weaves through the busy streets of Silver City, with no time for the luxuries he usually affords himself. The stout, dashingly aged man is weaving and nudging his path through the crowd of sellers and scamps alike. Today is the first in a plethora of days that he has entered the city in his true form; most unfortunate for those hunting him. The buildings behind him shimmer, as if they had been sprinkled in pixie dust. They look like a painting had been captured and preserved for all to see. Everyone here plays their part and no one here seems to care about the man rudely passing through. A few cast cursory glances in surprise when he passes, but that is due to hauling such an odd-looking assortment of things more than to his behavior. Beads of sweat form on his temples, glistening against the ebony skin. Another snort emits from him as he hoists the bag back up onto his shoulder. He is looking for someone intently. He glances to the left, then right, followed by over his shoulder to reassure himself there is no one following him in this pursuit.

"Blast it all, where are they? Think, man! Where would you go if you were their age?" He stops and sets the bag carefully on the ground to draw out a small handkerchief, dabbing at his temple. His thumb gently plays over the delicate fawn embroidered in the corner. His last evening with her made him feel euphoric and jubilant. He knew when they met that his heart would melt for her and he gently paws over her handy work. He hopes beyond a wish that her sister knows nothing of the evening's festivities.

By the storm brewing in the distance, he would bet all of the Aesopi Nation that she knows. He thrusts the cloth back into his pocket and retrieves his pocket watch, "I'm late," he mutters. His temperament swings like the pendulum of the tower's clock. With a loud click, he clamps the intricately built pocket watch closed and tucks it back into his vest pocket.

"Ah ha!" He crows to no one in particular.

The sack swings up onto his shoulder with a newfound strength as his great strides lead him to the North. The shops here fall more into pleasantries rather than necessities. Gowns, slippers, jewelry, and of course, wishes can be had for the right price. He snorts again at the thought of buying wishes. Anyone foolish enough to buy a wish deserves whatever predicament they find themselves in.

"Wishes," he grumbles. He stops dead in his tracks and his nostrils flare as he pulls in the surrounding scents. There is wheat, and honey, along with sweat and grime. There is no visible grime in Silver City, at least not for long. The court does not allow it. Never in a million midnights did he believe princesses would be so much trouble. He has Jakob and Wilhelm to thank for that, no doubt.

"Of course, how could I have been so stupid? They are always there. Foolish boys." Another glance over his shoulder and he turns into a seedy mark between the shimmering buildings, leaving the whirling whisper of autumn leaves in his trail. He trots down a cobblestoned alley to a small wooden door with a broken and faded sign above it. The words long wiped from legibility, but everyone knows the place, The Hole in The Wall.

The pixie dust is less glamorous here, and its true nature shines through. This place is older and looks to have been from a time before the glittering towers were erected. With a crashing thud, he slams open the door and squints in the hazy glow of the dimly lit tavern. His eyes adjust to the candlelight and his nostrils flare at the stale scent of honeyed ale again. The room bustles with activity. The tables are crowded with gnomes, fairies, humans, ogres, Aesopi, animals, and even a few Wonderlanders. He would be proud of this moment if he were not in such a hurry to be gone from here.

He is running late, after all.

For a flitter of fairy wings, people look up and size him at the door. A few angrily wave him off, and others continue to watch cautiously; a stranger in their midst is never a good omen. His stature is large and demanding of attention. His hands can easily palm a dwarf's head, and his eyes look like two dimming embers amongst an inky shadow. With a quick lick of his lips, he ignores their judgment and narrows in on a table supporting four young gentlemen. Of all the Grimms, these four are the most prominent. Wilhelm, Jakob, William, and Hans are beloved by the court, and princes in their own right. If it were not for their father's doing, they likely would have wooed away half the princesses to some less than wholesome storytelling by now.

They are huddled over their pints and laughing at the misfortune of young Hans, who cannot hold his ale. He sways dangerously, but is laughing with them. William, closest to young Hans, grins like the cat who caught the canary at his devious lesson in teaching Hans to not loosen his lips regarding the power of wishes.

"What is all this?" The older man growls at them.

"We are just having a bit of fun," Jakob chortles. To which, he gets a slow eyebrow raised response from the beast of a man.

"Hans has decreed that any Noddian who can out-drink him this eve shall be granted their most desired wish," Wilhelm adds with great gusto. Wilhelm, not being very well known for keeping his mouth still either, is rewarded with a suddenly quiet pub. So quiet, that the field mouse in the corner can be heard scuttling across the floor as she bolts into the tiny hole in the door. Much to his dismay, this did not warrant a good laugh, or an eye roll from the elder man. Wilhelm demurely settles down and shrinks as the man hovering above them visibly seethes in response.

All four young men grow silent and watch in awe as the elder man draws in a sharp breath. He does not need to make any motion at all. With a mere thought, he can erase all the memories of every soul in this pub, including his sons before him. However, making a point of showing them the price of their folly, he waves his hand in a slow circle above his head. A singular finger points to the ceiling. Slowly, and without any appearance of smoke, glitter, or whatever else magical creatures are supposed to create when they use magic, he traces an arc over his head.

It starts with the few that stood up to approach. They are momentarily dumbfounded, then seeing their own pints they quickly move back to them. The laughter and music resumes. The arguments, the rattle of dice, and jangle of coins all fill the air as it appears that not a soul had just heard that a Grimm was about to award wishes. Every single patron is lulled back into their mundane visit to the pub as his finger completes the circle it was tracing in the air. William starts to speak, but is silenced by a touch from Hans. The elder man leans onto the table, his clothes now sweat soaked and crumpled. The man's shirt is singed, and his hands tremble. Hans is up and out of his seat, drunkenly stumbling toward him.

"Father, what has happened?" He comes to the man's side and tries to usher him into a seat only to be shoved off and growled at by his father.

"Sit down, you fool. I am fine. I have no time. I'm late. Gather those things most precious to you that you can carry. No horses, no carts, and by Merlin, do not use magic! Meet me at Midnight. At the eastern gates to the Garden of Nimh. Tell no one. Bring no one. Do not be late."

Before any of them are fast enough to ask a question, the elder man clicks his heels three times and vanishes from sight.

As if summoned by the old man's disappearance, two Silver City patrolmen appear, slamming the pub door open. Their dark gray uniforms are only accented by the silver metal of their buttons and buckles, waist length cloaks with blood red underlining, and sleek gray caps. Their lowly rank is obvious to the onlookers since they do not shine in the dim light like newly minted pennies. Where the knights of the Silver Court look positively radiant in their armor, on their stark white stallions when they venture from the castle grounds, these two look darker and more sinister.

The two soldiers pull hoods back of patrons, jerking people up from their "slumber" of drink. They bark at the patrons in a most unbecoming manner. It is not commonplace for the Silver City patrolmen to manhandle citizens as such. The patrons murmur and gripe under their breath, all whisper about the rumors of Merlin's demise, their beloved ruler. How his daughters are ruining everything.

"Have you seen the storyteller?" is the only question they ask with each new assault.

The Sisters Three

The four young men look at each other and then back to the guards. William is reaching for his pocket-watch when Jakob shakes his head no. "You heard Father, no magic."

"I did hear him plainly. But it seems we are in danger, and you mean to tell me we are going to just sit here while said danger approaches?" Irritation at his younger brother sounds like a growl in his very rolling manner of speaking.

Jakob responds without hesitation, "I do. If they are looking for him specifically, they are not going to care about us." Jakob learned at a tender age that his father's creations hold to very naive logic. Logic his father had used to escape his captors in a place his father only will refer to as Lloegyr.

"Have you seen the storyteller?" The guard's barking tone makes Hans jump and come close enough to falling off his stool that Wilhelm snorts his ale.

"Excuse me, good sir. But to which storyteller are you referring?" Jakob asks. His tone holds an austere, commanding ring of a person who neither jests, nor means to be ignored. "For, I believe the last time I looked, this is a room full of storytellers, should you fill the pint enough."

The twinkle in his eye is enough to make Wilhelm snort his drink again. "Aye, and if you ask ol' Hubbard she will tell ye e'ery man who pays her for her time has a sordid tale as to how he cannot take his progeny with him."

There is a moment the guard looks at Wilhelm as if he is going to run him through with his shining rapier sheathed at his hip. The other gives the first man a tug and motions out of the bar.

"Let 'em be. Just hooligans that are too drunk to know better. I bet he went to the clock tower. The baker says he is always there, trying something out of one of his books. We will look for him there." The angrier of the two guards stares at the four young men.

All provide their most innocent and charming faces.

William's eyes widen as he realizes there is a foggy gloss to the guard's eyes, as if he could see, and not see, at the same time. That kind of magic is forbidden. The control of another's body violates the laws of Nodd. No Noddian is a slave to another. His father vehemently denies this power and punishes anyone foolish enough to try it. William is about to motion his brothers to the man, but they leave too fast for him to act.

The clock tower chimes the sweet piping ring through the city, six chimes in all. It is time for the sun to set and all the city's inhabitants to find their way back to their homes. The clouds of the impending storm block the sun from the sky, causing it to be darker than normal. The twinkle of lanterns can be seen along the streets as the leeries make their way out from the castle. The shimmering buildings shine like millions of stars mashed together. The Silver City never dulls, no matter how dark it gets. As if the entire sky disapproves of the existence of the sparkling city below, another clap of thunder can be heard, causing people to peer upward. Another clap of thunder follows quickly after and the wind begins to howl. Its cries are the sound of a mournful woman whose soul is being torn apart.

In the heart of the city is a castle. Large and vast, it could easily be a city itself. A canal encircles it with the purest waters from the Neverland Seas. There are four bridges, one for each cardinal direction that leads to the castle. The walls glow with an opalescent sheen. Different from the city, but full of color and sparkling light. The ethereal power that holds this structure together still awes the old man every time he sees it.

From a balcony hundreds of feet in the air, a young woman watches the sky in the West. Her green eyes are vibrant from the tears recently shed. Her unruly and untamed auburn hair ripples like a great banner behind her. Her skin is fair and flushed from the howling winds. To the unknowing soul, she looks frail and petite. Her features are delicate and innocent. To those that seek her virtues, she brings them new life, hope, beginnings, happiness, peace, and most of all, love. Nimh, the name her father gave her meaning maiden in the Noddian tongue, stands quietly as if she could tame the coming storm with her very presence. The youngest of the three, while hundreds of years old, is ever treated like a foolish child. She lowers her gaze as fear wells inside her. She has seen this storm before. It is how her garden came to be, a haven from the storm of her violent older sister. Her sister had conjured it in a fury over some petty slight. Nimh cannot even remember what the slight had been. Even though her sister is the favored, beloved daughter who gave birth to an heir to the throne, she rages with a malevolence that not even the Grimms dare to rival. Her sister will be crowned Empress of Nodd, so why is she so full of fury?

"Do you really have to ask that question?" Titania gives Nimh a bemused look.

She turns her gaze through the grand balcony doors and into a room filled with plush chaises, a harpsichord, intricate paintings, and every luxury a young woman could want. Slightly older, but no less vibrant, the second woman chirps from her perch in the center of the room. Her eyes are soft sapphire in color, serene and warm, looking up with an ever-present smile at her youngest sister. Everything about the woman is pristine, refined. She is the epitome of grace and beauty with the wisdom and kindness age brings. Her voice is the soothing tone of a mother. Her tempered mind is keen and clever. She is the current deciding factor on wishes. Of course, she is wise enough to allow her sisters to decide with her; but her father specifically gave her the power to grant them. The ever-dutiful daughter, Titania, is watching Nimh with a schoolteacher's reproachful gaze.

"Of course I do," Nimh whines, sealed with a petulant look back into the room. "She has nothing to be furious about. Why can she not just be happy?"

"How was your dinner last night?" The question appears to have nothing to do with why their sister would be furious. Titania is smirking at her sister while she turns her gaze back down her to her embroidery. She knows full well that Nimh and the old storyteller have been spending many a night in Nimh's garden. Whatever they have been doing, it has not been visible in the crystal balls, or through their father's water mirrors. Their sister is a jealous beast, if not a powerful witch. Titania inhales slowly as the lightning flashes, and the thunder booms loud enough to rattle the walls.

Nimh is not capable of keeping a secret from her sisters. Which means the storyteller has been keeping their actions hidden. Not very appropriate for a man about to become the Emperor of Nodd. There is also a hint of bitterness in Titania's posture. It was not so long ago that he whisked her off to fair Verona, and they counted the stars among the fairies there. She is positive not a soul outside the two of them hold those memories.

"It was lovely!" Nimh, does not get the point of why Titania asks. "He talks of a place to the South of here. He wants to call it Ozrail. It lies beyond the Wonderland Empire and Aesopi Nation. They have all these wonderful marvels of metal and gears, along with magic and flying monkeys!" Her enthusiasm bubbles up as her cheeks flush and she comes quickly to sit by her sister. Her clothing is much wilder and free moving than her sister's elegant gown. "He held me so close and hummed to me. I have never felt that way before. His hands are a lot softer than they look. Did you know his eyes change colors?"

"Oh, Nimmy," Titania sighs and pats her sister's knee. "You are a fool. A lovely, naive fool. How would you react if your true love were spending time with your sister and not you?" While Titania is smiling and shaking her head, she has a foreboding knot in the pit of her stomach. She knew this day would come. The storyteller is too clever for Nimh, and not cautious enough for their sister. She pities poor Nimh. "You should tell-," A crack of lightning snaps across the sky close enough the room reeks of ozone. The thunder roars soon after. It causes Titania to drop her embroidery. "Fiddlesticks," she mutters much to the gasp of Nimh who picks it up.

"Oh, this is so beautiful! Is this for the infant?" Nimh runs her fingers over the little drops of water and dragons on the cloth. The blues and silvers are as precious as any jewels the dwarves could mine.

"Tell me what," hisses the woman who appears in the doorway. Her eyes are the darkest of starless nights and settle on Titania. Where Nimh is innocent and frail and Titania is regal and composed, the third sister is sinister and wild. Her pale skin is shadowed by the mess of loose ebony ringlets of hair that float and flare about her like ink in water. As she moves across the room, the silk of her gown swishes with menacing promises.

Before Titania can respond, Maab settles herself on the other side of Nimh and pointedly twirls a lock of the youngest sister's auburn hair around her finger. The middle sister, in all her wildness, appears the eldest. When seen by the peasants, she is old, and decrepit. It is a cruel spell her father cast on them. He claimed it was for their protection. Maab believes it is to keep them prisoner here until he decides their fate. If it were not for the storyteller, she likely would have become a crone before knowing True Love's Kiss.

"Yes, dear sister," her sickeningly sweet tone is anything but sincere, "Tell me why you felt the need to sleep with my true love and steal him from me." Her fingers curl tighter on the locks of hair in her grasp, expecting Nimh to panic and to bolt.

The skies open wide in response to Nimh's fear and the scent of rain washes away the lingering ozone. Her entire body trembles and there is an audible hum around them.

Titania narrows her eyes and with a swift palm outward she sends Maab flailing back from Nimh, forcing her to release Nimh's hair.

"You will not harm her, Maab," she warns.

"Oh, and you, Fairy Queen, think you are powerful enough to stop me?" Maab snarls back.

"I am, and then some, you Toad Licker." Titania hisses.

Both women are to their feet.

Nimh follows a few seconds behind and is caught in the middle. The wind outside howls through the doors around the three women. This is normally the time when their father, Merlin, would intervene, but he has not been seen for weeks. Since the birth of his granddaughter, his daughters have been left to rule in his stead. His rules are strict, and he was adamant about how the world is to be run.

Without their father to keep them in check, the three sisters are poised for a battle that could level all of Silver City in its wake.

A Noddian Scorned

The rain falls on a slant as the old man looks toward the tower. His skin crawls with the prickly sensation of danger. He told Merlin this would happen. That old fool trusted them with too much power. Maab will easily overtake her sisters, destroying them before she realizes what she has done. The old man looks down at his sack. He needs another means of taking all this with him. "No time. No time to fix it. Think. Think. Think." He mutters and taps a thick finger against his temple.

His hair is graced with flecks of earth, giving him an even more animal-like appearance than usual. "You ass, of course!" With a snap of his finger, he snatches the bag up and like a small child, he leaps into a puddle. His entire body immerses into the water as if it is as deep as the sea. He lets out a gasp as he appears in a dry, stone courtyard. The winter air is crisp, and fresh. The waft of incense that comes from the building at the top of the hill brings the hint of joy to his heart. He takes care to not step out of the pool, keeping the portal open. "You there, girl! Tell your mistress, to keep these safe until I return for them." His appearance is the polar opposite of before. He is now a pale, aged man, burly and weathered with Druid markings painting his skin. His eyes are as blue as the water he is standing in, and he shoves the sack's top into her little hands. "Do not let anyone else touch these things. This part is important. Only me."

"Aye, I ken what you said,'' she responds with a high-pitched squeak. "No one is to touch yer soggy bag o' books."

He cannot help but smile, then falls back into the pool and lands with a resounding thud on the ground in Silver City. Since the discovery of water walking, he has been practicing, but he had not traveled that far before and it is taking its toll.

His original intention was to verify that no one from the other side could find their way here by accident. As the years passed, he discovered how to make the water work in his favor, but it comes at great cost to the traveler. Magic always collects, and his tab is coming due. He rolls onto his back and allows the icy rain to fall on his cheeks. His body trembles with the effort to breathe and he barely hears the chimes from the clock tower nearby. There are eight muffled rings amidst the howling storm.

"On your feet," the sharp tip of a rapier finds his chin. "And none of your funny business, old man. The crone wants you for questioning."

He opens his eyes to be greeted by Silver City patrolmen. He knew the price of using magic was to alert them to his presence. He is not sure how Maab accomplished the feat, but every bit of magic used in the kingdom by a Grimm is being tracked. His son, Lewis, was executed three midnights prior. He was accused of violating the laws. There was no trial, no questioning, just a brilliant flash of light, and his son vanished from the stones in a shriek of pain. Since then, he has told his other sons to keep their heads down, and to not use magic of any kind until he could talk to Merlin, or now Maab, as the case appears to be.

"I cannot very well stand with your rapier threatening to provide me with new ways to whistle, now can I?" He barks at them, impatient at their incompetence.

With reluctance, the patrolmen ease back, and keep their swords aimed at him.

The old man chuckles at their fear. They should fear him, but for now, he needs to be in the castle, and this appears to be the easiest way to gain access. With an uncharacteristic grace for a man of his age, he rises.

"Lead on, good sirs." He motions for them to lead him to their Empress as his foot taps against the slick stone underfoot.

The entourage turns and begins to move quickly toward the castle. It is a long and winding walk. If not careful, one could get dizzy climbing the staircases of the central towers. He whistles, in spite of the seriousness of the affair. It is off-putting to people when a person whistles for no reason. He knows a Cricket that whistles just for the sound of the music. The closer to the summit of this glittering tower, the quieter his whistle gets. The pleasant distraction gives way to genuine concern for what he can hear from afar. A booming crack whips the tower, and a sharp scream echoes from the doorway above. He falls into the wall and sinks down, clutching his chest.

"No," his voice croaks. "No," tears well in his star-filled eyes. "Maab, what have you done?" He cannot breathe. The pain in his chest is tight, feeling as though a great troll is sitting on him.

The guard hesitates, part in fear, part in surprise. The storyteller is visibly wounded, and not a soul has touched him.

He pulls his hand from his chest, frozen in place as he watches stardust floating from his fingers. "Nimh," his voice cracks as he struggles to his feet.

"Help her, you fools," he growls at them as he staggers against the wall.

They share a look and then abandon him to rush with weapons drawn to the door at the top of the stairs. When they round the corner into the room, they stop in horror. Where the balcony used to be, a jagged scar runs across the floor and the wall is a smoldering mouth gaping wound. The wind whips furiously around, threatening to rip from the wall the tattered and burning draperies. Flames dance along them with malicious glee, spurred on by the violent winds.

"No, Maab, stop," the old man's voice carries over the wind, but he is nowhere to be seen. "You are all one."

He closes his eyes as he tries to will her to stop. He believes he can do it. There has only ever been one Noddian he could not control, and he had made that man Emperor to buy his loyalty.

"Silence!" Maab's voice is shrill as she screeches to the air. "You are as guilty as she!" She whirls around to come face to face with the patrolmen. Her appearance resembles more of a wild creature than the next Empress of Nodd. Her hair whips about her, a ferocious, inky black cloud. Her gown flares and ripples as if it has a life of its own. Her hands are above her head, fingers outstretched. Blood drips from her left hand where she holds a tiny gem, pulsing brightly. A flick of her hand sends the patrolmen crashing with bone-shattering force against the wall.

Their lifeless bodies slump to the floor.

She floats into the air and thrusts her hands down to land on the marbled floor with a crashing thump.

"Be gone, liar. Take your stories and get out of my kingdom." A crack, hairline and fine, dances across the floor from where her fists had crashed into it. It darts from Maab, serpentine and wild, fleeing her like terrified prey until it reaches the edge of the stairwell, where it begins to crumble. It is a few pieces at first, then larger chunks, and quickly followed by whole steps.

His eyes widen and he turns, starting to stumble along the wall, tripping, and then tumbling down the stairs. The walls disintegrate as the wild winds suck the air from the fast-crumbling stairwell. He is sent ass over teakettle down. He cannot draw breath as Nimh's soul fades. His eyes close and tears fall at all he is losing. Nimh was so innocent, so pure, with her sweet kisses on his cheek, the tender feel of her skin under his, the way she believed in everything. It made his soul roar in pain.

How could Maab do this?

The loud thud of him colliding with a door on a landing knocks him out of his mourning stupor.

Maab appears satisfied with his apparent death and has disappeared back into the room at the top of the tower.

Barely able to see through the tears, he breathes hard and slow, forcing the air in and out of his lungs until he can feel his heart beating steady. More screaming and crashing come from above, but as no one appears in the doorway, he will have to deal with that later. For now, he must escape Maab's wrath. His shaky fingers grope up the door he finds himself at until the levered handle gives way, allowing him to crawl into the safety of the room behind it.

While the landing outside is full of terror and destruction, this room is filled with serene music and soothing imagery. The walls ripple in shades of blue, as if the depths of the Neverland Sea are contained within. From the center dangles a mobile of stars and the moon. Light shines down over the bassinet adorned with silks and flowers. He looks quickly from left to right. They are alone. His brow furrows, and then he chuckles. "Of course, she would not have a nursemaid for you. No one is good enough for her little moonbeam." He pulls himself to his feet and finally looks to his chest. There is an open wound where his heart should be, and he closes his eyes as he puts his hand over it.

"Come what may," he chokes back his emotions, "I promise to keep you in my heart."

The words are plain and simple. That is the trick. Powerful magic does not always require a lot of flair. Those foolish philosophers in Greece, where he was birthed, never understood that.

In his short sentence, he binds his soul to hers. His immortal gift of slumber over death. No matter what Maab does to her, she will live. It is not even magic he has taught Merlin. The wound on his chest seals in response to his promise. He wipes his hand on his trousers, and steps forward, towering over the delicate bassinet.

The pair of most lovely little eyes gaze up at him. They are as blue as the Neverland Seas, only to shift to the golds of Rumpelstiltskin's hay, and finally turn to the Ozian greens of their seeing glass. Her skin is a pale olive color, reminding him of sweet chocolate melted with milk. Her hair has the hints of the ebony curls, like her mother, so precious and sweet. Ten fingers and ten toes, sprawl up at him, or the mobile; he is not sure. Her face lights up at seeing him and she coos enthusiastically. There is no name for her yet. She is a Grimm as much as a Noddian. Names have meaning, and nothing has come forward to dictate her path.

His heart weighs heavy as he knows what he needs to do.

Thieves in the Night

"She will never forgive me," he murmurs to the infant. "But I cannot let her taint you." He reaches down and lets the infant grapple his fingers with her tiny hands, pulling them right to her mouth and drooling over them profusely. She is growing fast. Infants do not stay as such for long in Nodd. He hesitates in what to do. He could turn around and beg for forgiveness. He could soothe her wrath, save her sister, and reign over Nodd with her.

The words of Lewis's mother, who long passed back to Lloegyr, float through his mind, "What about my son?"

He snorts, shaking this morose behavior off and forcing himself to focus. He extracts his fingers from the infant to easily scoop her up into his arms. It is a matter of minutes to get her swaddled, and a small satchel of things for her. His free hand cups a small talisman. "You will remember one day. You will be safe. You will save us." His voice is barely a whisper and his eyes close tight. His fingers squeeze around the talisman, willing the future into it. Light glows from his hand and the air ripples around the room, as the magic of Nodd replies to his plea for protection. He opens his eyes and looks back at the infant as he slips the talisman over her tiny head and tucks it into her swaddled clothes.

If nothing else, her safety will be assured. He looks around to locate any way out with her. Water walking would drown her, and he does not have the strength to pinpoint where to meet his sons with it. They will have to risk it on foot to get her to safety. Another look around the room, and he pulls the strap of the satchel over his shoulder. Then, cradling her close to where he had healed himself, he looks back to the door. That way is not safe enough. Maab would hear him and be on him in an instant.

The tower shakes again, and the burning scent of ozone creeps closer. The prickly feeling of being watched makes the old man shudder. His eyes burn over the nooks and crannies of the room once more, looking for any shadow out of place.

"Blast you, Merlin." The old wizard always disappears when you need him most. Not that he would be much use to the storyteller right now, but there is something strange about this disappearance and he could do with an ally in this moment. "Get it together, man!" He growls into the air, and it elicits a startled cry from his passenger. "Shh, shh. It is alright," his voice instantly turns charming. "I will never let anything happen to you; I promise." A few gentle rocks and a reassuring smile, allows him to calm the infant.

He clicks his heels again, three times, and the two of them vanish in a whoosh, re-appearing just outside of the clock tower. He looks around urgently. The night is black and starless. A quick look down the street where there should be street lanterns, reveals nothing, not even the glittering hints of the buildings. Then the clock chimes. It is loud and ominous above him. The rain is pouring. He stands there, riveted to the spot by the chimes, until the infant is shrieking from the icy drops kissing her skin.

"Hrmph, it is just water little one," he grumbles as he looks down at her. His eyes widen and he watches her as she wails about this unsuitable existence. The rain, dancing to her will, parts to flow around her, while her entire body radiates a warm, faint light. If she were not his own progeny, he likely would have dropped her where they stand. To control the weather is no small feat, and only the most powerful of Grimms can do it as far as the world of Nodd knows. He is roused from his admiration of her abilities by the frantic sound of Hans.

"Father! Father! You are late!"

With a jerk of his head, he snaps his gaze up to Hans,

watching as the young boy closes the distance. "It is nearly the last stroke of twelve! The garden is burning! The Mother and the Crone are dueling. I have never seen such a thing. They are hurling lightning bolts, fire, and all other manner of elements back and forth. Maab is taunting her with some stone that gives her power. It is madness! Pure madness, father!"

"Then we had best get going, fool!" He thumps his son, and the pair of them take off, racing toward the eastern gate, the entrance to Nimh's garden. Just as Hans had described, a wall of flames roar toward the sky, only to be reduced to smoky plumes by the downpour. His heart breaks all over again, having just spent the evening prior in said garden. It is full of secrets and wonders that Nimh had created on her own. Now, most of those secrets are furiously racing to save their haven.

"By Merlin," Wilhelm gasps as he comes running from the North. Within seconds, all four young men, each carrying various bags and boxes look on in horror. "Is that a baby? Where did you steal a baby fr--? Wait! You stole *that* baby? Father, you've gone too far. She will have all our heads for this."

Jakob raises both brows, "I suppose it is not stealing if you half own it."

William frowns and looks between them. "Why do you have Maab's daughter in your arms? What in Verona is going on here?"

"There is no time to explain. We must get to the stones of judgment. It is imperative we get her to

Lloegyr." The old man bellows at them as he turns to begin the arduous trek.

"To LLOEGYR?" the young men ask in shocked unison, but they were already gathering up to click their heels.

"No! No magic you idiots. They are tracking us by our magic!" It is the first time he has said it aloud, but the ramifications of the Grimms being tracked registers with them like a wet blanket being thrown over the flames. "We must go on foot, and hurry."

"There they are!" The guards shout, not far in the distance. "Stop! In the name of the Empress!"

Any arguments about the distance and amount of work to travel it are instantly silenced. All the men look at the approaching knights, and with a graceful turn, press open the gates to race into the inferno that was Nimh's Garden. The old man cradles the infant, who is now shrieking in an inconsolable fit. Rain and smoke fill the air as the men press forward. Creatures of all sorts race back and forth to save their home. Some are standard woodland creatures, others magnificent and rare mythical beasts that only an innocent and pure mind could conjure.

The shrieking howls of the dueling women creep over the wind. The trees, vines, and all manner of flowers are teaming with life. They lash out in pain, and in anger. The creatures that can fly bring buckets of water. All around the Grimms the words, *I wish,* fill their ears.

"Ignore them. Get to the stones," the old man

commands. The young men follow dutifully. Wilhelm, fancying himself a swordsman, has his rapier drawn, expecting an ambush.

Wishes are a special kind of magic. It is not just a gift, or a trick. A wish changes you eternally. When granted, the Grimms will warn the wisher that wishes come true, not free. With a quick look back at the boys, he can feel their suffering as well. The Grimms are being tortured, knowing they can help, but will not do so. The "greater good" is a cruel and unforgiving mistress. The old man knows that he must let the garden burn if they are to have a chance to reach the stones. His sons' dissent in his command is coming, but using their power to save the garden and its inhabitants will cost them everything.

"It will be alright. The Garden cannot die." His words grate with anguish at the surrounding destruction. He is gentle now, taking the tone of a father to his sons. "I will not lose another of you. Do what I say, and we will all get through this." He looks from them, back to the gate, now so far in the distance He sighs, and thrusts his free palm forward, toward the stones looming in the distance, mere specks on the horizon. It is reckless, but there is no more time. The very fabric of existence changes. It warps and shifts in a grotesque swirl of stardust and color. In the center is a black hole. Nothing is visible save for the void of the surrounding chaos. Just as it appears, it gives way to a meadow of blues and greens in contrast to the oranges and reds of the burning garden. The boys rush through. Once they are safe on the other side, the old man follows, the void sealing behind him.

The guardsmen charged with protecting the Stones of Judgment mill about in boredom. This quiet clearing is a far cry from the madness happening in Silver City, or Nimh's Garden. The men nearest the old man's destination are brought to attention the instant the wind begins to whistle and whirl, a telltale sign of Grimms using magic. Weapons are drawn, and the men ready themselves for the fight of their lives. Before their eyes, the world bends and darkens, ripping open a large hole painted with an inky shadow. Fear fills the young men as the old man steps through, followed by his four most prominent sons.

The Stones of Judgment

"GRIMMS!" A young knight bellows, and it echoes across the field and calls to arms all those waiting, not just those nearest. "Do not let them get to the stones!"

"How could they know?" the old man frowns. He had hoped to not harm a soul in this escape. There are only two people in all of Nodd who know the stones are for traveling, not just magical rocks that reduce people to nothingness. They had to be activated properly, and with all these buffoons running about, that would be difficult.

"Father, what do we do?"

The old man is not sure which of his boys asks this of him, nor does it matter. They must push through. "Turn them to stone. There is no time to waste on them."

The brothers set their things down and stand shoulder to shoulder. One Grimm has power, but four are an unstoppable vortex of energy.

With a loud roar, Jakob calls the earth to grow up around the knights, grasping at them, and pulling them into place for his brothers.

Wilhelm rolls his hands in front of him as if a master clay-maker is shaping his molds with the soldiers.

Hans, with his eyes closed out of fear, chants in an old language he barely understands, "Factum est lapis de monte. Fortis et absque fœdere. Non tendens amplius frangere." The butchered Latin comes from his father's heritage. It would have proved more powerful, had he chanted in Greek, but he is too scared to attempt it.

William rests his hand on Hans's shoulder and lends him his strength.

At first, the knights rush forward, closing in to grapple and restrain the brothers, unaware of their fates.

Their father lingers behind them, watching the fight for any signs of who is in command.

One by one the knights yell and gasp as the ground itself comes to life. It wraps their feet and pulls them to a standstill. The grays and blacks of stone creeping over the silver armor begin to paint a grim picture. The wailing cries of men as their skin hardens and cracks fills the air. Their faces are in anguish. The echoes of their last breaths dance around them like moths dancing around a flame.

When Hans opens his eyes again, they are surrounded by stone statues, full-sized men trapped for eternity, or until the spell is undone. While possible, it would take a powerful witch to undermine a Grimm's spell, much less one crafted by four.

The entire meadow is silent, other than the four young men's labored breathing.

The fifty men sent to capture them are frozen in stone.

The old man stares into the woods, his back to his sons. A shrouded figure reveals itself long enough for him to connect the strands in the weave of this madness. His eyes narrow and he is about to march headlong into battle to put this whole thing to rest when searing hot pain slashes across his face. The ebony skin rips open to reveal the bone and muscle beneath. It is gruesome and violent compared to the hint of golden stardust that flutters into the air. The ground quakes under them, and the old man drops to his knees. He does not remember crying out, but he must have, as his sons rush to him.

"Father! Father!" He can hear them calling to him, and the infant is shrieking. Her wails cause him to look down at her, blood drops kiss her pale skin and cause her to wail more. "Titania," he breathes in grief. Tears well in his eyes and his face burns in vibrant colors from the wound. He struggles to draw breath. "Come what may, you will always be in my thoughts." He brings his free hand across his face, hastily sealing his wound to deal with it later.

The shrouded figure hovers in the distance, watching him.

"Take the infant," the old man opens his good eye to turn it upon Jakob. "Go through the stones. They will take you where you need to be. There will be a boat. Put her in the boat. Then vanish."

Jakob takes the tiny baby and the satchel his father has. "What about you?"

"Do not ask foolish questions. Do as I say, now!" The old man's fury grows as he feels more helpless than ever. His gaze settles on the shadow again, ignoring his sons.

It is Wilhelm who silences their protests by taking the baby from his brother and making a mad dash for the stones. He is not sure what will happen, but he trusts his father implicitly.

"Wilhelm! Stop! Wilhelm! You will be murdered! Stop!"

A brilliant strike of lightning, and a clap of thunder rip through the chaos as Wilhelm leaps into the air, right into one of the stones, vanishing from sight.

With only a second of hesitation, Jakob follows in the same fashion.

William, not so daring, but just as quick, runs headlong into the stones.

This leaves Hans, afraid and alone. "Wait for me! Brothers, wait for me!" He whines as he backs up and then runs head down into the stones. It is not the same sound as before. This time the stone lets out a ringing protest and cracks clean down the center, splitting it into a V shape.

The old man does not look, but he knows. He knows in his heart what has just happened, and he pulls himself to his feet, swaying from the nearly fatal blow of Titania being murdered.

"You cannot win. She is too powerful now." His words are slurred from the injury on his face.

The figure vanishes then.

The old man stumbles forward, unable to pursue. His body is heavy from the abuse of the day, and his mind is full of fluff. He swears his chest aches as if his very heart had been ripped from it. If he does not stop to rest, he will die. He stumbles to the nearest campfire from the guards and sinks down to stoke it with a nearby stick. The winds have quit howling. The rain has stopped. The thunderclouds have moved on, and the stars are twinkling above. He lies on his back and stares up at them. Tomorrow will be the worst day of his life since he came here. For now, he is going to rest.

"Sight unseen. Sound unheard. Peace for the beast within. I will meet you straight away another day." With the spell of protection cast, he relaxes, allowing himself to fully cry then. Two of his beloved Noddians had been murdered in one day.

While Maab is the culprit, she is not guilty in his mind. To the other Noddians she appears wizened and decrepit, but her existence is young in comparison. She is only a pawn in this treacherous game.

He knows the game better than anyone. What he does not know is the reason for such brutality. He does not know the shadow, and for the first time since the beginning of Nodd, the old man is terrified he has failed them all.

He knows Maab is in danger. He will go to her and do what he can, hoping he is not too late to save her. At least their daughter is safely away, albeit not with the son he wished to oversee the task. A smile creeps over his face as he closes his eyes to truly sleep. His face is already working to mend itself. His body is aglow with the stardust that is part of him. He can smell her sweet perfume, feel her gentle touch. He can hear her laughter at his rather crude method of thinking.

"I can save her," he murmurs to no one. "I can save you all."

His rest is unfit. Nightmares of death and destruction plague his slumber. The shadowed vision of a woman ripping Nodd clean in two plays like a horrific opera in his mind. Her voice carries across the winds and seas to tear her home into shreds. He screams awake. His entire body convulsing and being thrown about.

"No," he grits his teeth, and his fingers dig into dirt and grass alike.

"Maab," he calls to her in a plea. It is not a plea of forgiveness, but one of fear.

"I'm coming!" His gallant promise sails across the wind and he thrusts his free hand up into the air. She still lives, but he could feel her fear. He could taste the iron sweetness of her blood. With a jerk of his hand, he is up on his feet and the whole of the field shudders from the effects of him breaking the spell that held him. He dashes blindly to the banks of the nearby stream.

"I'm coming," he gasps out as he falls into the stream, his mind only on the massive bath he and Maab shared more times than he can remember. The hall appears in his mind and the sweet scent of oils and incense fill his nostrils. The water turns from the frigid stream to the steaming and scented bath. All of this takes shape as he falls through the water into the in-between, then as he falls into water in the new location.

With a gasp for air, he tumbles in the waters of the massive bath. Flailing and trying to get his footing, panic fills him as he still does not have his full bearings and only one good eye. Air fills his lungs, and he coughs, splashes, and plants his feet down firmly. He towers in the center of the waters, looking more like a wild beast than a man.

The ladies enjoying the bath scream and scatter to their various hiding places like a dule of doves before the hunting fox. He would laugh at this scene if this were not such a dangerous time. His steps are heavy as he moves forward, up the stairs, and out of the water. His mind is having a challenging time focusing. It is bouncing between pain, fatigue, and fury as he leans against the doorway. If Maab falls, there is no telling what will happen next, and for all his efforts he still has not saved the ones he loves most. The vision in the grove tortures him without mercy.

His thoughts drift to the woman he called wife,

struggling to focus on her memory. Her patient and clever wisdom is sorely needed tonight.

There is Always a Price

Pulled from his revelry, the old man sees four figures waiting. One as lovely as a Spring morning, her cheeks rosy and bright. Her beauty is unrivaled. Just standing in her presence, makes him want to draw her in and have his way with her. The vision of the woman is ripped from him as she is hidden behind the demure stature of a gentle-looking man. His eyes promise a great deal of pain to the old man if he follows through with his thoughts.

"Heh," is the old man's response as he turns his gaze to the other man. This one is tall and regal, old in appearance. Everything about him screams that he does things by the book, and only by the book. The third man, easily his counterpart, appears to be keeping them all in line. He keeps the order of the scene before them in check. They say nothing, but watch the storyteller with great interest.

He gives a smirk, assuming they have been newly thought of from his sons.

The young woman deftly moves around her protective counterpart. There is something familiar about her. The way she moves, the twinkle in her eyes, and then she touches him. Energy surges between them at her touch, like a bolt of lightning flooding his veins.

His eye widens, and he stares down at her in horror. Everything about her tells him she is Nimh, but she is clearly not. There is something different about her, missing from the girl he knew. "Nimh," his eyes well with tears and the young woman frowns up at him.

"Desire," she corrects him. "You must come with us. Maab is in grave danger."

He reluctantly pulls his gaze from her to the others, each expressing a varying range of fear, impatience, and indifference. He can feel Desire attempting to force her will on him. They are meant to detain him, and they are not from his sons at all. He curses himself for teaching Merlin the dangerous magic of creating life. The longer they stand still, the more he feels Titania and Nimh. The four souls before him each a shattered piece of his beloved women.

"Take me to Maab."

Desire recoils, swooning into her protective male's arms.

The old man shows her exactly how powerful he

truly is by rebuking her control over him. He is the first Grimm of Nodd, and her story is no more powerful than his. She will not usurp his will.

The elder of the four steps forward and takes the storyteller by the forearm, sending tendrils of pain down the old man's arm. "Law," he snaps before he is called Titania. "That is Order, and he is Saint. Now that pleasantries are over with," his free hand motions for the storyteller to move forward.

The storyteller obliges, and they begin their procession through the castle. People are hustling to and fro in avoidance of guards, picking up the pieces, and afraid. As the entourage continues into the main hall, the whispers are furious about the stolen infant, and the death of the mother and the maiden.

At every turn, a silver armored knight is posted, watching the frantic pace of the servants and advisors alike. Each of the lower courts have sent a representative to discern the meaning of the attack. No one will meet the storyteller's gaze.

He keeps his mind as focused as he can, feeling the strong pull to submit. Desire, Saint, Order, and Law work in tandem to subdue him as they walk in a diamond formation around him. Not a soul is talking about Merlin still missing, only about the garden, the fire, and the three de facto rulers of Nodd.

The main hall is grand, with crystal chandeliers dangling on the other side of a massive staircase made from the finest marble. The tapestries are woven with silver threads to sparkle as the light dances across them. Jagged burn scars from the battle between Titania and Maab blister throughout the room, up along the stairwell, and into the now half missing tower. Already, carpenters and masons are working to restore the glory of the building. Up the ornate staircase and across the veranda is the public hall where Titania formerly held court for wishes. As the monstrous oak doors swing open, it is quiet and serene aside from the inky menace pacing on top of the dais. Her clothes barely cling to her, tattered and singed, with hands stained brown from the blood of her sisters.

As the group approaches, she stops and looks right at him. Her eyes have gone entirely black, losing all signs of humanity. Starlight fizzles about her with a malicious promise to set anyone aflame who dares to touch her. She tries to come down to him, only to be thrown back by his captors. A screaming growl makes the four of them take pause.

The storyteller looks from one, to the next, as they stare at her and are unwilling to get any closer. When he looks back up to her, it is not the woman he loves more than life before him he sees. No. It is the gruesome scene behind her.

Floating in the air behind Maab are her sisters, each looking like porcelain dolls waiting to be taken off the shelf. No hints of their deaths are upon them. No scorched skin or gaping wounds. One, the epitome of maidenhood with her auburn tresses fanning out and floating like a sea of earth. Her gown made of golds and oranges, the embroidered leaves flitter, teased by an invisible breeze. The other sister is in purples and reds, her golden curls crowning her with the light of the sun. Her gown ripples with the hint of life, shimmers of children laugh and play amongst the pleats.

"Where is she?" The accusatory shriek pulls him from his stupor. "Where is *my* daughter, you monster?"

"She is safe, but I do not know where she is." He is thankful for Wilhelm's ignorant heroics, leaving him blissfully ignorant.

"LIAR!" The windows around them shatter as her voice rips through the air, sending shards of glass raining down upon all gathered there. Maab is beyond reason.

He knows better than to force her to calm down. For the moment, he is sure he only lives because she believes he knows where their daughter has been taken.

"I told you he would do this. I warned you, my daughter." From the side entrance, the shadowed figure from before is brought forward, flanked by two women. Their heads are shrouded and bowed, causing the storyteller to feel a dreadful knot form in his stomach. There is a dark and menacing force in the two women, which is echoed by the four around him.

The six move in unison to encircle Maab, leaving the two old men to watch in helpless frustration.

"Silence, you old fool. You allowed him to do this. You let him steal her and ruin our lives. Where were you when he was seducing Nimh and betraying our trust? How long did you let his filthy sons manipulate and destroy lives? Usurping our wishes for the citizens of Nodd? Before you will-" and her voice is cut short as a sword pierces her chest from behind.

One of the shrouded women holds firm as her lips move in an eerie singsong chant.

The other shrouded woman steps closer and plunges a dagger into Maab's neck. The four others sway and lock hands, all their voices joining the chant as Maab shrieks in pain.

Merlin stands, transfixed, and helpless.

The storyteller looks from Maab to Merlin, then starts to step forward. He catches himself and stops. Tears well in his eyes again as he takes a slow step backward.

"Help me," she cries as her decrepit form is shed to reveal the stunning, beautiful malcontent. Soft skin, ebony curls, and eyes as purple as jewels look wildly about for anyone to save her.

"Come what may," he starts, only to be thrust into a wall by an unseen force. He grunts in pain.

The two women hold Maab in place, the sword piercing through her while the dagger digs its way to its target.

He pulls himself up and feels his very soul being ripped to shreds. The wound on his face tears open, shredding his hasty repair from the stones. This is followed by the gaping wound above his heart also tearing free.

"Come what may," he chokes out and leans back

against the wall. "I will never forget this day. For your soul is my soul," the words are choked through a sob of his own anguish. It has been more than a millennium since he felt emotions as powerful as this.

"I love you."

He could say no more. He could feel his life-force ebbing from him. The stardust floats in the air. The visage of his three beauties dance around him. Maab's shrieking gives way to gurgles. The bond between the two is woven tight enough that by destroying one, it weakens the other. The very universe shudders in pain as the lovers are bested by these foes.

It would appear all is lost.

The woman shredding Maab's neck finally comes free with a gem in hand. Blood and stardust encircle her delicate fingers. Triumphantly holding it, she steps away from her victim.

The other woman allows Maab to collapse to the floor, the sword still firmly planted between her shoulders.

The two come together as the others circle around them.

Maab's eyes open wide as she stares into the nothingness, her blood pools around her.

He stares back at her and struggles to keep his footing. All of Nodd quakes as the very fabric of the universe is shredded by the two women tearing apart Maab's gem.

They raise their trophies to the sky, continuing the dark ritual as their chanting reaches a fevered pitch.

The room hums with a sickening tune. The old man's body shakes violently from the abuse of magic his is witnessing. He knows he should flee now, but he wants the assurance she will survive.

"There is always a price," he murmurs.

No Place Like home

As if the universe itself hears his plea, Maab's body shrivels before his eyes. Only the pile of tattered gown remains. Stardust floats in the air like the dust of a forgotten library's book giving way to a magical and brilliant oval of light. Seconds feel like eons as he watches the universe weave its spell. Once complete, floating in between her sisters, is the raven-haired beauty. No blood. No burns. No madness. Just a slumbering young goddess with midnight robes to accent her ebony ringlets. All manner of shadows dance and ripple over her gown.

"Thank you," he mumbles.

He is losing consciousness and knows that if he does so here, he will die. Why Merlin would let this happen, he is not sure. He always told the man to beware his own overconfidence. He uses the wall for support, until he can steady himself on his own two legs.

"Fate," the woman who stabbed Maab in the back declares with finality.

"Chaos," the younger woman giggles in madness.

Their names, Law, Fate, Order, Chaos, Saint, and Desire, burn into his mind.

They all turn and look directly at him, as if his remembrance of their names summons their attention. They tilt their heads in unison, studying him, and he flashes them a grin.

He clicks his heels three times. His body flickers and for a fleeting moment he believes his magic has betrayed him.

They quickly come off the dais, moving at a pace that would frighten the strongest of men. Some foul magic was trying to hold him prisoner here. His eyes turn to the statuesque Merlin again. It is then the hood of the old wizard falls back. A stony gray figure is turning, but much too slow to do any good. It barely registers what has happened to Merlin. The loss of his daughters must have weakened him as it has the storyteller. The fool had been caught like a fly in this dark web. He decides there is no saving Merlin and saving the Three is more important. He clicks his heels again.

"There is no place like home," he breathes out. Another flicker, and then his body vanishes; leaving young Chaos to slam into the wall as she tries to catch him.

When he regains his consciousness, he is face first in a pile of hay next to a poor excuse of a stable outside of an unkempt cottage. The Birds sing, and Horses chatter. There is a Pig bathing nearby, and young field Mice recite their alphabet on the only solid fence post in the yard.

None pay him any mind at first.

He always pops in and out without interfering in their comings and goings. It is no different today in their minds. Groaning, he tries to pick himself up, but the blood-slicked hay gives him little purchase. "Help me," he gurgles, and struggles to move from the hay again. He finds himself, for the third time today, on his back on the ground. He cannot help but laugh at the significance of three. Three goddesses, three powerful sons, three promises. All of it comes to the surface and overwhelms him. He allows himself to cry as he believes himself dying. He groans again, and this time a rosy, pink snout appears over him.

"Oh dear," her voice oinks at him. "What has happened? Send for the physician, at once! Come help me, Wilbur! He is in no condition to walk,"

The old man relaxes. He trusts all the Animals here implicitly. Not only are they talking, and interacting, they are living beings as much as the Silver Court. The Aesopi Nation is protected and sacred. Those who enter, respect its sovereignty above all others in Nodd. Even the three goddesses had respected it. His good hand shoots up, and he grasps her arm firmly. "The Rabbit, the Cat, and the Wolf. Tell them," he coughs and sputters up blood. "Tell them, it is the last midnight." With the message sent, he collapses into the fog of unconsciousness that has been slowly clouding his eyes.

Around him, the tiny farm is in chaos. The Pig and the Horse gather him up off the ground, getting him draped like a sack of potatoes over Wilbur's back. The old Horse no longer could shift into a humanoid form, but he can still talk and can carry the storyteller to a better place.

The door is opened by a Cat ornately dressed in boots and regal clothes, his tail twitches in agitation at the sight. He takes the old man from Wilbur and with the Pig's help, he carries him inside to lay him on the large table with an oak tree carved into it.

They make little work of his clothing and in from the kitchen bustles a Hen with a pot of water she hangs over the massive fire in the mantle. It is ever burning at the right temperature for a comfortable home, but grows in heat to bring the water to a boil after the kettle is placed over it. Behind her are smaller Hens all clucking their tongues in reproach at him bleeding out on the newly scrubbed table. Each take their stations and begin to administrate aid to him. The mother Hen comes to him and gently dabs at the wound over his heart. "You poor dear," she coos. Never has she seen such carnage, not even in her old age.

The door is thrust open, and the massive Owl of a man impeccably dressed and adorned with tiny wire-rimmed glasses fills the doorway. In hand is his black leather medical bag. "Step aside, ladies. I have this under control."

"You old hoot. You do your work, and I will do mine. But I'm not leaving him like this." The Owl, startled by the fact anyone would rebuke his command, that he stares, open-beaked, at the Hen for several seconds. "Move your arse or get gone. No time for your lallygagging." The Owl's eyes blink at her sharp tongue.

The Hens about her chortle and are cut short by her look. This is no laughing matter, and she is not about to be the one responsible for the death of the Creator.

The Owl, Nicodemus, jumps to respond to her command. He brings his bag over and begins rummaging about. His feathered hands begin to paw over the old man, evaluating the wounds with the tools he retrieves, listening to his breathing. He and the Hen, named Mrs. Haverdashal, work in tandem. This is not the first time they have saved a soul from their poor choices. "He is nearly gone," Nicodemus grimaces.

"No, he is just weak. He sent for the Rabbit, Cat, and Wolf. Nonsense about midnights. Likely over that girl he has been strutting about the Silver Court with."

Her matter-of-fact tone makes Nicodemus smile, but the words send a cold tendril of fear down his spine. If the old man was talking midnights, they are all in danger. He finally takes her hand in his, and motions to the old man's forehead. "There is no time for the nonsense in the bag. We need to stabilize him now."

She gives a firm nod and her hand slaps down on the old man's forehead while she grips onto Nicodemus' hand as tight as she can with the other. He draws in a deep breath and places his hand on the old man's heart. Animal magic is rooted in action, not words. Every action, from the placement of their hands to the motion of their bodies swaying above him, is what drives it. There is not a single word to be heard in the room. The other Hens join in and rest their hands on his body, creating a circle of feathered fingers around him. A breeze, carrying wild leaves with Autumn's entropic kiss upon them, blusters through the open windows. The golden leaves swirl in time with the healing circle, dancing to the rhythm of the stomping feet of the Aesopi. In the distance, the beating of drums can be heard in time with their dance as the news travels the breadth of the Aesopi Nation.

The old man's body glows and steam rises from the table, misting around them. His breathing steadies, and his wounds begin to seal. The fresh skin is jagged and rough. The scars to remember his arrogance form to remind him of the price of his magic. The Hens in the circle are paying their price for this magic as they begin to faint, one by one.

"Enough," Nicodemus finally breaks the circle, and they all stare down at the old man. He listens and watches to count the number of breaths from the old man. Once satisfied, he preens, and begins barking orders again. "Get him to the bed and let him rest. He should not be up and about for three days. You should rest too, Gertrude. It appears to have taxed you a great bit." He steps forward and gingerly helps her to a large, cushioned chair.

Her response to him is a loud cluck.

This makes the entire room stop moving and stare in horror. Even Nicodemus takes pause, She clears her throat and begins again, "I will be fine. Get him to bed, girls." She is trembling. To act like an animal, meant a great deal to an Aesopi. They pride themselves in being Animals. Animals are proud and strong people who have embraced their primal heritage. The other, animals, are pets and creatures used for labor, feeding, or other menial tasks.

Nicodemus frowns at her but says nothing else. He learned a long time ago that Mrs. Haverdashal is not to be argued with. Leaving her to her Hens, he follows the movement of the old man to his bed chambers. He gets him settled in, takes his vitals again, and he ushers everyone from the room. While the Hens fawn over Mrs. Haverdashal, he paces and waits for the three summoned men to hopefully deter them from whatever task the old man sets them on.

The Last Midnight

The first to arrive is the Rabbit. He is tall, slender, and pristine in appearance. His mind is one of the sharpest minds in all of Nodd. Ever punctual, ever fair, he is often sought after to settle disputes, and prevent war. His long ears are gently tied back like two tails of hair behind him. As far as Aesopi go, he is considered the Regent of the land. When the old man is away, he is the effective ruler.

Seconds behind him is the most devilish looking man you will meet, the Cat. His skin is dark and soft, with fur tufts sticking out from his clothes as the only clue that he is in fact Animal. His eyes are emerald today, though they change with his mood. His body is muscular and strong. He is the kingdom's most feared enforcer. Many believe he is an assassin, but none are brave enough to accuse him of it. His toothy grin can unsettle even the fiercest of warriors, and often does.

Finally, with little ado arrives a massive beast of a man, the Wolf. His body is reminiscent of the Greek Gods, muscled and toned. His hands are the size of a lesser man's head. His fangs are sharp, and his eyes glow the fierce amber of his wolf ancestors. His nostrils flare as he eyes the other two. He is the Captain of the Guard in Aesop, leading the Aesopi army, which contains mostly a canine assortment of predators.

Nicodemus approaches them and holds up a delicate, feathered finger to stop them. "He is not well. We did all we could for him, but take what he says with a grain of salt."

"I will judge for myself his state, you old hoot," the Cat retorts.

"What my colleague is meaning to say is," the Rabbit begins to smooth over the ruffled feathers, "The old man sent for us. It matters only that we meet with him. It is for the good of the nation."

Nicodemus raises his brow and shifts uneasily, looking to the Wolf. The only response he gets is a menacing look as the man eases forward. "Alright! Alright! The thanks I get!" He mutters in anger and steps aside, allowing the three to enter the room where the old man rests.

The room is tiny and dimly lit. The bed is made of feathers, sealed in a soft cotton bag large enough for the old man, with an ornate headboard, four posts, and some of the softest linens skin has ever touched. In the center of the bed is the old man, looking frail and ravaged. His body is riddled with scars and his skin holds the ashen color of death. He appears to be sleeping soundly, as if he had not arrived in a pool of his own blood. The walls are lined with bookcases. The books and scrolls that once neatly rested upon them, are half missing, disheveled, or on the floor. A wardrobe is tucked ominously in the corner, its doors cracked open for spying eyes to peer through. A large mantle fireplace provides the glow in the room, and crackles with the happy promise of comfort.

The closer the three get to the bed, the more worried they become. They share a glance, and there is a silent dilemma of which unlucky Animal will wake him.

Brave and true, the Rabbit rests his fine, ghostly-colored hand on the old man's shoulder, "Father Aesop, you sent for us," he sounds more like a frightened boy than a quiet man. At first, there is no response, not even an acknowledgment of their presence. Again, the Rabbit nudges Aesop. He gives the Cat and the Wolf a concerned look. "Father Aesop," his tone grows a hint louder and firmer as panic starts to well in him.

"By my whiskers, you are as quiet as a mouse," the Cat steps up and with a firm nudge that nearly sends Aesop sliding right out of the bed. "We do not have time for your games, old man. Wake up!"

"Oh, why not just slash him with your claws while you are at it, Chesh." The Wolf chuckles, but there is something strange about this room today, a terrible, dangerous feeling, that makes the Wolf want to be anywhere but here.

"What do you propose we do? He said the end of the world is coming, and we are supposed to sit here and watch him sleep? I could be halfway through a bottle of milk right now."

"You know milk makes you gassy," the Rabbit gets his verbal jab in. "Besides, if it is the end of the world, what do you intend to do about it? Perhaps our mission is to sit here and watch him sleep."

"How anyone can sleep with you three prattling on like a Hen, is beyond me," Aesop cracks an eye open and looks up at the trio. His smile is soft and sad at the same time.

"My three most loyal friends," he begins as he pushes himself up.

The trio immediately move to make sure he is comfortable.

"I'm not an invalid, you fools. Just worn out." It takes several minutes, and a few tries, but he eventually gets out of the bed. He moves away from them to paw over the mess of clothes the Hens left piled on the floor. His bare ass moons the three, who have the good manners to look away. The treasure he is looking for is freed from its confines, and he staggers over to the water basin where he claims the pitcher before making his way back to the bed.

"You are to take these gifts. Use them when they are needed most," he holds up his hand to forestall their questions.

He turns to the Cat, "You, Cheshire Cat, I gift you your smile. Use it to disarm, to charm, to distract your prey as you carry out your deeds. Beware of lost girls who want to go home."

He turns to the Wolf, "You, I dub the title Big Bad, and give you your breath to blow your enemies down where they stand. You will be feared and revered. Use it wisely. Avoid red cloaks."

He turns to the Rabbit. "White Rabbit, my most trusted friend, I can only give you this," he raises the pocket watch. "It will always lead you to your destination on time. You are clever enough to figure out the rest."

Reluctantly, he lets the trinket settle in the pink padded palm of the White Rabbit. He then pours the water on the floor at their feet, causing the three to growl, hiss, and twitch their noses, respectively. He does not care for their irritation. It will make the passage much easier. Guilt fills him as he has purposely not explained what has happened. The less they know the better, and the easier it will be for them to go undetected.

The cuckoo clock on the wall begins to chime. The little canary carving flits out and chirps a sweet note. One chime, followed by another, then another. He touches the Wolf and in a dazzling burst of light, he vanishes.

"What?! Where did he-," the clock chimes a fourth, fifth, then sixth time, and the Cat is sent spiraling into the ether, sucked through a wormhole created right behind him.

This leaves the Rabbit and Aesop alone in the room. The seventh chime, followed by the eighth, then the ninth, and he reaches up, pulling the Rabbit into a hug.

"I wish," the Rabbit begins, and then he too vanishes in a cloud of stardust.

Aesop turns to face the clock as chime ten rings, then eleven. Tears well in his eyes, but he knows what must be done. His voice is soft, and gentle when he speaks again.

"The last midnight calls. All the tower falls. Peace for our nation free. Only now you are enslaved to me. Never do you live. Never do you die. No more talking. No more walking. Animal is now a beast. With me the king of this feast. Until the heir that is true comes to rescue you."

The twelfth chime rings and echoes throughout all of the Aesopi Nation.

A wave of stardust ripples out, starting from him.

His entire body is thrust into the air and he bellows out a dreadful guffaw. His ebony skin is spiked with fur pushing through in its place. His nose and mouth reconfigure into a snout with teeth comically large for the mouth. His head elongates and his ears stretch like taffy pulled from the pot until they are pointed and flicking. His body curls as ribs crack, and haunches form. His fingers mold together into a fist that gives way to a hoofed foot. When he finally returns to the ground, all that is left in the room is a pudgy black furred donkey, braying angrily into the air. The other room houses a gaggle of hens clucking about on the floor. The piles of clothing where the feathered women once stood are being trampled by the little birds. On a perch near the fireplace is a large barn owl, hooting angrily.

By the time the chime dies away, all the Aesopi within the nation's borders have been turned into animals, cursed to live eternally in this state.

Throughout the rest of Nodd, their brothers and sisters, free of the curse, cry out in mourning.

In the Silver City, the clock tower's face fizzles, then pops, as steam rolls from the edges. It has struck its last midnight.

Gifts Without Givers

The puff of heavy breath forms a cloud around Wilhelm's face. The infant is wailing her displeasure for all to hear. His ears are ringing, and the distinct burning smell of being kissed by flames clings to them both. His body feels heavy, and he recognizes nothing. The sky here is different. The stars seem further and duller. The ground is rougher, and not the perfect lush greenery of the forests in Nodd. He stumbles out of the stone circle while he ignores the baby's displeasure. "Jakob," he hoarsely calls out. "William! Hans!" He looks around in a panic. There are no stone soldiers. Even the stones of the circle look different, their surfaces are weathered, pitted, and overgrown with deep-rooted vines.. The only response to his frantic pleas are crickets and frogs. He turns his head this way and that, much like an owl, but he is alone. His brothers are gone. Panic floods him and he barely manages to shift the infant aside as he vomits. There are trees all around, but they did not sway with life as proper Noddian forests should. His breathing is shallow and quick, and his heart hammers a mile a minute in his chest. He shuffles further from the stones and instantly his body is heavy and refusing to walk him forward. His stomach does flips as it tries to empty itself again. There is still no answer to his continued call for his brothers. His breathing is labored and his muscles ache.

Where are they?

"Where are we, little one?" He is trying to soothe her and himself at the same time. It is then he notices his hand. His skin has changed to an olive color with darks green and blue tattoos traced over his skin.

"By Merlin," he murmurs. His eyes follow the changed hand to take in the furs and deerskin leather bag on his shoulder. He drops to his knees, cradling the babe to his chest, albeit awkwardly, as he tries to comfort them both. He cannot remember what his father said. Was it to find a boat and take her somewhere? Or was he supposed to give her to a person on a boat? He needs Jakob for all this remembering. Why did he grab the child? Father had given her to Jakob for a reason. His gaze traces the tree line hopefully, looking once more for the return of his kin in vain.

He finds himself at the edge of a massive lake, mist covered and blacker than Maab's soul. A figure shimmers in the dark mists, and he strains to make out the hazy visage. He watches, unable to pick himself up and flee, growing aware of a force holding him where he dropped. The figure grows larger, reminding him of a lazy crocodile until it bumps against the bank ten feet away, and reveals itself to be a boat. It is a tiny, empty, wooden boat with no oars, no rope, and no hints of a person around. He swears the visage he saw was of a person. Wilhelm sways and almost collapses as the weight is lifted from his shoulders. He turns to flee, only to feel as if his body is stuffed full of rocks once more. The infant stares up at him, quietly suckling on her talisman. The tiny moon on her forehead causes him to raise a brow.

"That is new," he says to her with an accusatory tone. The absurdity of him accusing the infant he has been cradling all this time of somehow transforming them into these tattooed vagabonds in the night is not beyond him. They are not in Nodd anymore, that much is known. There is magic here, but it is strange and wild. He turns back to face the boat and narrows his eyes at it.

"Never trust a gift without a giver," he grumbles, taking a cautious step toward the boat. Much to his chagrin, he finds himself unhindered in approaching, but completely hindered in moving away from it. Sighing, he looks at the infant, as if she can give him the answer to this riddle.

"I bet you're enjoying this," he mutters. In the distance, he can hear hounds and men shouting. It is not a language he understands; guttural and growled, much akin to the noise the hounds with them use to communicate. He takes a moment and weighs the risk of the hunting party versus the risk of the boat. How he wishes his brothers were here to tell him what to do. Wilhelm has never been good at thinking solutions through to their conclusion. Rather, he always acts before he thinks. The baying of the hounds draw closer, and the men sound unfriendly. He has had enough of unfriendly men to last him a lifetime.

"Boat it is," he nestles her into the boat and pushes off from the foreign shore. The little boat teeters and totters steadily once they free themselves from the bank. The fog grows thicker, and he keeps yawning. The infant has already returned to slumber as the steady cradle rocks soothingly on the water. There is a sense of peace in the air, in spite of not being able to see more than a few inches in front of his nose. Shifting the infant to the side, he lies down next to her. "At least they cannot shoot an arrow into me from here," chortling at his cleverness. He gazes up at the haunting gray mists that engulf the tiny boat. Silence wraps them as he listens to the hounds and men draw near to the shore and then leave. While he is sure the hunters cannot get to them, he is not going to tempt fate by making superfluous noise. The steady breathing of his tiny traveling companion next to him and the gentle lap of the water against the rocking boat are the only sounds he hears now. Try as he might, he finds his head nodding into the crook of his arm.

"Please do not be a trap," he murmurs to the mist. Giving up the battle, he falls into slumber. His arm drapes over the infant, and his robes providing a comforting warmth to the napping pair.

The tiny boat drifts and rocks along the water; giving the watcher the impression it is a happy little old man teetering as he walks. The sounds of the night fade away into the lapping waves against the wood, along with the heavy breathing of Wilhelm. The minutes pass into hours as it bubbles along its winding path. The fog, thick and damp in the air, does not hinder her sight of them. She no more uses her eyes to see them, as she does her soul. The child radiates like a lighthouse over the sea.

When Aesop first sought her counsel, she called him a madman. He acted like every other Druid that roamed the lands on the other shore. How he even found her island is beyond her comprehension. That had been eons ago. Then he vanished as if she had conjured him right out of the water and it poured back into the lake, which protects the Avalonians. Now, she stands on the cliff, watching the tiny boat approach with his progeny in its soft embrace. The infant is the only one she welcomes. She will deal with the outlander trying to protect her in due time. It was supposed to be Aesop who brought her the child, and even then, he would have known better than to come to her island. He had been frantic in his plea for her help.

"It is a matter of life and death for all of us that you protect her," his words echo in her mind.

Her choice to help is much simpler than that. She is aging, and the infant is powerful. She had cast the bones and burned the sage wraps. Both pointed to the moon and the sword. A great warrior queen dominated the visions. A young woman so fierce that kings bowed to her whim. A frown crinkles the old woman's lips as the tiny boat reaches the shore. Turning and walking down the path, her bare feet make no sound. Her robes of faded blue and silvers, ripple with the light breeze. Her hair is wild and unruly, silvers and grays kissed with hints of ebony stubbornly lingering from a lifetime ago. Her alabaster skin is covered in the runes and symbols of her kind. Teal and blue lines weave over her as if each tattoo on her skin manifested itself and changed on its own whim. Well-worn hands take hold of the edge of the boat and pull it further up the shore, until it will not drift away on its own. Surveying the young man and the infant, she raises both eyebrows in surprise. The resemblance in the features is unmistakable. Canting her head to the side, she admires them fondly. Her anger at Wilhelm's presence fades as she watches his sleeping form still protectively cling to the infant. Reaching into the boat, she gently brushes his hand aside and scoops the infant out. She pulls the small girl to her bosom and coos to her. "Shh, little one. You are safe now," she smiles warmly in the morning light. Easing the swaddling away, she hums a serene tune.

It is enough to rouse Wilhelm from his slumber. At first, he blinks and stretches. Then he remembers the horrific night before. "What? Where? The baby!" He struggles and twists, having forgotten he is on a boat.

The woman ignores him as he starts up like a rocket only to lose his balance. The teetering little boat finally tips him into the icy water and she grins while continuing to coo to the infant. She takes a seat on a nearby tree stump as she waits patiently for him to gather his wits about him.

Like a drenched cat, he drags himself up onto the shore and peels himself out of the robes. His breath is visible on the air, and he is regretting stripping down as soon as he has the robes off.

"You will be fine, boy," she chastises. "Tell me why you did not follow the instructions. You were not to come with her." Blue eyes bore into him, peeling back the layers to see every deep, dark secret he holds.

Growing shy under the scrutiny, he runs his fingers through his mess of brown curly hair and looks for any small piece of familiarity. Even his own skin is foreign to him. Her voice, as clear and sweet as any muse, is speaking to him in a language he does not understand, but he is not about to admit that to her. Furrowing his brow, he mimics her sentence back to her, only his is a question.

She laughs and shakes her head at the young child in her arms, feigning ignorance of him once more.

"Well, at least she did not attack me," Wilhelm grumbles, his eyes darting about to orient himself.

"Attack you," she asks with an incredulous tone in his language. "Young man, you are lucky I do not feed you to the dragons for invading my home uninvited."

"Invade your-. What? I am not invading! There was a boat," he looks around and points dramatically towards it. "That boat! Madame, unhand my," he hesitates, unsure what to call the infant. Damn his brothers for not being here when he needs them.

"Your what? Daughter? Sister? How do I know you did not steal this infant?"

"Steal her?! Now you listen here you old hag, that is my ward and by the stars, I will not see her harmed. Now unhand her this instance and we shall be on our way." His arm gestures wildly in the air as he makes the demand.

The old woman returns her gaze to the child, stands, and walks away, her back to him. The power reeling from the boy is strong and alluring. There may have been a time, in her youth, when such a prize would be worth the price. The infant and he have the same magic. She could feel the infant far more than the boy. There is something about the power the child holds that makes the old woman fear for her. All those born with great power are destined for great suffering.

10

Fairy Who Lives by the Sea

"Stop, you! That is my infant! Hey! Do not walk away from me!"

He rapidly grabs what he can from the boat and discarded robes to pursue after her. No matter how he darts to and fro, he cannot seem to get close enough to her to take back the infant. It is infuriating and taxing, as they climb the cliff via a winding path. It is not until they reach the stone circle at the top of the cliff that he slows in his pursuit. Unlike the rings of standing stones, this is a circular slab with intricate runes and carvings embedded into the crest of the hill overlooking the lake below. As the woman's feet touched the stone, it glows. It is enough to make Wilhelm stare in awe. Rune magic is forbidden in

Nodd. His father had said there was too much power in runes, and the people who wielded them are not to be trifled with. Fear creeps over him and while he wants to run right back down the cliff side and flee, he steps forward to do his duty and protect the child.

"I must insist. She is all I have left." Spoken with sincerity and sadness. "Please," he swallows hard to fight back the tidal wave of emotions ripping through and bites his lip in anxiety.

She stops walking away then and turns to face him across the circle.

He dares to meet her gaze. The stern blue eyes of the wise woman both unsettle and bring peace to his soul. He knows she will not hurt either of them, though he could not explain how he knows this. Her unwavering stare makes him uncomfortable, and he turns his gaze away in defeat. Rubbing his nose to stave off the blubbering his brothers would tease him about, he sniffles and shivers which reminds him that he is in fact bare before her, other than his trousers.

"I am Nimoway, the Lady of the Lake. You are in the kingdom of Avalon. For thousands of years, not a single outlander found their way here that I did not allow. Until your father stepped out of the fountains." Her tone is firm.

Wilhelm feels the guilt of having done something terribly wrong, yet he knows not what it is he has done.

"He asked only for refuge for the infant. This island, and its teachings, are forbidden to men. I cannot allow you to stay. I will grant you respite as reward for escorting her, but only until the moon is full in the sky. At which point you will be sent back to the shore from which you came. The infant stays with me, as per my arrangement with your father."

Wilhelm takes a page out of William's book and nods graciously. His brother always goes on about how the pen is mightier than the sword, and how words cut deeper than any blade forged by mortals. Brute force is not the answer, so he will make every effort to learn what he can about this place and steal the infant away when the time is right.

The old woman does not budge but gives him an impish grin. Almost as if she had read his mind and knows full well what his intentions are. She turns from him again, walking up the stone steps to the temple looming in the distance.

His eyes widen. He has seen this place before, once when he was small enough to be carried. It is several seconds before he pursues after her again. Fear and excitement fill him.

Avalon, she had said. Avalon, the kingdom of water. The Lady of the Lake had been instrumental in helping Aesop create Nodd. Wilhelm cannot remember how, or why, but he remembers this temple. Stumbling along, he finally catches up to her.

"What name has the infant been given," she asks casually, as if she had not just treated him poorly.

His brow furrows, and he does not answer immediately. Names are of monumental importance.

Each named creature has a power only they can wield. No two creatures of Nodd have the exact same name and the wrong name could seal a terrible fate for its owner, but they were not in Nodd any longer. Should he give her another name from this place? Would it matter?

"Morgan," he blurts out suddenly. "Le Fey."

"Fairy who lives by the sea," she replies in amusement. "Morgan le Fey?" she coos in question to the infant.

In response, the baby gurgles, and slobbers over the talisman in her little clutches, completely oblivious to the old woman.

"It is a good name, boy." Stopping at the doorway to the temple, she turns and faces Wilhelm. "This is where we leave you. You cannot enter the temple. If you follow the path down to the stables, Imogen will find you suitable quarters for the time you remain here."

"And the infant?" Wilhelm does not budge from the doorway. He will not abandon the child after all he has witnessed. His heart tells him that all is well here, but his stubborn mind tells him that his time with Morgan is not at an end. How could he abandon her after all the efforts his father went through? A small frown appears on his otherwise jovial countenance. He still wants to know what happened to his brothers and father.

"All will be well, young Wilhelm." Her free hand moves to his shoulder and gives him an uncharacteristically strong squeeze. "She is under my protection now," her tone is soft and motherly.

He can feel the magic flowing into him from her touch, and fights it with all his might. There is a mental struggle between the two. Wilhelm breaks into a sweat as he tries to fend off the command she imposes on him.

Then she smiles, and leans in close, her voice a sweet whisper to him. "You will never overtake me, son of Aesop. I am the beginning and the end of all that your father knows. My magic is older than the tallest tree and stronger than the largest mountain. Now go." The rumble of thunder gives a menacing promise as she forces her will upon Wilhelm.

For a fleeting moment he sees what kind of being she truly is. He has only read about her kind in his father's books. They are legends in Nodd. The very fabrics of all the veins of magic stemmed from her kind. Then they vanished without a trace. Some Noddians even believe Aesop, the Father of Wishes, imprisoned them deep within the confines of the Aesop Nation, and that is where his power came from.

Wilhelm nods in acquiescence. Although his mind is aware of him not wanting to abandon the child, his body jerks its way down the path. His brow drips with sweat as he takes step after step. Screaming internally, he now knows why his father forbade this kind of magic. The helpless feeling of knowing what you are doing and being unable to stop yourself would break lesser minds. He struggles to grip onto anything in his path, only to find his hands will not raise from his sides. His teeth grit and his body trembles as he exerts every ounce of his power into stopping the forward motion. He can feel her eyes on him, watching his struggle. He will not give her the satisfaction of grunting in frustration. He succeeds to a degree and remains frozen in place. It takes all his concentration to keep his body in that spot.

From the doorway, she shakes her head. He could stand there, frozen, until he passed out for all she cares. She eases the door open and slips in, letting it click closed behind her. "See he is fed, bathed, and that he is gone by the full moon," she commands without even looking at two women near the door, swathed in soft blue robes of Grecian homage. Their heads are shaved and the colorful runes that kiss their pale skin are of war and wisdom. Each, adorned with a sword and shield, nod and are out the door without a question. Moving up the stairs on the other side of the room, she sends two young serving girls into a flurry of preparations. They draw her bath, light candles, strip away the clothing from the old woman and the baby, and guide her into the large pool of water that steams. Taking the infant with her, she is careful to wipe away the grime of the little one's adventure, and to ease away the pain of using so much magic in one go. Watching the infant, she leaves her floating in front of her and smiles at the child. "Fairy who lives by the sea," she murmurs softly.

Maelstrom of Emotion

"What do you mean you cannot find her? It is an island. One she does not know how to escape from," the old woman's tone is censorious. Each priestess looks from one to the other, then back up to their mistress in anxious frustration.

"She is quite clever, Milady."

Rubbing her temples, she draws in a heavy sigh. She could no more punish them than catch a moonbeam. Morgan has proven every bit the troublemaker her advisors warned her she would be. "Find her. The ceremony is in three days." She has an inkling as to where the young woman has gotten to, but Morgan Le Fey is nigh impossible to find when she does not wish to be found. "Try not to get hurt this time," she calls to them as they hurry from the room. Turning to face the statue of a motherly figure she shakes her head. "I am sure you are laughing at all of this," her tone is bemused and intimate, like sharing in the confidence of an old friend. The entire island is alive with the news. The Great Hunt has not taken place in most of their lifetimes. This ceremony will choose the next Lady of the Lake. There are rumors of a budding kingdom in the Druid lands, and she knows they will need the vitality and strength of youth to survive against it.

Meanwhile, in the densest part of the forest on the island a young girl is on her hands and knees, her face smudged with mud. Her hair is unruly and unkempt as it escapes the single braid down her back. Bare toes wriggle as she works meticulously through the plant life before her. "Why can I not use magic to make them glow and pick them?" She does not look away from the task, as if she is arguing with herself. Her delicate fingers pluck up the little mushrooms with finesse and deposit them into the basket next to her. Moving on, she begins her search again in the next patch of underbrush.

"Because, Morgan, magic is not the solution to all problems. Having a strong back and swift hands are just as important as the ability to bend reality to your whims. Some day, you may find yourself in a situation where showing you can wield magic is not the wisest answer, and simply doing it yourself is." His voice is both irritated and amused. He watches her work her way through the patch from his perch in the old tree he calls home these days. It is high enough to let him see anything approaching with enough time to hide. The tree is ancient and rotted by all appearances. Its bark had sloughed off and revealed the ashen trunk long ago. Its leaves barely bloom these days, but the branches are strong and its crown is a twisted, crooked maze of barren limbs. At the base, a large gaping hole leads down under the tree and into where the roots once held strong, leaving a large cavern underground.

"I think it is you are just too lazy to pick your own, Archimedes. I would be done by now if I used the spell. Then we could be learning something new." Petulance and defiance radiates from her as she holds no belief that there will never be a time where magic cannot solve the situation. She does not stop picking the mushrooms manually.. She learned that lesson the hard way when she was little. Archimedes does not cater to tantrums and does not keep her company unless she does as he asks.

"I am, and it is a valuable lesson. Not those, pay attention, silly girl," he hoots back at her.

She looks down and frowns. They look close to the ones in her basket, and she does not believe him at first, so she brushes away the vines growing over them, only to see what he means. Under them are dead little slugs. Their slimy tails are curled sharply from the cramping of their insides until they were no more. Leaning back on her calves she looks up at the owl. "Tell me again, why do I have to be the Huntress?" She changes subjects without warning and is staring straight up at the large barn owl scolding her.

He throws his wings out and hoots with great frustration. "Morgan le Fey, you know well enough why. Nimoway chose you. You are the most powerful and the cleverest of girls. Who better than you to lead all of Avalon?" He pities her. There is nothing about this matter that he agrees with. He has wanted nothing more than to whisk her away and take her back to Nodd. Until the blood moon was in the sky. He had been soaring high over the island when he felt the strong and steady pull of his kind. The draw of Noddian magic is distinct from the draw of the Druid magic. He flew as far as the island's magic would let him and that is when he saw the man, older now, but no mistaking him; Jakob Grimm was alive and well. If Jakob had not returned to Nodd, then it was still not safe. He did not approach him, but made sure to be seen. He has been making preparations since. "Listen, my little fairy, there is something important I need to tell you." He pushes off his perch and easily glides down to settle on the fallen tree next to this little meadow.

She swipes her hand across her face again, trying to brush hair out of her eyes, but she nods. She shifts her weight around to sit comfortably and does not retort about dumb rituals.

He had been waiting her whole life to reveal himself and tell her the truth. It would risk everything. The moment he reverted the spell Nimoway would know that her command had not worked. He fluffs his chest and shifts uncomfortably.

"What is it, Archimedes?" she reaches up to gently brush her fingers along his chest and soothe him. Her eyes are a dark blue, like a clear star filled sky just after sunset. Her skin is pale with a hint of olive. All the other young women here are covered in runes, but her skin is relatively free of them. A tiny crescent moon graces her forehead, and the hints of vined-together runes at her temples, snaking up into her hairline, are the only hints that she is Avalonian.

Over the years, with intense eavesdropping and quite a severe amount of thievery from the temple's library, he has learned the meaning of the runes on their skin. Unlike the other girls, she does not gain further runes. He guesses it is a testament to her power. The runes are the key to the magic for the other girls, but Morgan simply need utter the word, or pass the thought, and her will is done.

"You can tell me anything, I'm your little fairy, remember?"

"Fiddlesticks," he curses. As if the other young woman approaching intentionally interrupted them, she comes into his line of sight before he can tell Morgan the truth. "Not today, little fairy. Come back tomorrow night and I will tell you then." He pushes off and flies back to his perch high in the mazed bough.

Morgan frowns, and looks from him, then to the direction of the now quickly approaching young woman. "What do you want?"

"The Lady of the Lake sends for you. She said I am to

bring you home, even if it means cursing you to obey." The other young woman, Elaine of Uther, gives a malicious smile. She very much wants to have a reason to curse Morgan.

"I would like to see a fat cow like you try to curse me. Why not go chew on some grass instead?" Morgan flicks her hand in dismissal.

The other girl begins to turn, then stop and jerks in a horribly awkward fashion as she fights off Morgan's hex.

The owl hoots angrily, chastising Morgan.

Then, as if the universe agrees with Archimedes that Morgan needs to be brought down a peg, she is moving to her feet and Elaine is the one standing still.

"Stop it!" Morgan snarls at Elaine.

"It is not me! You started this. Release me at once!."

Morgan comes alongside Elaine and takes her hand.

"Make it stop!" Elaine sounds more frightened than angry this time, and Morgan is breathing hard as she tries to will herself to move away from Elaine.

Another angry hoot and the two girls are jerked toward the temple.

"Morgan! This is not funny! Stop it!" Elaine tries to wrench her hand free but cannot. Morgan draws in a deep breath and struggles fiercely against the control that is washing over the pair.

"I... I cannot," Morgan finally whimpers in defeat. "I ... I do not know who is doing this." She looks over her shoulder, to see if she can still see Archimedes, but he appears to have vanished in the canopy. Tears well in her eyes, and she looks back to Elaine, who is crying as well.

"Stop your blubbering. See if you can walk to the temple."

"You are one to talk." Elaine mutters as she takes a step, then another in the direction of the temple. When she gets at arm's length from Morgan, she can move no more, anchored by the firm grip on the other woman's hand.

Morgan tries to move away from her, only to find her feet cannot move at all, like she has sunk into quicksand. This only results in her squirming in place. Finally, she moves close to Elaine, and finds herself free to step again. Another step, and they are side by side.

Moments later, after trying to escape each other, the two are walking together toward the temple. Neither girl can let go of the other's hand and they can only follow the path back to the steps at the main entrance, where Nimoway is waiting with crossed arms and a raised brow.

Once they stop, Morgan jerks her hand in frustration and is surprised when it comes free from Elaine.

Elaine wastes no time in capitalizing on her freedom and flees from Morgan and Nimoway. She will get Morgan for this, even if it is the last thing she does.

"Morgan, you are making an enemy of Elaine. You would be wise to keep her close. She is likely to be your dragon master when the time comes."

"Assuming I even participate in the Hunt, Mother."

Morgan rolls her eyes.

Before she can even finish the dramatic teenage action, Nimoway is standing right before her and has her by the chin, lifting her off the ground as if Morgan is a chalice, not a teenage girl. "Listen to me, daughter of mine," her tone is feral. "I have had enough of you shirking your duties. You will perform in the hunt, or I will send you to the Druids with nothing but the clothes on your back. No magic, no memory, no name. Do you understand?"

Morgan's eyes narrow and while she is terrified, she is not about to show her mother fear. Her cheeks flush as red as cherries, and her fists clench. There is a lightning strike in the distance, and the thunder booms loud enough to cause the ground to shake. The wind, which had been non-existent, raises to a furious gale around the two of them. It whips Morgan's face with her hair, and Nimoway looks more like an ethereal ghost than an old woman standing before her daughter.

Nimoway does not back down, holding Morgan over her, determined to put the girl in her place. She lets Morgan rage. The skies open up with rain and hail crashing against the two of them hard enough to leave bruises on their skin.

A Truth Spoken

The other women near them flee for shelter. Another bolt of lightning strikes, lighting the ground not far from the pair on fire. Nimoway does not flinch. She watches Morgan's eyes shift from a serene blue to an inky black. The rage and maliciousness that Nimoway has tried to slowly lock away has released itself and is threatening to tear into them at any second.

"Morgan le Fey," Nimoway calls in a booming and firm voice. "This is not our way. Listen to your heartbeat. Listen to my voice. Come back before the storm overcomes you."

The young woman lets out a cry of frustration and anger. Struggling in her mother's grasp, she flails and claws at Nimoway's wrist to no avail. Nimoway is the rock the wild wave of Morgan crashes against.

"I am the beginning and end of all you know. You cannot hurt me, but you can hurt the others." Nimoway's hair crowns her glowing visage in the winds of the storm. "Your friends, your teachers, even your beloved Archimedes."

The creature of a woman in Nimoway's grasp turns her inky black gaze down to her and looks astonished.

"Listen to my voice. Fight the darkness. Come back." There is another crack of lightning, which reduces a temple gargoyle to nothing more than dust. The boom of thunder that follows causes her old bones to ache, but she holds firm.

"That is enough, Morgan le Fey," his voice is furious, louder than Nimoway's and it is not a request. "You will not use your power to bully your way out of your responsibilities. Calm the storm before I calm it for you." Behind Morgan, in all his splendor, stands Wilhelm Grimm. Dressed in robes, and wild looking himself, he holds a satchel strap. He dares not move as he believes he might have to dodge both women. Men are not allowed on the island of Avalon, and Morgan has only ever seen him as Archimedes. His words seem to have hit home. Between the startling realization her mother knew of her secret friend, and that friend is at the temple yelling at her draws her away from the darkness in her soul.

The hailing rain stops, followed by the wind dying down. The clouds in the sky give way to the bright and sunny afternoon it was prior to this exchange. Morgan trembles and sobs in her mother's grasp. Nimoway lowers her to her feet, but keeps firm hold of the younger woman, gazing deep into her face. She watches Morgan's eyes as she shifts back from the monster to the maiden. Her other hand flies out to her side and she holds Wilhelm in place, not sure which to deal with first.

Wilhelm plays his part and does not move, but is no more controlled by Nimoway than he could be by Morgan. Morgan is not the only child of Nodd who has learned the ways of the Avalonians. When he sees Morgan swoon, and he is to her in the blink of an eye, forgetting the farce of letting Nimoway believe she has control over him. He scoops her up in his strong arms and he looks at Nimoway. Holding the girl protectively to him, he expects Nimoway to do something foolish and emotional in this moment and hopes his Morgan shaped shield will stave off a reprimand for breaking her laws. "I told you I was not leaving her," he finally grumbles, not daring to look away from those crystalline eyes.

The guards finally burst forth to surround them. Six massive women point their swords at Wilhelm and Morgan.

Nimoway raises her hand to stop them and keeps watching him. She had suspected as much. Since he had kept to the forest and stayed out of sight, she had let him linger. It has been good for Morgan to learn things the temple cannot teach her. Now that he has revealed himself, she will be forced to banish him a second time. Their laws are absolute. No man can stay on this island; it says nothing of male animals. She motions for him to enter the temple, which elicits gasps and whispers from the onlookers that now are coming out from their hiding places. This entire spectacle irritates her.

Wilhelm turns and moves up the stairs with the unconscious girl and frowns as he reaches the top of the stairs, knowing they were about to forbid him from entering. He is going to have to leave her without saying goodbye and is preparing an argument just for that case when Nimoway steps around him and eases the door open.

Even the guards take pause. No man has ever set foot inside of the temple. The gathered onlookers shift, ill at ease, and the whispers quiet down as they collectively hold their breath. Breaking the laws could bring evil upon them.

He lowers his head in deference and steps into the massive building. Carrying Morgan the entire way, he gently sets her on the pile of pillows and blankets that are her bed. His fingers gently brush her hair from her face as he looks fondly at her more akin to a father than a brother. His heart is breaking as this is the last day he will probably ever see her, and she can never know why. "I have to forget this place," he says quietly.

"That is not necessary," Nimoway replies. With a wave of her hand, the three of them are left alone in this room.

"It is. I now know why Father forbade us from getting into that boat. I am a beacon, drawing those who look for her." Wilhelm runs his fingers through his hair in an anxious motion.

Nimoway says nothing in response. Even she cannot deny that someone is looking for Morgan. The two men that have tested the lake have proven persistent. Unable to discern their origin, or their intent, she fears they may be the culprits he is afraid will find Morgan. She leaves him by Morgan's side and steps into an antechamber before returning with two little mugs and a small pot of heated water. "You cannot leave without saying goodbye, Wilhelm. You saw what happened today. Imagine if you just abandon her." She opens the little container and pinches leaves between her thumb and forefinger to drop into each mug. Repeating the process with another container in each of the mugs, she then fills them with water.

"Come, sit. She will not wake for some time," she settles into a chair next to the table where she has prepared the tea. Stirring each mug with her finger, she offers him one, and takes the other.

With reluctance he collapses into the chair opposite Nimoway. Eyeing the tea, he takes it, but does not drink.

Nimoway laughs genuinely, and it sounds musical to Wilhelm. "You fool, I am not drugging you. It will merely calm your nerves. Altering one's mind takes far more than herbs and honey." She jests about what he has asked of her, but does not deny she can do it. With a small sigh, she looks back to Morgan. "Her power will be unrivaled once she takes the mantle. I am having my doubts on passing it on to her as he temper gets worse."

"She must take it. Your time is ending and will return home soon. If your histories are correct, your other half has already returned and is waiting for you."

Twice in one day, Nimoway is completely surprised by Wilhelm. "I see that you have decided to violate all of our laws then." She sips her tea to cover up the anger and fear at being told she is dying. He is not wrong. She has kept the entropy of her body from showing. With each harvest moon since the child arrived, she wanes in power and presence. Her soul is tired. Both hands curl around the mug, and it gives her the youthful appearance of a child enjoying a sweet treat.

He cannot help himself in smiling at her. She comforts him, even with the abrupt manner in which she treats him. He could get lost for hours talking with her, he is sure. Her knowledge, her tricks, and everything about this place fascinates him. Sadness fills him at having to leave what has been home for the past fifteen years. As Morgan's sixteenth birthday approaches, he fears for her safety.

Meanwhile, Morgan's dreams are filled with shadows. Figures chant around her and the winds howl. Fear and sadness overwhelm her with every breath. She stands alone in the stones as she casts to the wind. It causes her to gasp awake and sit upright, looking around her like a startled rabbit.

"Shh," Wilhelm coos as he comes to her and brushes her hair back from her brow. "It was only a nightmare, my little fairy."

"Who... Archimedes?" Looking at him she shrinks in fear.

He nods in affirmation, not pursuing her; nor does he correct the name she uses. The less she knows of him, the better, Nimoway and he had decided.

When he does not leave, and does not harm her, she settles down, looking from him to Nimoway. "What happened?"

"You behaved like a spoiled girl, that is what happened," he scolds. "Morgan, I was trying to explain to you this morning. You are about to take on a great deal of responsibility. With that comes sacrifices," he hesitates briefly before a big grin cracks his face, "and benefits. Nimoway is dying. She must name an heir for Avalon to survive."

"What? Dying? Mother, is this true? What has he done to you?" Morgan looks from Wilhelm to Nimoway for confirmation, eyes wide and head shaking in disbelief.

Brotherly Love

Nimoway joins the pair on the bed of pillows and gently takes Morgan's hand. The vision of an elderly woman dissipates to the frail and hallowed looking soul of Nimoway's true visage. Her skin is shriveled to the bone, her hair wispy shadows of the wild mane. Her eyes are no longer the soft hue of blue that reflects the lake, but a dark silvery sea of stars. The vision lasts for a heartbeat before she is back to the timeless old woman. "We are all dying, Morgan. Some slower than others. Your coming was foretold long before you were stardust in your mother's heart. I had hoped to have more time with you. To see you grow into the Lady of the Lake, and to rule Avalon, but the stars did not align as such."

Morgan feels as though she is about to vomit. This morning it was just her mother being angry at her insolence. Now, she finds out her mother is dying. Tears cling to the corners of her eyes, and she shakes her head in disbelief again. The night sky swiftly darkens with black clouds heavy with rain. The rain drops plunk against the stone walls in solidarity with the young mistress who summoned them. "I'm not ready. Not yet. Can we not do something for you?"

"You *are* the something, sweet girl." Nimoway pulls Morgan close to her and rocks her gently. "Life and Death are one, Morgan. You cannot live without dying and you cannot die without living. When you finish the Great Hunt, I will become part of you and you will inherit my magic, and my soul will go home to be made whole. Without this ritual, I linger here and suffer." She kisses Morgan on her temple. "You are anything but cruel. I trust you would not let me suffer."

"No," a hiccup escapes Morgan's lips as she manages to reign in her emotions. "I would not." Her gaze settles on Wilhelm. "And you will be with me, right?"

Wilhelm bites his lip and looks down, fingering the pilled blanket on her bed. "I cannot stay, little fairy. I am needed elsewhere." He braces for the backlash he is sure to come.

"What? Why? I need you here. You belong here," her protests are petulant and demanding. "I command that you stay." Raised by the Lady of the Lake, she feels entitled to command everyone around her.

He snaps his gaze up to meet her eye to eye. "You do

not own me, Morgan le Fey. You would do well to remember you own no soul but your own. People are not property." He sounds very much like Aesop and can hear his father's voice roaring in his ears. "I am leaving to protect you. That is all you need to know." Wilhelm stands and moves away from the women before he changes his mind.

Morgan lunges to reach for him, only to be held back by Nimoway. "No!" She cries louder and the room shakes with the crash of thunder that echoes her.

He whips around and points his finger at her. "That is enough of that. You cannot destroy everything around you with the weather when you do not get your way. Now stop behaving like a fool Hen and come give me a last hug goodbye."

His chiding words and widened eyes catch Morgan by surprise at how closely he resembles Archimedes in human form that it snaps her right out of her concentration.

Nimoway feels the thread of magic that the boy used to usurp her tirade and watches with fascination. Wilhelm is such a dramatic boy. He could have easily slipped away with none of this drama while the Great Hunt took place. Instead, he chose to work her into a fit, only to swoop in to calm her down.

Morgan goes to him.

He pulls her into a tight hug and kisses her temple. Breathing in her sweet berry scents mixed with the earthy scents of mud and grass, he can feel her heart beating fast as he holds her tight. He fears his heart will burst if he lingers longer, and finally steps back. "We will meet again, someday, my little fairy. Do not come looking for me."

Tears streak down Morgan's cheeks as her arms collapse back around her, silently warring with herself to keep from binding the man to her. Her eyes widen and jaw slacks open as he clicks his heels three times and vanishes in a sparkling poof of stardust. Blinking in shock, she thrusts her hand forward to see if he truly disappeared, then looks back at her mother for an explanation.

"It is called fast travel," she replies. "And he is an ass for using it."

Morgan looks at Nimoway as if the woman has grown a second head. Then, gathering up her robes, she clicks her heels together three times. There is a flicker, and Nimoway's brows furrow as she hopes that man had not taught her another bad habit. The girl is already hard enough to control, and giving her the freedom to travel as she wills is dangerous and reckless.

Another set of clicks, and another flicker, but Morgan stops abruptly. She turns and vomits into the chamber pot. The abuse of magic exacting its toll on her.

Satisfied that Morgan has not broken through the wards inhibiting her magic, she pushes up off the bed. "You should finish your studies for the hunt. I need rest."

In a cloud of stardust, Wilhelm comes tumbling down the hill to land with a grunt at the base of the very stones that brought Morgan and him to this place. A pair of over-sized hands clamp onto his shoulders and he is hoisted to his feet as if he were nothing more than a sack of potatoes.

"Unhand me," he barks in the Druid tongue, as his hands rise to brush off the brute that would dare to manhandle him in this fashion.

The other man laughs in response.

There is something familiar about him. No matter how Wilhelm twists and turns he cannot seem to get free of the man holding him, as if the man knows his every move before he makes it. Then Wilhelm turns himself into an owl.

The comedy and urgency of the man attempting to contain a full-grown barn owl makes his companions laugh and give themselves away.

Wilhelm can feel himself breaking free. Just a few more well-placed claw swipes and he could soar away.

"Brother, calm down," the man growls as Wilhelm breaks free, only for the other men to throw a fisherman's net over him.

All his flapping and flailing does is tangle the net around him until he is forced to the ground. Hooting and struggling he returns to his human form. "I am not your brother," he growls.

"Well, I am sure our father would box your ears if he heard such nonsense." Jakob's grinning face comes into full view and Wilhelm's eyes widen. He stills, and the overwhelming sadness he felt in abandoning Morgan is now replaced with the joy of finding his brother.

"Where is William? Hans?"

He attempts to extricate himself, only to tangle the surrounding net more.

The men with Jakob erupt into laughter again.

Wilhelm, indignant, finally succumbs to being entangled before calming his thoughts and wriggling himself free. Standing up, he dusts himself off and takes another look at the mob of men. His brow furrows. Druids, all of them. The burly and heathen men of war, as Nimoway describes them, look every inch the barbarians they are, Jakob included. While Wilhelm holds the markings and robes, his figure is wily and wiry. He looks more like a boy than a man next to these brutes. His brother's hand clamps again firmly on his shoulder and he grimaces with pain.

"Come, I have much to tell you. Where have you been hiding all these years? What is beyond the horizon on the lake? You must tell me why you are flying around as a barn owl." He guides Wilhelm away from the stones towards the horses tied nearby.

"You have not answered my questions, Jakob."

"In good time, brother. What happened to the infant?" Jakob's look is queer and sinister.

It is enough to give Wilhelm pause in mounting his horse. Holding the reins in one hand, and patting the horse, he keeps his eyes locked with Jakob. "In good time, *brother*," he mounts giving no further answers. He could curse Nimoway for not making him forget. She put them all in danger with her arrogance. He will just have to do it himself once he is alone. As they ride along, the night sky is bright and shimmers above them. It reminds him of the night sky in Nodd. How he longs to be there now, nestled comfortably in his harem of followers. Looking ahead, he keeps to the steady walk the rest of the party has adopted and he watches as the path winds into the forest. None of them talk, and there is a heaviness about them that makes him shift in his saddle. Subtly, he ties his reins into the horse's mane as he prepares to take flight should this prove a trap of some sort. A small grin breaks across his face as he chastises himself mentally for being an old distrusting hermit.

As the night wanes to the hours before dawn, he sighs with relief to see the small village come into view. It is remarkably similar to the village on Avalon island, only there are men and women bustling about in the wee hours of the morning. The smell of fermented drink, and roasted animal fill his nostrils. Approaching, they each dismount and tie off their horses. The others disappear into their own huts and tents, leaving Wilhelm alone with Jakob.

The pair walk in silence to the building Jakob has called home for some time now. Easing back the leather in the doorway, he reveals a warm and well-lit circular room. At a tiny wooden table, a man sits hunched over, pouring over scrolls and texts.

"William!" Wilhelm is to him in a flash and draws him into a hug.

"Posh! Will you unhand me! You smell like an animal! Where have you been? What did you do with the infant? Where is Hans?" His questions berate Wilhelm as if they had just parted and Wilhelm is the culprit of everything that has gone wrong.

"Happy to see you too, brother," he continues to avoid the whereabouts of the infant. "If Hans is not with you, then where could he be? He has not been with me all this time."

The three exchange looks. Accusation and fear weigh heavy in the silence until finally Wilhelm breaks the tension.

"Maybe he is with father," he says meekly. There is heavy doubt in his tone. He had been so reckless that night that he did not think of the repercussions of his actions. Now, what should be a time of joyous reunion, is filled with awkward silence. He looks from one brother to the other and the pitted knot in his stomach pulls tighter.

What has happened while he was gone?

"Father is missing," William finally snaps.

"William..." Jakob warns.

"Do not take that tone with me. You know as well as I do that he knows all about the unnamed heir and is keeping it from us. For all we know, he murdered Hans and abandoned us to this filthy hell." William leaps from his seat and moves angrily towards Wilhelm.

Jakob plants himself between them, facing William.

Wilhelm's eyes widen and he shakes his head in disbelief at William as his brother starts after him again and is staved off by Jakob's sturdy hand.

"He is our brother. He would not murder Hans or

keep from us the one thing that would make Nodd whole again." Jakob's voice rings in his ears, muddying the sound of the crackling fire in the background.

"*Run*," The soft murmur is pitched for Wilhelm's ear alone and he blinks as the word cuts through the fog growing in his ears.

The Fog of War

Wilhelm's head jerks to the right, expecting to see Nimoway there. Instead, all he is greeted with is a wash basin on a stand, full of water. The water ripples softly in the still room.

"*Run. Now,*" her voice commands again as if it comes from the ripples of water.

Wilhelm stumbles back a step, unnoticed by his brothers who are engaged in a quite dramatic argument. His brow furrows, and he studies them, still easing away from them while looking at their body language and their mannerisms. These two are not William and Jakob at all.

Who are these men?

He turns and runs. His feet move fast and sure as he

heads for the edge of camp. Not looking back, and not caring who sees him, he runs hard and fast. Cries of alarm raise behind him and he puts his head forward to run faster, leaping over the tiny stone wall at the edge of the village.

He stumbles as he lands and gasps for air. He throws his arms wide, takes one step, then another, until he is flapping his arms frantically, rising higher and higher as a barn owl once more. The harder he pushes, the higher he soars. Arrows whistle by him. Banking hard, he feels one rip at his wing feathers. He manages to get over the tree canopy and beyond their sight. Horse hooves beat behind him, and he keeps flying, heading back to the stones visible on the hill near the lake. He could fly back to the island. He knows the way. If he could only get through the fog.

I am sorry, son of Aesop.

Nimoway's voice sounds melancholy in his head. The fog engulfs the shore, racing towards him. Thick and damp, he realizes too late that she is shielding him from their attacks but also preventing him from returning. At the bottom of the hill, he plummets, transforming back into a human. "No," he begs. "Please let me come home. I will protect her. Please. I take it back. Do not do this."

From the mists, a woman appears so beautiful that even the stars above dim in jealousy. Her hair, raven in color, ripples down her sides and back. Her skin is as pale as the moon and as radiant as new fallen snow in the morning sun. Her fingers splay out and the mists form about them, hiding them from his pursuers.

"Do not do this, I beg you. I take it back." Tears well in his eyes as fear grips his heart. Her hand takes his, and he stands, following her like a bridegroom to his bride, and the pair move up the hill to the stones.

"She is all I have left. She is everything to me."

She leads him to the center of the stone circle.

He can hear the men barking orders their horses neighing in the distance. The sounds of the impostor Grimms barking orders fills his ears. He cannot look away from the woman before him. His chest is heavy, and he gasps for air feeling like he is drowning in the mists swirling around them at the top of the hill. Tears stream down his cheeks, and he shakes his head no. No matter how hard he tries he cannot break free of her.

"In your heart she will remain. Forgotten love is your pain. No name shall she hold. No image will be bold," she paints a daub of rabbit's blood on his forehead.

"From the highest mountain to the deepest sea. Search you may, but never will she be," his eyes roll into the back of his head as the memories of Morgan le Fey are singed from his memories.

"Her name ever slipping your tongue. Your fondness fades like a song. Home and heart torn asunder. Avalon forgotten like distant thunder. This I bestow as my last gift ere you go." She places both hands on his head and pulls him forward, kissing his forehead where she daubed the blood.

Wilhelm, sobbing in her grasp, jerks and is ensconced in shimmering light. His memories of Morgan and her whereabouts fog over, lost to the mists that protect the island. Once his body quits trembling from the force of magic, he stares blankly at Nimoway. His heart feels empty and hollow. He knows this witch has taken something from him, and the ache in his heart gnaws at him like a rabid wolf. His features droop and it is as if she sucked the very life out of him.

She sheds no tears, but her heart is leaden with the pain of what she had to do. She had hoped he would not have needed this protection. She lets his hand slip from hers, and he slowly turns toward the stone in the center.

"Think of them, and you will find them," she encourages. "They are safe, all of them, but you must go now. Before you are found."

With his back to her, he squares his shoulders and grunts. He wants to wring her neck, and force her to give him back what she took. Her chanted words echo in his mind louder than a roaring wind, taunting him. He will never forgive this witch for her curse. When he finally turns his glare over his shoulder, she is no longer there. There is only mist around him. He blinks slowly, looking much as the owl he had been for years. Had he imagined the whole thing? A sense of urgency nags at him, but all he can remember is that he wanted to get to the lake. Why would he want to get to the lake? The sense of danger fills him as he hears his name called through the mists by unknown entities.

"William, Jakob, and Hans," he murmurs as he turns to the stone before him. "William, Jakob, and Hans," he says once more, with more authority. He closes his eyes and steps forward, hands up. He chants the names of his three brothers like a protective mantra. His entire body burns with energy as he steps into the stone.

Howling winds burst forth from the stones, sending the Druids chasing him ass over teakettle as the mists dissipate. The pretenders stare at the traces of stardust settling silently around the center stone in shock. Wilhelm has slipped through their fingers.

William shudders and shakes to give way to a wild beast of a woman, ebony eyes to match ebony hair. Madness clings to her person like leaves to a tree.

Jakob is much less dramatic in his shift, the visage simply melts away to reveal a large man, well-kept and meticulous. He stands as the polar opposite of his feminine counterpart.

"You let him get away," she cackles. "Oh, Law will be furious. You failed to capture Aesop, and now you failed to capture his sons." She is beside herself with joy because Order will suffer for this.

"You failed as well, wife," his tone is biting and crisp to her singsong madness.

"Killjoy," she mutters and the two of them vanish into the mists as if they are born of it. The Druids scatter for the far woods, freed from their grip.

In the distance, the sound of horses can be heard. Not the wild and free-roaming horses of the Druids, but the steady pace of soldiers and men. The sun is rising in the east, and the fog from the lake gives way to a beautifully haunting morning. Horns blow in announcement of the knights' approach, their king triumphant and proud in the center. "Make camp here. Tend to the wounded. Rest," the king decrees upon reaching the large empty field.

Within a few hours, the entire field becomes a city of tents, with women and boys fetching water for cooking and healing. Knights strip out of their armor with the assistance of their squires. The wounded are being cared for near the water, while the war council meets further inland.

The young king, no more than a boy himself, enjoys a soak in his tub after days of travel. They are no more near the end of the war than they were yesterday, but he could at least afford his men this break. Their victory three days prior allowed distance between him and the invading army. He wishes sorely for that old wise man to return. Merlin's magic had been key to the battle. Whatever that black liquid was, it was enough to turn the tide in that bloody mess.

"We should be pressing on. What if they regroup and follow us?" One of his advisors hisses from the next tent.

"Then we shall give them another thumping, as the likes they had three days prior."

He smiles at that retort. That burly old knight could fight in his sleep and be happy.

"We should have pursued them and crushed them all under the might of Pendragon," a third voice corrects the other two.

The young king sinks under the water, wanting to

drown them out, only to find they are getting louder and angrier.

Why can they never agree on a single course of action? Why do I always have to choose?

He lets them linger on in their bickering for several minutes while he scrubs the grime away. Finally, he steps out of the tub to pull his robes about him and runs his fingers through his unruly golden curls. He looks more like a lion than a dragon, he surmises. The old wizard will find that hilarious, that he compares himself to a lion.

"Perhaps we take a few minutes to enjoy the victory, replenish our strength with food and ale, then talk our next steps. There are grieving widows out there, along with orphaned boys and wounded warriors. Without our people, we are nothing. Now go," he snaps to the gathering of men.

Their bickering stops long enough to see who spoke, then each bow with respect and glare at their counterparts. They give way to young ladies bringing him meat, fruit, and ale.

He has little eyes for women these days and summarily dismisses them as well. He studies the map sprawled out on the posts in the ground. Since his uncle's passing, all Lloegyr has been in an uproar of who shall be king. With no heir, there is no lineage. Arthur is the next eligible relative, but as a boy himself. Were it not for Merlin, he would have been murdered long ago. Whatever the old man did to the others makes them believe he is king, as if it is their destiny to

hints of flickering fires across the water. The day is as clear as the waters below them. Whatever magic her mother uses to keep the island hidden she will know soon enough. This gift gives them the advantage of seeing their enemies without being seen, but she no more fears the world of man than a child does a toy.

"You have three days to hunt the white doe. Fail this task and the crops will not grow. Trees will not bear fruit. The fields will wilt in the sun, and the island suffers. The burden is on the three of you to learn to use your skills as one for all of Avalon."

That snaps Morgan from her stupor. There had been nothing said about working together. Until this moment, she and Elaine had been competing for this. Elaine's stunned look back to Morgan says Morgan is not alone in this thought. The third, Isolder, tries to stifle her giggle with a cough.

"Together," Nimoway commands from her throne. "No ruler survives without her people, Morgan. You need Elaine's keen mind and sharp skills to help protect you. You need Isolder's healing touch and kind heart to guide you. They need your power and your strength to lead them. Our lives are woven together like tapestries. When one of you fails, you all fail. When one succeeds, you all succeed." She eases of her throne and makes her way down the stone steps to the three girls who turn to kneel before her.

Morgan frowns as Nimoway is barely standing on her own. She cannot see the true form of her mother, but she knows something has happened, and it is worse today than before. As Nimoway rests her hand on Morgan's head, she can feel the power waning from her faster. She wants to pull her mother close and hug her tight, to will strength into her.

Nimoway chants softly in the Druid tongue, giving each girl the final gifts they need to conquer their prey. A bow with a single arrow is set before each girl.

The other women chant and bang the drums to signal the beginning of the Hunt. They are raucous and terrifying to both those who know what they hear and to those who do not. Their very existence depends on the three maidens kneeling before the Lady today.

Morgan can feel their fear, their excitement, and the beating of their hearts with the steady drum. The sounds of the courtyard are drowned out by the deafening roar of Elaine and Isolder's hearts next to her. All three girls gasp in surprise at the silence as they are transported. When their vision clears, they are kneeling together in the middle of a meadow, the temple nowhere to be seen.

"Right, I'm going to catch that doe. See you in two days," Elaine chirps and snatches up her bow and arrow. She starts to walk off in the direction she believes the doe would most likely be.

"Elaine, you heard the Lady. We are to work together," Isolder scolds. She reaches down to pick up her bow. "Besides, you have not looked for tracks. You are going the wrong way. See here," she points to the trampled grass and muddy hoof prints.

"I do not need your foolish ways. I can smell them.

They are this way."

Morgan is left standing in the middle, frowning. If she chooses Elaine, Isolder will think she has no faith in her skills. If she chooses Isolder, Elaine will think it is to pick a fight. Morgan chews against her lower lip in worry, watching the two of them grow further apart. If it were up to her, she would sit right there and wait for dusk, when the animals are more active. It will be easier to get sight of the doe before she gets wind of the girls.

"Stop," she commands. "Come back. We need to be smart about this, so we do not get too tired we cannot fire our arrows." At first, neither girl responds to her. She narrows her eyes and there is a rumble of thunder in the distance.

Isolder stops then and looks back at Morgan, fear in her gaze. She had witnessed the scene in the courtyard the day prior. It was terrifying and destructive, and they are in an open field.

Elaine shakes her head. "Just because you can make thunder and lightning, does not mean you can dictate what we do here."

"I am telling you, Elaine, we are going to end up walking for hours with no reward if we move now. We should wait. Let the animal come to us," Morgan takes an exaggerated breath to quell her temper. "If I am wrong, at dusk, we will follow your way."

This wins a huff from Isolder. "Her way? She could not smell her way out of a chamber pot!"

Morgan cuts her a look to silence her, but it is too

late.

Elaine moves with all the grace of a warrior until she is face-to-face with Isolder. "Say that to my face, you herb picker." Her bow is in one hand, the arrow resting against it, ready to be drawn.

"Herb picker?! At least I am not always covered in dragon dung!" Isolder's high-pitched shriek carries across the field.

Morgan rolls her eyes and moves to get between them before they hurt each other. "Stop! We are supposed to be working together. Ow!"

The two girls have dropped their bows and arrows to claw at each other. Their naked bodies collide with Morgan's in a flurry of long flowing hair, rune covered bodies, and squawking noises in the battle to determine their pecking-order. Three teenage girls who have been competing their entire lives for the chance to be the next Lady are now venting those frustrations out on each other.

Nimoway, from her perch, watches with dismayed amusement as flashes of her own Hunt flit through her memory. She owes Imogen two silver for the girls holding out until they were away from the temple to start bickering. Fear and doubt creep into her mind that they may not work it out. Morgan could end the fight easily with her abilities and force her will on the two others. She is proud that it is not the case, as Morgan is merely getting it out of her system just like the others. It might not be such a dire situation after all.

In short order, the girls will learn the truth of the Hunt, and finding the white doe will be the least of their concerns. She has faith they will learn their lessons in time, trusting they will do the right thing she will return tomorrow to see if they are ready. She does not see the other onlooker in the tree line.

Arthur had had enough of his bickering advisers and slipped away to gather his thoughts. Merlin had told him that often the best plans came when in the woods. He is standing stock still, eyes wide, and mouth agape at the sight that greets him. If those were the kinds of "best thoughts" Merlin meant, he would need to wander alone in the woods more often. Three wood nymphs are brawling in the field like the barbaric Druids. That is all he can figure they are, since they are without clothing and covered in odd script. At least until he hears them screaming at each other in the Druid tongue. Their words are off from the ones he knows, but it is still the same guttural sounds of those barbarians. That means only one thing: Druid priestesses. His hand rests on the handle of his dagger as he hugs tighter to the tree.

"Spoiled princess! I bet you cannot even cast the bones," Elaine bites into Morgan's arm, which results in Morgan growling in pain and punching Elaine's face.

Isolder is trying to crawl out of the fray, her eye swelling closed, and her nose bleeding while the two stronger girls continue rolling around as if their lives depend on who wins this fight.

Morgan finally rolls to pin Elaine under her and her

fists rain down like hail, one after the other, closed, then open. Tears stream down her face and her eyes flood with inky darkness.

Elaine, while stronger than Morgan, is at a disadvantage and is forced to block and defend while trying to buck the hurricane of an emotional girl off her.

"Morgan! Stop! You are hurting her! Stop! Stop!" Isolder comes back to them and tries to grapple Morgan into a bear hug, only to be thrown off her and sent flailing back, landing with a loud thud on the ground several feet away.

The moment Isolder goes unconscious she stops swinging at Elaine. Trembling, bleeding, and crying, she rolls off and lands on her back, breathing hard to get herself under control.

Elaine says nothing and rolls with her back to Morgan, curling up. She felt Isolder too and is hiding her fear while she also tries to regain her composure.

The silent onlooker is not sure what to do. One is badly hurt, and the other two seem to have come to a truce or have battled themselves to a standstill. Should he attend to them, or call for help?

Three Wood Nymphs

Arthur's chivalrous nature takes over, and he eases from the trees to sneak to Isolder. He kneels next to her to check her wounds and frowns as he blushes fiercely at her nakedness. He unclasps his cloak and drapes it over her, his hands gently brushing her hair from her face. That is when he notices the blood trickling from behind her ear. "Oh no," he murmurs with a sense of urgency. He scoops her up and bolts towards the tree line, heading back to his camp so he could get her to the healer women. She is dead weight in his arms. Just as he is about to disappear into the trees with his patient, an arrow comes whistling by his temple to sink into the tree. Shying from it, he looks back over his shoulder to see his attacker in all her glory, standing about a hundred paces away. He blinks in shock and stumbles to a stop.

She stands there, raven hair flowing in the wind, pale skin reddened from the physical battle, covered in mud, scratches, and the blood of her fellow combatants. She looks other-worldly.

He pulls the unconscious girl closer to him as the other stands and looks every bit as out of place as the first, drawing her arrow and taking aim. "I am trying to save her!" He shouts it at the two girls.

Girls! They are just girls! Naked girls in a field with arrows.

He curses himself for not realizing this is a trap. That the Druids are about to murder him because he could not leave well enough alone. He could try to run with the unconscious girl, or he could put her down and save his own life. There is no choice to be had. He grunts and takes off at the fastest run he can muster with the girl in his arms. The other two women would have to shoot through trees and forest canopy to hit him. Merlin would be chastising him if he were here. With Arthur's mind not focused on his task, and more worried about phantom wizards, he does not see the vines pop up out of the ground like two hands peeling out of a grave, fast as a whip crack. One snakes around his hand and tugs it back hard while the other coils right around the would-be rescued young woman, holding her aloft while he crashes to the ground. He rolls and his hand goes for his boot, retrieving the small dagger stashed there. He slashes at the vine only to find it has a mind of its own and jerks his leg right into the path of his own attack, leaving a nasty gash across the top of his thigh. Arthur gasps in pain. Another vine whips out of the dense foliage to wrap around his wrist, forcing his hand open and dropping the knife. His body contorts and twists as he futilely fights the vines encircling him until he is held upside down from an old tree and with the vines covering his mouth. He struggles and squirms as he tries to break free, only to feel the blood rushing to his head. Grunting and growling like an animal in a snare, he looks at the girl lying on the ground, helpless, and now uncovered.

Moments later, the other two girls come crashing through the brush to their friend. Ignoring him, they drop their weapons and toss his cloak aside. One quickly moves about the area on her hands and knees, looking for something, while the other cradles the unconscious girl in her lap. Her fingers sprawl over the wound on the girl's head as blood washes over her porcelain skin.

"Leave the plants. Come, lay your hands on her and repeat after me," Morgan demands of Elaine.

"But the root will stop the bleeding. Why did Isolder have to get in the way?" Elaine whimpers. "I cannot find it."

"Because we are not on the island," Morgan says. "Elaine, I need you. Please, come help me."

He stills as they speak, straining to listen only to find himself unable to understand either of them. He thinks he catches the names Isolder, then Elaine. He groans and struggles again, trying to tell them he can help, that he has healers, but they are still ignoring him. He watches as the darker one gives up her quest and comes to the other, kneeling over the third girl.

Her hands also sprawl on the girl's forehead and the two begin to chant. At first, the chant is nothing more than a murmur, but grows louder as the pale one teaches the chant to the other, until they are in harmonious unison. He has never seen such a sight and his noisemaking falls silent. Whatever they are, they are beautiful, magical, and naked. He stares at the three of them, awestruck.

Morgan's voice is steady and calm as she chants.

Elaine's voice is less confident but clear.

Minutes pass as energy flows through the three of them. The slick, sticky liquid flowing from Isolder's head slows to a trickle as Morgan feels the gash knit under her fingers. Finally, the two of them fall silent at Morgan's nod.

Elaine slumps back on her haunches, eyes barely able to stay open.

Morgan relaxes as well, her hands trembling as she releases her healed friend from her grasp. She swoons as the exhaustion from using too much life magic takes its toll upon her, but she forces herself to stay awake. She has other problems requiring her attention before she could fall into the soft embrace of sleep.

Silent as a mouse, he stares at Morgan, from the curve of her hip to the pout on her lips, he has never seen a woman so beautiful in all his life. All he can think of is how he longs to feel her touch and have her worry for him as she does the other girl.

Isolder gasps awake, sitting upright, and letting out a cry of shock and pain. She looks around, trying to get her bearings. "I hate both of you," she whines, and the three of them break into tears of joy and relieved laughter.

Elaine is too weak to move from where she has collapsed.

Morgan is still trembling, but steady. "We should not linger here. Where there is one, there are more," trying to sound like the authority on men, despite none of them had seen one until the day prior when Archimedes revealed himself. The foreign landscape, and easy appearance of a man confirms they are not on the island anymore.

Isolder and Elaine nod in agreement and Isolder helps Elaine up as the two of them stumble their way back to the meadow. Once gone from sight of the man, Isolder lets Elaine sit propped against a tree while she hunts down their bows and arrows.

Morgan turns and faces their captive.

She is a wild she-devil beauty with her skin splotched in ruddy browns from the drying blood, and her eyes are the darkest blue Arthur has ever seen. He cannot help but gaze at her.

With being from an island full of magical women, Morgan knows nothing of the sensibilities of the rest of the world and is not shy as she approaches Arthur. She comes closer and cants her head to the side, half smiling at him. His eyes flutter as he tries not to faint from all the blood rushing to his head.

Squatting down, she gathers up his dagger in her hand, turning it over to admire it. It is ornate and silver, with jewels she finds as fascinating as the tiny dragon symbol on it. Frowning at the symbol of the dragon keepers of Avalon on this man's knife, anger blooms at the idea that he might have hurt one of her people. "Where did you get this?" She demands of him as she stands.

He shrugs and tries to point to his ear to show he does not comprehend what she is saying, but finds himself still tightly bound by the vines.

With a wave of her hand, the vines let him fall to the ground, but do not unbind him.

Arthur grunts as he crashes into the hard earth and tries to avoid rolling his slashed thigh in the dirt.

Morgan narrows her eyes at him, commanding the vines to roll him fully onto his back as she takes hold of his chin to force his gaze to hers.

He feels the strain and is about to burst right out of his britches with the way her naked body looms over his prone form. Embarrassed and miserable he groans in pain.

That makes her look at him curiously, and then her eyes grow wide with the realization of why he is behaving the way he is. She peers deeply into his eyes, judging him.

He swears he can see the night sky swimming in

them. The longer she holds his chin, the more he wants to tell her he would never hurt her, even if she did try to murder him a few moments ago. The seconds feel like eons as he gazes deeply into her eyes.

Then she giggles, her cheeks flush pink, and she shifts away to focus on his thigh. She places the palm of one bloody hand against the wound and begins to chant once more in the odd Druid language.

He can feel warmth seeping into his thigh, and the pain dulls to a small ache. Arthur is convinced he can feel every little tendril of skin weaving itself together. Never has he witnessed such a wondrous way to heal people, and this woman has not only done it once, but twice in as many minutes. He wriggles to see what she is doing to him, getting ever closer to her.

She smells sweet, of berries, the sea, and a hint of lilies, mixed with the iron twinge of blood and muddy earth. Her smile never fades, but she says nothing to him. She keeps giggling and finally eases back from him to stand. She keeps the dagger as she turns to find her friends.

"Morgan, hurry, we should get moving," one of them calls in the distance.

He only understands the word Morgan, and he promises himself to never forget her. He moans in panic as she turns away, trying to get her to untie him.

With a coy smile she pauses to look over her shoulder at him before turning back and leaving him to work himself free of the vines.

His body feels heavy, and his brain muddled with

lustful thoughts of the wild nymph that healed him as he rolls back onto the ground still bound by plant life.

As she reaches Elaine and Isolder, they are exchanging knowing looks and biting their lips to keep from laughing at her.

"What?" Morgan snaps at them.

"If you smile any broader your face will crack," Elaine chortles and Isolder snickers.

Morgan thumps Elaine hard in the shoulder and then helps her to her feet, her cheeks starting to hurt from the silly grin still plastered on her face.

Not All Compasses Point North

"Come on, he will not stay bound much longer," Morgan says.

The three girls wander back into the field while Isolder looks for tracks and other signs of wildlife. The trio keep searching, tracking further into the woods and away from the camp of warring men and women.

Morgan keeps casting glances back the way they came, where she left young Arthur. She felt the spark, the little whisper that his tapestry weaves with hers. Archimedes had talked about when you meet certain people they will forever alter your destiny. She could not see much of his future, but she saw herself in it. There is a strong tug at her wild heartstrings to run off and learn about the people here, to forsake the Hunt she did not want, followed by a pang of guilt at the idea of abandoning her duties. Her mother's death is looming nigh, and here she is thinking of adventures with a boy.

"I need to rest," Elaine finally confesses after hours of walking through the woods. "I do not feel well. Morgan, how are you not affected this way?"

"Because I am stronger than you," Morgan quips without hesitation.

"Says you," mutters Elaine.

"I will start a fire," Isolder flutters about the tiny grove to gather up wood.

Morgan clears away moss and grass to dig a hole for the fire to sit in.

Elaine settles down and hugs her knees to her chest. She is trembling and looks pale. They all look as though they had been in a massacre. Blood, sweat, and grime cover them from head to toe.

Morgan does feel ill, but puts on a brave face to keep them from worrying. She looks back the way they came, as she is not sure they are on the right path. The White Doe is not a regular animal. The majestic creature is smart and knows her time is coming. Wandering off to forage for food, she leaves her sisters to rest. Berries, or mushrooms, will do, but she smiles when digging about in the dirt the fungi appear. She checks them over and sniffs them to make sure they are safe to eat. She gathers a handful, and then returns to the now glowing fire.

"Eat these," she offers them to Elaine and Isolder,

taking none for herself. Her mind is far from here, thinking about the curly blond-haired boy they encountered. She would have murdered him to protect Isolder and Elaine, and wonders if he realizes how close to death he came.

Elaine speaks up after inspecting their bows and arrows. "We only have two now. Will it be enough?"

"It will," Isolder offers in a hopeful tone.

"I took his dagger," Morgan reveals the ornate weapon.

"Do you think you can run fast enough to catch the White Doe?" The skeptical look on Elaine's face tells Morgan what she really thinks.

"If we are smart, she will come right to us. For tonight, I only want to think about sleep. We will plan in the morning. We have to be careful to not be caught by that man again, or anyone like him." Morgan ignores Elaine's jab as she tries to reason with them.

"I'm not sleepy," Isolder sulks.

"Then just lie there and rest," Morgan growls in response. She flops down and puts her back to the fire, trying to end the discussion.

"Her royal highness needs her beauty sleep," Elaine jabs, but she too is settling down to munch on the mushrooms. The warmth of the fire leaves a comforting glow on the three girls.

******

Wilhelm stares up at the night sky. The stars shine bright and clear in the sleepy little village, bringing his tormented soul comfort. His eyes are heavy from crying, and his chest aches from the lost feeling of forgetfulness. He yearns to know what that woman took from him, but as his father would say, "No use in crying over lost stardust. What is the story you can tell?" He ponders that and with a firm nod, he kneels and draws into the ground a simple compass. When his handy work is done, he moves to a nearby tree and plucks a few twigs off it. He returns to the compass with the twigs and looks to the stars again, "Stars bright, shining light, guide my hand with all your might." He lets the twigs fall from his fingers to land on his drawn compass. With a light bounce, they settle in two different directions. One points towards the village's clock tower. The other points towards the woods.

"Fiddlesticks," he grumbles. He is not about to go traipsing in foreign woods, where something terrible and deadly might be. Nothing good ever happens in the woods. So, he turns to the village.

The center of it has a clock tower, remarkably similar to Silver City. What he would not give to deal with princesses, fairies, and dwarves right now. He frowns as his hands come into view. All the Druid markings are gone. He also realizes his clothing is better fitting and more suited to his liking, not the flowing robes of Lloegyr. He gives his vest a tug as he cautiously moves into the village proper, and to the clock tower in the center. As he approaches, he can hear the mechanical innards of the ever-present dictator of the day grind their way through time itself. He loathes time and its hold on people. His father had been obsessed with time; going on and on about how it could be traversed or even alter the pace it keeps altogether. Wilhelm rolls his eyes as he recalls his father's loony rants about how crucial time himself is to everyone. The clock tower, itself, is not his goal. The compass only shows you the direction the path goes, not when to turn.

He stuffs his hands into his pockets and abruptly turns to his right to observe the buildings clustered together. No lights, or movement, indicates the shops are closed for the night. Another quarter turn and he clicks his heels together without thinking about it. The large building across the way glows with the warmth of home and hearth and the hum of idle chit-chat calls to his ears. A smile crosses his now owl-like features as he steps forward with a small bounce in his step. The sensation of having lost someone important to him still weighs on his heart, but he has a mission to see through. Besides, his brothers will restore what has been stolen from him. He eases the massive wooden door open, and is greeted with the sweet scents of beer and roast meat. A survey of the room gives him a pleasant first impression. This tavern is not graced with odd misfits of creatures, or less important citizens of an otherwise pristine race of beings. Instead, it is full of farmers, shopkeepers, wenches, and the occasional seedy looking fellow. A jovially plump young woman with honey brown ringlets pulled up to allow a healthy view of her voluptuous assets pauses and gives him a wink. In German, "Sit anywhere ya like. We will get you settled right." The sing-song lilt of her words stir a deep sense of nostalgia in him, then she is off into the crowd of patrons again. Reluctant to look away, he watches her bob and weave with all the grace of a delicate flower avoiding being plucked by greedy hands.

Finally, he shakes his head and looks over the patrons with a sharper gaze. If he had plans to stay in this village for any length of time, he would spend his nights here. Much to his dismay, there is not any person who openly reveals themselves to be his brothers. He takes a seat near the massive fireplace, props himself up, and waits. His vantage point gives him the best view of the entrance, as well as most of the room. While there is another room around the corner, he feels this is the best place to start. His stomach agrees with a loud growl, convincing himself he had swallowed a bear cub in his adventures. The sounds of a tambourine, a lyre, and hand drums fill the air. Steady and lively, the music engages the men in the room to cheer and whistle. It is not the type of music he would think of for the people he sees around him, but he likes it. It reminds him of his childhood, and of a woman he has long not thought of, his mother. He reaches into his vest, grimaces, and pats himself as he searches for a lost trinket. When he does not find the item in question, he drums his fingers impatiently on the wooden table next to him.

"Aha!" he exclaims to himself. He thumps the left vest pocket with his right hand three times. The vest begins to bulge, and he gingerly reaches in to pluck out a leather satchel, no larger than the pocket itself. It grows as he pulls it further out until it is large enough he must settle it on the floor next to him. The bag bulges with all the possessions he knew he would need for this journey. It does not occur to him that this place does not teem with magic. A few of the patrons witness this inexplicable act and their eyes widen as they gossip to each other while pointing in his direction. Shoving his arm into the bag he rustles around in it for several more moments until he retrieves a small pouch of coins. While they are Noddian silver, they will transform to the coins of this place when one of the locals touch them. Never, in all his days, did he think he would have need of that spell.

He is cast into shadow by the lovely silhouette of one of the wenches. She has full, pouting lips, her hair braided loosely down her back, and her clothes crumpled, but clean. Her skin is flush from the beer and her slurred German is making him squint up at her. While he does not understand a word she says, he gets the idea of her intentions. With a careful eye, he watches her sway and giggle as she takes another swig of her beer. He smiles but declines her tempting offer. With a grunt, she moves on, not wanting to waste valuable wage-earning hours. She is soon followed by the barmaid who greeted him. She is holding a handful of empty steins in one hand and a tray of empty bowls in the other.

"What would you like, stranger?"

He clears his throat and replies, "I do not speak your language," but his words match hers.

She laughs heartily at him, "Are you sure about that?"

This gives Wilhelm pause. This tongue is not one he knows, yet he speaks it fluently. This terrifies him, as he could agree to marry a goat, or something far worse, without having a clue to what he says.

Lost & Found

"Food and drink. And a place to sleep," he barks, the foreign words rolling off his tongue.

Without a word, she is off again, disappearing through the door to the kitchens.

He rubs his hand over his face in frustration. Stuffing his coin purse into his vest pocket, he crosses his arms and teeters on his stool, trying to figure out the best course of action for communicating. She clearly understood him, even if the sounds coming out of his mouth had been nonsense.

The woman reappears with a bowl of hot stew, a large roll, and a pint the size of Wilhelm's head, which she clanks down without spilling a drop. She swats away the hand of a toothless old codger that mistakes her for one of the wenches without taking her gaze off Wilhelm.

Before he can pick up the spoon for a bite, she snatches it from him. "Nothing is free, stranger," her tone makes him look at her in confusion, until she holds out her other hand, palm up.

"Ah, yes. I apologize," he reaches into his vest and retrieves two coins, dropping them into her hand.

She lights up, plops the spoon back into the bowl, and pockets the coins before he can realize he has paid four times the cost of this meal and drink.

He pays her no mind as he devours his meal, as if he had not eaten in days. The truth of his famished state is that stone travel is dangerous, taxing, and wildly inaccurate. One wrong thought and you could be torn asunder. Too much metal on your person and you could be set ablaze as you tumble out of the stones on the other side. If the stone gets destroyed while you are traveling, you might find yourself thrust into the wrong time, much less the wrong place. He can only assume that witch in Lloegyr picked this place on purpose. Whatever thoughts she put into his head when she stole the others brought him here.

Think of them, and you will find them.

Her voice echoes in his ears. She had been panicked. He could remember that much. Even as he clings to the image of her face, he struggles for the details. He does not want to admit to himself he is forgetting her, but she will soon be lost to the fog along with whatever she stole from him.

After a large chug of his pint, he relaxes. His belly is full, and the beer is strong. The music is soothing and rhythmic from the other room. Wilhelm leans back and taps his booted foot in time. The rest of the room leaves him be.

A young boy, dirtier than the laziest hog in the stables, peeks around the corner in his direction. A man who had witnessed the bag retrieval jerks the boy up from his crouch and whispers angrily at him. The boy's eyes widen, and he bolts from the tavern. Wilhelm watches the interchange from under hooded eyes. His free leg slides his bag under the table to prevent it being easily snatched up. He tries to keep tabs on the spindly man, but the beer is strong and it is not long before the man slips from his watchful gaze. When nothing of significant importance happens, he relaxes and fumbles around with his large satchel, trying to shrink it. He chuckles at himself when he fails horribly on the first try. On the second try, the bag shrinks down but the items inside do not, causing the bag to fill the room with the sound of the seams popping. He scrunches his face in concentration and firmly places both hands on the bag, completely ignoring the rest of the patrons. A pointed count to three and there is a loud pop as his satchel shrivels itself up properly and plops onto the table, looking like a doll's accessory. "Much better," he mutters to himself as he plucks it up and tucks it back into a vest pocket for safekeeping.

Wilhelm stands and rests his hand on the table for balance. He gets an impish grin on his face and motions to the barmaid for another. Within moments, he is happily bouncing along to the music in the other room, stein in hand. The merry little troupe stirs more half-forgotten memories of his mother once he lays eyes on their festive garb. He takes it as a sign that he should wait here, despite not getting anything accomplished.

I have been a monk for far too long.

Before he can decline, he gets drawn into the crowd of wenches, all giggling and pawing at him like kittens for attention. He is not worried for his personal things as anyone foolish enough to reach into his vest uninvited deserves to lose their hand.

The minutes turn into hours, and then even the merriment subsides to the peaceful hum of a few remaining drunkards and wenches. The farmers and shopkeepers have long gone home. Those not three pints in talk in hushed tones to plot nefarious adventures. Wilhelm beguiles a young wench with a glorious tale of defeating three bears with wit and cunning, no longer caring for the comings and goings of others. He has faith that who he needs to find will make themselves known when the time is right.

A tall and lean man steps into the tavern. He is well dressed, and the barmaid gives him a more revered greeting than she did Wilhelm. "Master Jakob, what brings you to our humble establishment at this hour? Is everything well?"

"Feuring said there was a man acting as though his mind is touched. I have come to collect him."

Her brow furrows in thought, and she shakes her head. "No one acting odd that I know of. You are welcome to look around. Would you like a pint to warm your innards?"

"No, thank you, Gretal," he gives her a gentle smile and begins to survey the remaining patrons. He takes great care to not get too close, nor to let his gaze linger too long. The last thing he wants is to cause trouble and spook the person he is hoping is here. He is also trying to stay his anger. The number of years he has wasted hunting for Wilhelm are not forgotten. If it is him, Jakob will make sure the fool suffers for his reckless choices. He steps into the pub proper and immediately he is drawn to the man boasting about bears. Crossing his arms, he leans against the wall, waiting for the tale to end. His appearance is nothing like it was in Nodd, and he will not reveal himself until he is convinced the blowhard is, in fact, his brother.

"You, sir have not kept this bed in proper fashion! I grumbled at the Bear. Accusing the Bear of making his bed entirely too hard for my liking. The look on his face was priceless."

The women with him giggle to stave off sleep, hoping to get at least one coin out of Wilhelm before the morning light comes creeping through the window.

"And that, my lovely little birds, is how I escaped the clutches of the great Bear." He had given up trying to understand why he did not know the language coming out of his mouth. The people responded to him properly. He goes for another gulp of his beer, only to find the shiny damp bottom of his stein instead. This prompts him to look for the lovely woman who has been keeping it full. She is nowhere to be found. His gaze is pulled to the man against the wall, staring at him. He tips his stein to him in acknowledgment before resuming his quest for a refill.

Wilhelm extracts himself from the wench who pouts adorably as he stumbles to the entryway that leads back to the side room, closer to Jakob. He scowls when there is no barmaid to be found.

"They stopped serving hours ago, my friend." Jakob's voice is silver-tongued with a sweet ring, and holds an air of command.

It is enough to draw Wilhelm's attention. The confused, squished look he gives Jakob makes the elder brother laugh.

"I think you have had enough, my friend. How about I take you to where you are staying?" He moves away from the wall and comes close to drape his arm around Wilhelm.

With drunken fluidity, Wilhelm ducks under the looming arm and stumbles back from the other man. The last time comforting arms tried to guide him anywhere it proved nearly fatal.

"I am not your friend, sir. Where is the barmaid? She is to show me to the room I purchased." Wilhelm sways another step away from Jakob and shifts the stein in his hand to use as a weapon should it come to that.

"Then you have been duped, friend," he shakes his head and chuckles, "As there are no rooms here. The inn is at the outskirts. Come, I can take you there on my way home." Jakob deftly moves again and takes Wilhelm by the forearm.

Wilhelm swings his stein up with all the force he can muster.

Jakob easily jerks the arm he is holding to throw off Wilhelm's balance.

The cartoonish motion leaves the younger brother all legs and arms as he juggles between freeing himself and clinging to Jakob to keep from landing on the floor.

"Unhand me, fiend!" Wilhelm slurs.

Jakob rolls his eyes. "You have always been an insufferable beast when drunk." He gives Wilhelm a shake and rights him. The familiarity with which he speaks unnerves Wilhelm. The remaining patrons of the tavern are watching this interlude keenly. A few have even moved to assist Master Jakob should this stranger get too unruly. "Come with me, and we will find you a place to sleep off the drink. We can discuss why you are here in the morning." He does not let Wilhelm respond. His will is imposing and strong.

Wilhelm shakes his head and tries to free his arm. Between the beer and the traveling, he is no match for his brother. The pair exit the tavern in an awkward stumble of limbs, and the night air is cool against Wilhelm's flushed cheeks. He inhales sharply and regrets this decision. The town reeks of farm animals and makes the beer in his belly churn. With a great heave, he turns and bends, vomiting into the bushes.

This brings a hearty laugh from Jakob, who lets him

go. Jakob offers his handkerchief to Wilhelm, patting his brother's back roughly.

"Thank you," Wilhelm breathes out as he takes it and dabs at his mouth. His hands rest on his knees and he remains hunched over until he is sure he will not vomit again. His temples throb with the remnants of the night's merriment. The mix of apprehension and excitement radiating from the other is enough to make Wilhelm take pause. There is a niggle of hope in his own being that he has, indeed, found one of his brothers.

Stranger Danger

The two men walk in silence down the dirt road leading to the North. Wilhelm can only think about how tired and sore he is.

How far is this inn, anyway? Have I been duped again and about to meet my end in a dark little village?

Jakob has been silent, working through how to bind this stranger to the town so he can question him properly. He leads him to a worn down home, large and looming in the darkness.

Wilhelm takes pause as its size registers through the cloudy haze of drink and shoots a distrusting glare at the other man.

Jakob eases open the gate, motioning for Wilhelm to enter first. He meticulously closes the gate behind him and guides the other man toward the building.

"This does not look like any inn I have ever seen." Wilhelm grumbles.

"It is inn enough for what you need. What is your name, stranger?" Jakob tries to sound casual in his question.

Wilhelm hesitates. There is power in names. William used to always ask what was in a name that made it so powerful. Their father claimed names are the root for the only magic that cannot be undone. Once named, the named object is immortal, and holds the magic that only the name can possess. "Dieter," he finally replies. "Dieter Morden."

Jakob's brows raise at the foolish nonsense coming from the man's mouth. In his attempt to read the man for truth, or lies, he cannot discern either. So Jakob decides to force the issue by squaring up with Wilhelm and placing both hands on his shoulders so he can invade his mind.

Wilhelm has seen this before, though he is failing to recall where. The feeling of déjà vu makes him look away first.

"Very well, *Dieter*," testing the name on his tongue to evaluate its validity. "Welcome to my home, Mürrisch Manor." His grip on Wilhelm's shoulder firms, exerting significant effort to keep Wilhelm from bolting. The prolonged contact has made one thing crystal clear. Someone has altered this man's mind. He lingers, muddling through thoughts clouded by drink and mist as he attempts to learn more about this visitor.

Wilhelm looks back the way they came, then to the house. His very core tells him he can trust this refuge, yet his mind cannot fathom why. "Very well, lead on good sir." He convinces himself that should he find himself in a pickle, he will escape.

A gentle smile appears on Jakob's face as he leads them up the stone steps to the door, thankful he did not have to fight the man.

******

The morning dew sparkles in the sunlight filtering through the grove. The fire has long burned down to embers. Crickets chirp and birds flit about their daily routines, ignoring the three sleeping beauties curled around the cold fire.

Isolder is the first to rise. With a stretch and a yawn, she brushes off a determined line of ants attempting to conquer her. Her fingers reach up and tenderly feel where her hair is matted and caked in dried blood. There is not so much as a sting or a bump from yesterday's fight. She spies movement and rolls onto all fours to crawl near Elaine. Slowly picking up a bow and an arrow, her eyes never leave the foliage. They each have one chance to strike the doe.

Another rustle of underbrush and the doe comes into Isolder's sight. The lovely creature is cradled in the early morning sunlight, causing her coat to glow with an iridescent sheen.

Isolder takes aim with trembling hands. Her emotions are wild. She could send them all home. She would be the Lady and things would become far more peaceful.

Their eyes meet and Isolder's heart is pounding in her chest. She has never really hunted before this, as her skills lie more in healing and gardening. Her muscles twitch from holding the heavy draw of the bow with all her might. She draws the shaking tip to center on the doe and lets the arrow fly.

It whistles through the air. The doe bounds off into the woods, leaving the arrow to sink with a thud into a tree.

Isolder sighs and nudges Elaine. "Get up, the doe was here."

"What? Who?" Elaine groans and sits up, rubbing her eyes. She is cold and has forgotten where they are. Sleep laden eyes look at Isolder, then the bow, then back up to Isolder. "You wasted an arrow. Now we only have one." Her tongue is sharp as she scolds Isolder for trying to do that which she wants to do. "Which direction did she go?"

"That way," Isolder sulks. "Good luck finding her. She bolted."

Elaine pushes up and takes the final arrow along with her bow. "I will catch her. Do not wake her highness."

Her glare stills Isolder, keeping her from arguing, and she nods. "What do I tell her when she wakes and you are not here?"

"Tell her I will be back, and to wait."

"You know she will go after you!"

"And you will get lost. Just stay here. I will not be long." Elaine leaves the camp to conquer the doe, her body crouched as she inspects the tracks left by the doe.

Isolder fusses and frets as she watches Elaine vanish into the woods. None of them know these woods. How will any of them find their way anywhere?

"Is she finally gone?"

"She is... No. Just... Elaine is," Isolder stammers for what to say as Morgan sits up and watches her with a bemused look.

She heard the entire conversation and is sure she will have to find Elaine to bring her back. Lucky for them, Morgan has magic to aid in hunting. She preens and lets Isolder fluster through her thought.

"She said to not go anywhere," Isolder mewls, finally giving up on trying to cover for Elaine.

"She will miss. The Lady specifically said we must work together. None of us will overtake the doe on our own." Morgan suspects there is more to this Hunt than she is ready to face. Part of her wants to fail in finding the White Doe. Morgan's eyes are on her childhood friend, studying the fear roiling off the other girl. There is so much pressure on the three of them that any normal girl would crack. "It will be all right, Isolder. If she does not come back before the sun is directly above us, we will get her."

"What about the arrows? If she uses hers and misses, we are out of arrows."

Morgan frowns at this news and picks up the dagger she stole from the boy. "I imagine we will have to use this." The weight feels foreign to her. There is death and destruction linked to this dagger. A high-pitched ring drowns out all the surrounding forest's sounds, leaving Morgan panting and lost in the vision. Morgan closes her eyes, grits her teeth, and tries to force herself to release the dagger. When the dagger finally drops to the ground, the ringing subsides. She can feel sweat beading on her brow.

"What was that?" Isolder whines as she comes to tend to her friend.

"I do not know," she murmurs, not really hearing her companion. She knows full well it was a vision and refuses to reveal that she can see glimpses of the future. People would behave differently, and it would also bring trouble if what she saw came about different from how she told it. She leans on Isolder for comfort. The two girls sit in silence for quite some time before Morgan finally nudges Isolder. "We should get some food and then start after Elaine. I think there are berries that way."

The two girls get up and brush themselves off. Isolder's fretting is soon forgotten as she and Morgan work out from their little grove to find berries, and an apple tree. They grab enough to carry back to the grove, giggling and crunching through an apple when Morgan stops Isolder in her tracks. She lets the gathered fruit fall from her grasp. The scent of sweat, with hints of metal, and a twinge of excitement is the only warning they get. She swallows her bite and her eyes flick to the side, watching the man fall from the tree above them. Without hesitation, she wraps her arm around Isolder, and they move at the speed of thought to the other side of the grove. Another man drops near to them as the first curses, and Morgan looks to the dagger.

Isolder brandishes an apple as a weapon, and the men follow Morgan's gaze. A quick look between the two of them, then back to her, and all three of them leap for the dagger.

Isolder screams and hurls the apple at the nearest man.

Morgan grunts as she lands first, her delicate fingers curling around the hilt of the dagger. She is nearly crushed as the weight of the two men collide with her. The three of them roll about, a pile of limbs struggling for control of the blade. Their gloved hands grope and paw at her to free the dagger from her grip.

"Hold 'er down," one barks at the other.

She very much knows their language and redoubles her efforts. These Druids are not about to defile her person. She bucks and squirms as she wildly flails the dagger at them. The blade bites deep as she connects with a shoulder.

"Ow! You filthy wood nymph!" The smaller man stumbles back, and the other moves to pin Morgan down.

Her strength is too much for him and she bucks him right up into the air, allowing her to roll over and scramble away.

His hands slide along her bare body and is about to get a firm hold on her leg when there is an eerie crack in the air.

"Unhand her you... You... You dog!" Isolder looms over the swaying Druid with a tree branch that is half her size, held ready to swing again.

"Again!" Morgan cries out.

She obliges, swinging with all her might. Another sickening crack fills the air as bone and flesh collide with bark and sap.

The larger man falls back, his nose broken and mangled. Blood oozes out as he gurgles in surprise, toppling off Morgan to twitch on the ground.

The smaller man growls, full of rage as these two women murder his friend. He coils and strikes out at Isolder, tackling her to the ground. His hand rears back to pummel her delicate face when he freezes in place. The entire grove is quiet, aside from the panting girls and gurgling of the dying villain.

Morgan stares in shock at the arrow sticking out of the man's eye socket. The hawk's feathers for a tail, and the silver metal for the tip meant it could only be one person. "Elaine," she breathes out in relief. She scrambles to her feet towards Isolder who is pinned under the dying man. With a grunt, Morgan pulls him off her and he claws futilely at Morgan.

"Slit his throat, Morgan," Elaine's voice is cold behind her, but firm. "He can survive the arrow."

A Reckoning

Morgan looks down at the man and frowns. The idea of slitting his throat seems drastic.

"No, leave him be. Let us just go, please," Isolder's voice begs from the other side.

"We cannot risk them being found alive, Isolder. There are men all over these woods looking for three women without clothes." There is no remorse or pity in the cold depths of Elaine's voice.

"How do you know this, Elaine?" Morgan's voice is breathy, as if she is in a dream and far away. She watches the man paw at her leg and the blood streaming down his face. She cannot yet bring herself to commit this heinous act. To take a life exacts such a high price, and the last thing she wants is to be banished from Avalon.

"When I could track the doe no further, I heard a group of men talking. There is a reward for finding us and taking us to someone named Arthur, or King, I am not sure exactly. Their speech is off-putting, and the spell I used to understand them only half-worked." She feels ashamed to admit that she is not as good at magic as Morgan is. "You are making him suffer, Morgan. Put him out of his misery and keep us safe."

"Just leave him be," Isolder begs again.

Morgan turns her head slightly to Isolder, then to Elaine. She closes her eyes and prays, "Mother, forgive me." With firm resolve she leans down, plants a knee in his chest to still him and uses the dagger to silence his groans of pain. Wiping the blade clean on his shirt sleeve, there is a darkness shrouding her heart. A tiny part of her enjoyed spilling his blood. "Take any weapons on them. I will deal with the others." Morgan stalks away, in the direction Elaine came from. The dagger weighs as heavy in her hand as the guilt even heavier on her heart. She flits through the trees, hunting those that would seek to harm them. The drumming sound of her heart drowns out any logical thought. The sun is high in the sky before Morgan finally reaches a point where she can see the path below her. There are men on horseback discussing the best method of searching. She raises her hands high in the sky, whispering a spell she has only read of before this day. The words are fast and her tongue trips over the strange words. She can barely breathe as her heart hammers in her chest.

The spell is a simple hiding spell. It befuddles the victim and causes them not to see what is right before them. However, Morgan has taken a life and her magic reminds her of the price she must pay until she can make amends. When the spell is through, there is a rustling of leaves, and a cold breeze kisses her naked skin. She looks down at herself and where there should be pale white skin she is instead met with a brilliant golden glow.

"Up there!" A young boy shouts triumphantly. "There is one of them!"

Her eyes widen and she stumbles back, looking for an escape.

The horses snort and snarl in effort as they work their way up the hill towards her.

She turns to run and stops short. Isolder and Elaine are at the bottom of the hill and they are looking at themselves in wonder, their bodies also glowing with the radiance of the sun. They had not waited for her and now they are all in trouble.

"What did you do?" hisses Elaine.

"I... I... Tried to hide us! Run!" Morgan hurries by them, and an arrow whizzes past Isolder's ear.

"Hide us? You made us as bright as the sun! They are going to see us no matter where we go. We cannot out-run horses!" Isolder wails as she bolts after Morgan.

"We can water walk and go somewhere they will never find us. We just need to find a stream, or puddle." Elaine gasps as she runs to keep pace.

"Right, because we have so much time to look through every nook and cranny of this place for that," Isolder bitterly retorts.

"Elaine is right, Isolder, but I do not think we are near any water. We must find a place to hide until the spell can be undone." Morgan tries to keep her thoughts straight as she leads them deeper into the woods.

"Over there! This way! They are heading to the hollows!" The rallying cry is followed by the bray of a horn and hounds howling in response.

The three girls run with all their might.

The men hunting them cut them off, trying to encircle them.

When this happens, the three girls latch onto each other and blink away from the men. Morgan only uses her magic once this way. Instead of moving away from the men, they find themselves deeper into their ambush when she tries to move them.

Elaine and Isolder have to work in tandem to flit them away in time.

Terror grips the hearts of all three girls, Morgan most of all. As her fear runs rampant, the skies open in a torrential downpour. The rain is heavy and cold. The sound of drops hitting the leaves is like the roaring of young dragons. The more they run, the worse it gets. The ground grows muddy and slick making their trek treacherous as they slip and slide through the muck. Covered in mud, bruised, broken, and feeling as though they are about to meet their makers, they huddle together in the hollow of a large oak tree. The gnarled shell of a tree having long ago lost its will to survive provides shelter from the storm. The sounds of men and hounds echo in every direction. All three girls shiver, their breath misting in the freezing rain. Their ornate ceremonial decorations are gone, replaced with blood, brambles, and dirt.

"This is all your fault," Isolder yelps at Morgan as she tries to find a single dry spot to get any semblance of fire and warmth for them.

"My fault? Elaine started it!" Morgan knows she sounds petulant. Thunder rumbles to echo her words.

"Me? I'm not the one who shirks all her duties to go running off in the forest with some stupid owl!" Elaine hugs her knees to her chest and rocks.

"I am sorry," Morgan whines. Another thunderclap grumbles in the distance. The wind whistles through the grove of dying trees as it picks up, slashing ice-cold tears of rain at the three girls seeking shelter. "I am sorry I am not as good as you at everything you do! I am sorry I want to explore and learn new things! I am sorry I'm different! I am sorry she chose me! I never wanted to be the Lady of the Lake! Never!" Morgan curls into herself, tears hidden by the rivulets of rainwater washing down her face.

Isolder gives up the search for a dry spot as the machine gun tapping of sleet pelts their hollowed shelter.

Elaine's eyes widen in surprise, and it stings to hear Morgan say such things. She never thought in a million years that Morgan le Fey ever felt that way. She also feels guilty for making things harder for Morgan and starting rumors to get the other girls to turn against her. She wipes rain and tears from her cheeks in a useless effort and tries to think of something comforting to say to Morgan. "For what it is worth, I think you will make a good Lady."

Isolder pauses as the deafening roar of ice against the tree subsides. "No! You are an ungrateful, spoiled, princess!" She slaps Morgan. "You do not get to just say you are sorry and wave a hand to dismiss just how unqualified you are to lead us!"

Elaine stares, slack-jaw, at Isolder. She never raises her voice, much less her hand, in anger.

The world blooms to life in blinding white as lightning rips a tree mere feet from them apart. The deafening roar that follows causes Elaine and Isolder to flinch.

When their vision clears, Morgan's eyes have shifted from their normal dark blue to inky black. Her pupils are devoured by the sea of darkness that hides within her soul. "What did you say?" Dark malice lingers on every word.

Isolder squares her shoulders, blaming the trembling in her limbs on the cold, and gives Morgan a shove. "You heard me. You led them to us on purpose, just to see one of us get hurt. You do not care about anyone but yourself! You never have!"

"Isolder! Stop!" Elaine's voice is firm. While Isolder's anger is righteous, Elaine does not see the wisdom in not drawing out Morgan's fury. It is the talk of the island the way Morgan's emotions affect the weather. For once in her life, Elaine opts not to act on her first instinct and lets this scene play through.

Outside, the men that had been pursuing them have been forced to abandon the horses and track on foot. The hounds have lost the girls' scents in the hellacious storm. Lightning strikes have sent trees crashing and burning to the ground and the rain has turned to ice, pelting against their skin like tiny daggers. The wind is howling and none of them feel that the three girls could survive a storm like this. Their voices grow distant and the baying of the hounds no longer tear through the sky.

Morgan, lightning-fast, snatches Isolder by the throat, drawing her in close. It looks as though she is going to devour her when Morgan's eyes widen in shock.

Isolder just as deftly placed her hands upon Morgan's temples and the two freeze in place. The weather whips around in furious confusion, but none of it invades their shelter. They are in the very eye of this storm, a calm and quiet vacuum compared to the world around them.

Morgan blinks in disbelief and keeps watching Isolder, who holds firm and does not back down. It is Morgan who releases first, gasping and trembling. The weather dies down from the maelstrom to steady rain.

"Thank you," she whimpers.

Isolder squeaks as Morgan pulls her into a tight hug.

Elaine looks between the two in confusion and sulks. She feels left out of something important, until Morgan pulls her into the hug. Elaine can feel it then; the magic coursing through the three of them. The closer they are, the more powerful it feels. Morgan's feelings and thoughts are a hurricane of chaos, while Isolder's are of warmth and understanding. Elaine's own feelings of strength and cunning balance out the three. It takes several seconds before she realizes Morgan is chanting.

The prayer for forgiveness and to carry the soul of that man on to his next life is strong and sure. Then, Isolder's voice mixes with Morgan's, as they bind to each other. Before long, Elaine can hear her own voice echo the others. The three of them sway under the dead oak tree until the storm is completely gone, and the forest resumes its slumbering existence under the clear evening sky. The three girls finally break the circle. They are whole. Each can hear the other without speaking. They can feel the other's presence and how the power flows between the three of them. Isolder finally gets a fire going for them as the last beams of sun fade away. The entire day has been lost to this awful pursuit by men. "It will be all right," Isolder offers while she stokes the little fire.

"What if it is not?" Morgan gnaws at her lip as anxiety wells in her soul.

"We will find the doe," Elaine offers, but her confidence is bravado at this point.

The White Doe

As dusk gives way to nightfall, the three girls drift into a heavy sleep.

Elaine makes every effort to remain vigilant in case the men come hunting again, but eventually succumbs to her exhaustion.

Once they are asleep, the doe appears on the other side of the hollow. Her steps are gentle and calm as she makes her way closer to their little shelter and kneels on the ground. She could not be prouder of the three girls. They learned how to work with each other, and for each other. They will have a long road ahead of them, but in this trial, the trio succeeded. In the morning, she will pass the mantle on to Morgan. Elaine will inherit the powers of the Dragon Keepers, and

Isolder the powers of the Apothecaries. Each will live eons with their knowledge and power. Avalon will prevail, and she can finally rest.

Morgan's body aches and is stiff when she blinks her eyes open. The air is damp, and the fire has gone out. Not even the tiny embers pretend to give off heat. Her skin is clammy and hair damp against her temples. The only warmth to be had is from the two bodies pinning her between them. Their slow and steady breathing tells her neither is awake. She had been dreaming of the boy with his piercing green eyes and the unkempt fuzz on his chin. She could feel his war-worn hands on her skin and hear his heart beating like a steady drum. She squirms as she tries to get comfortable and sneak back into the dream. Her movements are enough to wake Isolder.

Isolder pulls herself upright, every muscle in her body sore from the treacherous gauntlet they faced the day before, and rubs the sleep from her eyes. She sees the doe sleeping outside their shelter and freezes in place. "Wake up," she whispers.

Morgan does not move, but Isolder knows she is awake.

"Come on," she nudges her with her knee, never taking her eyes from the sleeping doe.

With the nudge, Morgan finally rolls over and is about to snap at Isolder when she follows the girl's slender finger pointing at outside of the hollowed tree.

"Elaine!" she hisses. "Get your weapon."

At once, Elaine is awake and with weapon in hand.

Morgan stays her and motions. The doe has not moved, nor indicated she hears the three girls doing a terrible job of keeping quiet. As they emerge from their hiding place, they encircle the doe.

Morgan clings to the dagger she took from Arthur.

Elaine wields a short sword taken from the men who attacked them.

Isolder grips her bow like a club.

Each girl steps forward cautiously until they close the circle to a five-foot diameter. Each kneels, lays down their weapons, and draws their fingers through the soft mud while whispering chants to bind the doe. The dirt moves itself once out of their reach to form the seal as they concentrate on the ritual. The runic circle glows blue in the dim morning light.

The doe's eyes open, and she stares at Morgan. Up close, all three girls can see the runes that shimmer over the doe's body, hidden under the fur that glitters in the light of the dawn. Her eyes are as blue as the lake that surrounds Avalon.

Morgan realizes she has seen those eyes before. The chant keeps flowing from her lips, but she hesitates to do what is asked of her.

The doe makes no effort to run, nor does she stamp about in fear. Instead, she shifts to allow Morgan to enter the circle.

The other two kneel, facing the circle, and they continue to chant the binding spell.

Morgan slowly rises from her position to stand before the doe. The fanciful emblem bites into Morgan's palm as she grips the dagger too tight. Of the two, Morgan looks more a beast than the doe. Her breathing is labored and tears well in her eyes. The light mists of the morning become leaden and heavy, eventually giving way to a light drizzle. It is not the harsh monsoon of the prior day, but a steady and dreary drip that reflects the mourning in Morgan's heart. Entranced by those blue eyes, Morgan sees the doe's true form in front of her and she shakes her head no. "I cannot. Please do not make me do this. Please," she begs of the doe.

Isolder closes her eyes while chanting. Unable to break the chant, she tries to push her calm to Morgan.

Elaine follows suit, lending her strength to Morgan.

The two of them can only see the doe, but Morgan sees her mother.

The frail shade of her mother is standing before her, bare as the three girls on the Hunt. Nimoway smiles warmly as she eases closer to Morgan.

Unable to control herself, Morgan raises the dagger above her head. The doe rears up onto her hind legs and Morgan's hands are white knuckled, holding the dagger. "No, please, no. I cannot do this. I need you. I will do whatever you want, but please, do not make me do this. Please." Morgan's entire body trembles and is held in place as she resists Nimoway's silent wish to complete the ritual.

Isolder and Elaine sway as the words and power of the ritual takes full hold of all three girls.

Unable to stop, even if they tried, they are also

imposing their will on Morgan's heart. Elaine's anger at Morgan's insolence wells up, as does Isolder's pity.

Morgan can see Nimoway's presence fading. With, or without Morgan, she is going to die. The rain comes down harder now, to match the emotions of the sobbing young witch in the circle. "Oh, Mother," she blubbers.

A clap of thunder, natural, not from Morgan's emotions, booms loud enough overhead that it rattles Nimoway, causing her to break her concentration on Morgan.

Morgan does not dare move as she finds herself free of Nimoway's control. She could flee and throw herself at the mercy of that boy, knowing she would never look upon her friends and family again.

The desperation in Nimoway's eyes, pleading for release and for salvation, are what stays Morgan's retreat. There is a sincere desire to die by the older witch, and Morgan can barely feel her life in this circle. The doe does not move, and the two girls chant louder, as the strength of the circle wanes without Morgan to help keep it.

Morgan closes her eyes and forces herself to not think about what she is going to do. She plunges the dagger into the doe's chest. There is no blood to stain the blade. A cry of surprise escapes the doe, then she slumps as Morgan drops to her knees with her. Her hands come to rest on the doe with every intention of saving the creature's life. She could not let her mother die by her own hand. "Please do not leave me. Please.

Please. Please." She sobs pitifully.

The doe fades to stardust floating in the air and sparkles in the raindrops.

The three girls become engulfed in it as it whirls around the circle.

Morgan falls forward on her hands, having let the dagger go. She cannot breathe. No words come to her mouth to cry out. All she can hear is the roar. Animals are crying out. People are wailing. There is water everywhere, and Morgan is sure she is about to drown in this hollow.

Elaine convulses on the ground. Blushing and rosy skin turns into silvered scales that cover every inch of her. Her body shifts and contorts until there is barely any sign of the young girl who had taunted Morgan for all her childhood. Now adorning her body are the robes of the Dragon Mistress, giving her a menacing and fierce appearance.

On the other side of the circle, Isolder is lifted high into the air. The vegetation of the hollow springs to life and clings to her delicate skin. Her soft pale locks are interwoven with leaves and branches. Her ears elongate to point high along her head. Her skin gives way from the reds and pinks of a fair maiden to the greens and browns of bark and branches. Her naked form is now covered with the mossy greens of the Earthly Heart of Avalon.

Both girls look down at Morgan, who is still on her hands and knees, struggling to breathe. Each watch with the new wisdom of their positions. Neither girl holds fear any longer, and they are unwilling to leave Morgan's side.

The crescent moon that adorns Morgan's forehead grows larger and more vivid. Hints of runes on her skin shine and shimmer, then fade, leaving her skin pale and soft. The grime and blood of the past two days fades from existence as the stardust whirls around her. Robes, soft and silver, form around her person, giving her the look of a Grecian goddess. The silver bands of the Lady spiral up her arms. She is lifted and left standing between her friends.

Her eyes swim with stars, clear and crystalline blue. Her ears ring with whispered prayers to her mother. No, to her now. They beg for success in the Hunt, or to seek guidance, or deliverance from their troubles. Morgan's head swims as the deluge of desires, wants, and needs crashes through her. The water calls to her soul. The wind kisses her skin. The earth caresses her feet. The fire within her soul burns bright. She gasps deeply, drawing in the last of the stardust with the first breath of her new life.

Quiet settles around them as they stand staring at the empty circle. Slowly, the sounds of the wildlife returns. There is an overwhelming sense of relief from Isolder and Elaine.

Morgan, however, is racked with grief. She says nothing as she turns from them and begins walking to the East.

They share a concerned look and follow a few steps behind her. They can feel her sadness and understand that to begin anew she had to end what was.

Where three naked girls fled into the woods, now the three leaders of Avalon begin the slow trek home.

Drums of War

Arthur stands over the two dead men, concerned etched across his young brow. They have been cleaned and laid to rest with their arms crossed over their chests. One's face is mangled and caved in. The other's throat gapes in a mocking smile up at Arthur with the broken stub of an arrow poking from the remains of his eye. He fumes, torn between blaming the men for their foolishness or the women the other men claim did this. "They were naked, Gawain. I keep telling you the three girls I saw were naked. They only had bows and arrows. If they had wanted me dead, they would have killed me where I stood."

"Yes, Arthur, but you are to be king of all Lloegyr. You cannot just go traipsing about the woods to encounter mythical naked beauties who can make the vines grab you up and bring people back from the dead," the older man standing next to him casts a sideways glance at Arthur.

"When you say it in such a manner, it sounds far-fetched, but we both know there is magic here. The Druids believe in all manner of rituals and fairies. You have met Merlin, as well. The old wizard is far from mythical." Arthur is defensive and petulant as he tries to reason with the older man. Gawain is a gentle soul that prefers wisdom and reason over brute force and bloodshed. Arthur's retort leaves the two men staring down at their fallen soldiers again.

"Someone has to answer for this, Arthur. They were murdered. It was not an accident, or bandits. If those women are out there, and they did this, they should be punished."

"Is it right to punish them? How do we know they did this? These are men who have seen the blood of battle more than once. The three of them could not have been strong enough to cave his face in. Nor did they have any weapons that could slit a throat."

Gawain holds his retort as the other six men who had gone hunting are brought before them. He rests his hand on the hilt of his sword as he examines them with a practiced eye. All look as though they have just come from the battlefield. Arthur frowns at the sight. Their armor is dented from the hail. Their cheeks burned from the winds and stinging rain. All of them are muddy and exhausted. He gives a pointed look at

Arthur, who shrugs in response.

"Who made the decision to leave the camp?" Arthur tries his best to keep his tone even, but he wears his heart on his sleeve. His fury at the tragic loss bubbles to the surface. They are at war to claim Lloegyr. Any life lost is monumental to him. Finally, the bickering amongst his advisers falls silent and one steps forward.

"My king," the man tentatively starts, "It was my decision. I was concerned for your safety when I heard of your encounter yesterday. I only wanted to secure the women in case they were spies." His sycophantic tone tries to placate his king as he exaggerates bowing before Arthur.

Gawain watches with a bland expression upon his face. Unlike Arthur, the older man's face does not betray the rage boiling beneath. Arthur had only told a few men of what had happened to him in the woods, and this lord was not one of them.

"Did I tell you that I want them found?" Arthur snaps.

"Well..." the snake of a man lets the word hang as he searches for what he thinks his lord wants to hear, "not in so many words, your majesty. I just thought--."

"You just thought you would use them to worm your way into my good graces, and now two men are dead from the affair. Two men wielding swords for our cause. Two men to plow the fields after we achieve peace. Two men who trusted me to protect them. Now, they are dead and lost to all of us." Arthur's voice rises as his eyes flash in anger.

Gawain is impressed by the boy's grasp of how precious life is.

"Honor your dead." Arthur snarls as he turns from the hunting party.

Gawain raises a brow and follows.

"I want them with the spears in the next battle," Arthur seethes with righteous fury.

"Arthur," Gawain protests.

"Am I not king here? I want his horse and title stripped. He will fight with the foot soldiers. Not only did I not tell him to send a hunting party, but he has shown we have a weakness in our confidants. I only told you, Roderick, and Manchester about my misadventure. If you were the one to spread the tale, I am doomed in this quest." Arthur gives his old friend a side glance. "If you did not tell, then it would have to be one of them."

He huffs as he works through the puzzle. "I trust the three of you with my life, and it would long have been claimed had I not. I do not think they would betray my trust, especially for a lickspittle like that." He runs a hand over his face, scrubbing away the tension growing on his brow. "Which means he most likely was snooping around my tent. Remind me to double the guards and to make sure they are men we can truly trust. Damn it all, I wish Merlin were here."

"Really? That is your wish? I would have bet your wish was for your mythical women to whisk you away with them," Gawain teases.

Arthur, who wants nothing more than to sulk and

brood over the day's events, grunts a response. A smile tugs at the corner of his lips at the older man's teasing. The vision of Morgan keeps dancing through his mind. The way her skin glistened, how her eyes looked like the night sky full of stars. The image of the girls glowing with light as they brought their friend back from the brink of death will forever be etched into his memory. He can still feel the shameful, hot desire burning inside. He longs to feel those soft hands on him again. He has not shown the scar on his leg to anyone, nor revealed the loss of his father's dagger. Once safely deposited in his tent, he sits at his war table and runs his fingers idly over the scar. Under his leather britches, the red line is smooth and healing. When she touched him, something happened between them, he is sure of it. What he would not give to see her again. He needs to shake this foolish boy's dream off and focus. They are going to battle tomorrow, and he needs all the skill, power, and luck he can muster.

******

The three women walk the winding path out of the hollow, through the forest, and away from the rising sun. Morgan has not said one word.

Isolder nudges Elaine, motioning to Morgan's back.

Elaine shakes her head and returns the nudge.

The two glare and pantomime at each other and Morgan ignores them. She is preparing herself to face the other Avalonians.

How could they follow me knowing that I have murdered the Lady? Why must it be this way? Could mother not have just granted the title to me and move on?

The tears flowing from Morgan's eyes had stopped long ago. Now they just feel puffy, but her mind still swims with concerns and questions. The sun glares overhead, daring to dry up Morgan's storm.

The three emerge from the forest canopy to find themselves standing on the edge of the field where the Hunt began. So much has happened that Morgan can barely believe it has only been three days. She pauses and peers in the direction the boy had come from.

Elaine and Isolder silently follow her gaze. In the distance, they can hear the roar of men and the clang of metal.

Morgan watches the serene skyline with a mix of fascination and sadness. She has never heard the sounds of war before.

Elaine rests a hand on her shoulder, and Isolder gently turns her toward the path leading to the water.

"My Lady, there is nothing we can do for the world of man. They must settle their petty feuds on their own. We must think of our sisters first." Isolder's voice is gentle and full of sorrow.

"She is right. The world of man does not deserve your protection. They will only bring us death and destruction," Elaine adds.

Morgan can hear the men crying out in agony. Their souls beg for miracles they cannot have. There are strong and steady women there as well, all praying to the Mother, to Morgan. They want strength. They want wisdom. They want to save them all.

Morgan closes her eyes and draws in a long breath, silently granting what wisdom and strength she has to those that believe. When she opens them again, she nods curtly and turns, leading them down the path to the water's edge. The rocks and mud are thick here as the lake's waves ripple against them. In the distance is a tiny boat bobs happily towards the shore unaided by any normal conventions. The tiny boat is just barely large enough for the three women waiting to be ferried home.

Elaine steps into the water and pulls the boat the last few feet to the beach when it reaches them.

Isolder climbs in and then offers her hand to Morgan, who takes it and gracefully moves to the center.

Elaine pushes it off into the water and then she too climbs in.

The two women sit while Morgan stands. She faces the East still. The lake, as if in response to the boat daring to trespass in its waters, soon becomes ensconced in fog. The two women watch the endless wall of white mists as they drift aimlessly.

Morgan knows better. This is the final test. When the boat stops, she will have to part the fog to grant them passage back to the island. The barrier is ancient magic that not even her mother knew. The constant bombardment of the pleas of the people calling for her attention is overwhelming. Couple that with the very life force of the island pumping through her heart and she struggles to keep from vomiting. The battle worn

Lloegyr faintly sings to her as well, as if she belongs to that world too. Morgan stands stoically, facing the direction of the island, oblivious of the peril the three of them are in. She neither sees nor hears that which is around her. Her dark eyes are lost in the haze of seeing too much. Her ears are drowned in the sea of voices begging of her. Her tongue is held as she fears answering will only make matters worse.

23

When You Believe

"She cannot do it," Elaine hisses at Isolder.

"Give her time. She has to concentrate."

"Time!? We have been here for hours, drifting nowhere. No island in sight. No land behind us. Nothing! We are lost on this lake and will never get home."

Morgan blinks hard and looks down at Isolder, who is biting her lip with anxiety. The sunny sky has given way to sunset, and Morgan is tired from standing too long, having lost track of time in her silent revelry. "I'm sorry." With a wave of her hands, she parts the fog, like opening the curtains to the bath in the temple. The fog, thick and white creates a direct corridor shooting hundreds of feet into the sky on either side.

The island looms on the darkening horizon. The boat picks up speed as it dashes toward the shore, as if it is not sure Morgan can keep the fog parted. The lake ripples in displeasure behind them.

Elaine turns back to see the fog closing in on them and nearly falls out of the boat as it teeters.

The boat slows and turns before stopping alongside the rickety wooden dock.

All three stand on the shore, looking up at the massive temple they call home. The island feels wondrous and new to them.

Isolder can barely contain her excitement and the plant life grows and radiates about the area in response.

A screeching roar can be heard overhead as three male dragons circle in the air. Elaine's heart sings to them.

Morgan is sure that if Elaine could sprout wings to fly to them, she would. A soft smile blooms on her face as her two friends hurry off to begin their duties. Morgan stays still, paralyzed with fear and dread. Three days ago, she wanted nothing more than to run away from Avalon. Now, she stands as its ruler. All the knowledge of all the Ladies passed on to her in the binding blood of her mother.

Tears well in her eyes again, and she can feel Nimoway's presence. She can feel the love the woman had for her. She knows the truth now of Wilhelm, or Archimedes, as he called himself.

She lingers, basking in the lore and knowledge

bequeathed to her, absorbing it into her very being. Where she was riveted to the spot before, she now runs. Running as fast as her bare feet can take her up the stone steps to the stone circle, past the Fountain of Truth, and along the path to the temple. She blows by the guards who greet her with curt nods and into the main hall, pausing only long enough to focus her thoughts. Then she is darting up the winding stairs that lead to her mother's chambers and shuts the door behind her. Out of breath, she looks around the room. It is quiet, with none of the hustle and bustle of the island. Morgan realizes she cannot hear all the voices and pleas. Her mind is free and clear of all the power that comes with being a deity. At first, she is terrified it is all a trick, that she is not truly the Lady of the Lake. She closes her eyes and scrunches up her face, soon hearing the whispers again. Once, sure she is still the Lady she opens her eyes and moves to the center of the room to gaze up at the ceiling.

The ceiling is alive with the stars in the night sky, giving way to walls covered in tapestries. The large bed is soft and welcoming. Books and scrolls are scattered throughout the stone carved shelves, holding vast wealths of knowledge. At the far end of the room is a tiny fountain fed by the hands of the stone representation of the Mother. When Morgan was little, she often found comfort in seeing Nimoway's form in stone. Only now, as Morgan inspects it, it is her likeness, as if her mother had never been, which causes her to frown. She rests her hands on the hands of the statue, draws in a deep breath, and pushes against the stone.

Nothing happens. The only sound in the room is Morgan straining from the effort. Redoubling her efforts, Morgan feels it give way, scraping as it slides along a track cut into the floor. Morgan had always assumed the crescent track represented the moon reflecting up from the water, never realizing it was a cleverly hidden door to a hidden room. Once the statue stops, Morgan stares at items she had only heard about in the old tales from Imogen. There are ancient books and scrolls, baubles, goblets, strange little dangling objects that tick, and a sword. In the center of this trove is a lone amulet. As she moves closer, it comes to life, attempting to float to her, only to be held at bay by the perch it dangles from. Morgan's fingers reach out and tentatively curl around the stone and metal talisman. The amulet warms her hand and reminds her of a dream, of an infant crying up at a beast stealing her away. She plucks the amulet from its prison and slips it over her head.

Nothing happens again and she is dejected at this anti-climactic scene. She thumbs over the jewel in it, as flashes of Nimoway's thoughts dance behind her eyes, watching as she takes the necklace off the tiny infant with raven black hair. Now that she has been reunited with it, she feels the tension between her shoulders loosen for the first time in her life. With that done, she paws through the rest of her treasure. She starts with one a large tome and thumbs it open. The words are elegantly drawn, and in assorted colors of ink. She has never seen something so beautiful in a book before. She cannot make out the words. It is as if they are deliberately blurring themselves from her. Flipping the pages carefully, she tries several times to discern what the book's secret is, but gets no satisfaction. After checking a few of the other books and scrolls to find the same result, she leaves them be. She feels echoes of her grumpiness from each of the previous Ladies of the Lake when they found themselves in the same position.

Her attention finally turns to the sword. It calls to her. Grasping the heavy weapon she turns to leave her trove, and approaches the entrance where she spies the hidden level to close the wall. Using her free hand, she pulls it and returns the statue to its original position. With a bounce she plops down on her mother's bed and tugs the sword into her lap. With the hilt in her left hand, she firmly takes hold of the scabbard with the right and tries to pry it free. The long sword is too much for her, refusing to budge. She tries another tactic by trying to woo it with magic. No luck for the second attempt either. With a huff she turns it over in her hands to see if there is a spell on it. When she sees the hilt, she furrows her brow at the funny word carved into it.

πιστεύω

While Morgan has never seen Greek, she can feel her mind piece together the word's meaning from her newfound knowledge.

She holds the sword for the ruler of men who believe

in Avalon. Her mother had gone on and on about how important of a symbol this lost sword is to the people of Lloegyr. The last ruler of Lloegyr to wield it died centuries ago, and only one of his line can unsheathe it. Morgan is reminded of the horrible actions of those men in the forests.

The sounds of battle and bloodshed flood into her mind. Closing her eyes, she focuses on the sword, trying to see its future, and hers. The drumming sound of Druids preparing for battle grows louder. Screams of women and children echo through her head. She can see a shadowed figure watching her. His shoulders are square, and his presence is fearsome. Everything about his aura screams savior. He thrusts the sword high, the chaos instantly silenced as he stretches his hand out to her. Then there is darkness, shadows, and pain. Morgan feels as if her soul is being ripped from her body. The shrieking wails of an infant fill the air. Then death, sudden and painful, swallows Morgan like a fish gulping an unsuspecting bug on the water.

Morgan lets out a cry and drops the sword, scrambling back to hug her knees to herself and rocks. Her eyes wildly stare about the room as if all that had just happened in that very space. Her gaze finally lands on the sword again, and it is gleaming on the floor, a hair's breadth of shimmering steel exposed. It calls to her to pick it up and carry it to its master. The longer she stares at it, the stronger the call becomes.

Cautiously, she climbs off the bed. She snatches one of her mother's shawls and wraps the sword's hilt before gently lifting it like a viper about to strike her. Her steps are quiet, and she moves gingerly, with the blade held at arm's length. Placing it carefully against the fountain she makes sure it will not fall. In retreat she turns her back on the sword. Falling back into the bed, she refuses to deal with her vision. She will rest and start being the Lady of the Lake tomorrow.

The Path is Treacherous

"What do you mean you still cannot find it? It is an entire nation of Animals parading about like the rest of us. According to the Grimmerie, it is exactly three days walk South of here," Law, sitting at the head of the table, thumps his fist on the mahogany top to emphasize his displeasure. The young man before him is known only by his profession.

"I would not dare to presume I know more than you, your Grace. I can only tell you that something is amiss. I walked the path that leads to the Aesop Nation, and I found only a dangerous forest in its place. It is the same every year when you summon the huntsmen. I am the last of my order, and only by my wits did I return to you." The Huntsman shrugs.

"Be gone from my sight," Law growls.

The Huntsman bows graciously before vanishing from sight. The Six, as they are commonly known, sit in awkward silence. The three previous rulers of Nodd float precariously above them, eternal in their slumbering prisons. They had been a distraction in the public hall, so they are kept here until the Six can discern how to finish the job they started hundreds of years ago. Time, in Nodd, has been made fluid. No one knows why Time is fluid. Some days are hours, some are weeks. Three midnights could mean in a few days, or in a few years. Father Aesop would tell everyone it is because Time waits for no one, but he only knows when Time began to change, not why.

"How does one man manage to hide an entire nation? How? Saint," he shifts in his seat to look at the younger man to his left. "Why could you not find it again?"

"I have already answered you a hundred times over. There is an enchantment too powerful to break. I can feel it calling to me when I step foot in the forest. It causes me to grow weary, and it disorients me." Frustration at the constant badgering flashes in Saint's eyes.

"And you," turning to Fate, "This is none of your mischief, is it?"

The radiant woman with eyes as piercing as a hawk narrows them at her husband. "My love, if I wanted to have mischief, I would. I have no clue as to why you cannot control our kingdoms. Perhaps it is the will of the universe that you are not Lord over all of Nodd." Her tone is as biting and sharp as her gaze. Where he abides by rules, and demands all else to do so, she acts from the wild passions of her whims. The angry grunt from Law is enough to make her smile and settle into her seat, awaiting the long diatribe about the importance of unity.

"Have you heard from the old wizard?" Desire's question rings sweet and sincere across the room, interrupting Fate's fun, causing the other woman's smile to sour. She adores Merlin. He behaves like a doting relative to her. While he was instrumental in orchestrating this mess, she alone is convinced he is on their side.

"I sent him to negotiate peace with the witches of Oz. Since their Wizard's mysterious disappearance," the title twists her tongue as if Fate believes he is a wizard as much as she believes the sky is orange, "they have proved most uncooperative in becoming part of the realm. Their military is far superior to that of Wonderland and obtaining that knowledge will help put an end to this hundred years war."

From the night the infant disappeared, Nodd has been in chaos. With the Three absent, the Council of Six has stepped into fill the void and implemented new laws. The old guard, or at least the ones that had not been turned to stone at the circle, were dismissed. Highly efficient knights and mercenaries have been recruited to be the military arm of the Six. The first order of business with the transition of power was to hunt down all Grimms. The Grimms have become fairy tales themselves. Only the oldest and most knowledgeable of Noddians remembers them clearly. The power the Six hold is temporary. Every so often, Noddians' memories of that fateful night return and they rise in rebellion. Without Aesop and the infant, the true power of the Three forever remains out of their grasp.

"Tell us, oh wise Oberon," Chaos's screechy, unhinged voice chortles from her perch. "Just what do you expect? You cannot even keep the peasants of Fair Verona in check. Was it not the first to be brought under your infinite wisdom? Their sovereignty collapsed under the petty bickering of their own royal houses. There has been nothing but bloodshed and mourning in the wake of the annexation. It is now a haunting city of dreary souls. Their stories are full of dark plots, death, betrayal, and only the slightest hint of magic. The vines that intertwine the walls of Verona have long stopped blooming their flowers. The festivals in honor of Titania have given way to the rituals of Oberon, and the penalty for disloyalty to the *church* is death." Her flare for dramatics exaggerated as she throws herself back and brings her hand to her head with her monologue.

"Please," her dramatics drop as her tongue sharpens, "You are an inept ruler that cares more about the blood you write in than the power we should have. We should just burn the forest and everything in it."

"How is that malevolence working for you in

Wonderland, dear wife?" The contempt in Order's voice rings over her irritating giggling at Law's ineptitude. "The two queens had ruled there for eons in peace. Now, the Red Queen holds the throne. Her vanity and cruelness are only matched by the viciousness and cunning of her chief assassin, the Cheshire Cat, who *she* claims has never failed to catch his prey. Yet, the entire nation is in civil war and the White Queen lives." His voice is even and driving, never varying in tone or pitch. "Yes, The White Queen, the delicate little flower pining for her champion from Lloegyr to come and save them from their broken fate whom you claimed would be nothing more than a memory years ago." He ignores the daggered glare Chaos sends his way.

"With Red Heart's betrayal to her sister, the Suited Army was all but decimated. How are we supposed to rule without an army to keep everything as it should be? Had you let me finish cultivating the relationship with both Queens, we would not only have Wonderland, but we would have an army and could end the obstinate resistance from those damnable witches of Oz." He slaps his hand on the table to get his wife's attention again.

"Even with the thought of the White Queen being dead, her followers are ever bolder to rise against the Red Queen, yet we cannot even confirm or deny *that*! The only sign of the White Queen we have is her trusty ambassador, the White Rabbit, who is ever in a hurry for important business, or so he claims. He and the Cat are the only Aesopi left outside of Oz and must know what that cursed beast has done and how it can be undone. We should force it from them, once and for all." He turns his even gaze towards Law this time, blaming him for the lack of success in this endeavor.

Desire rolls her eyes at Order's prattling. He is always going on about how the right way to do things is the only way to do things, and how he should be the chief ruler of Nodd. "Of course, you think that. I mean, you are ever in line, licking the boots of our Emperor." Desire's voice stings like the thorn of a rose. "After all, Saint and I were able to secure the Labyrinth with none of the turmoil the four of you have caused."

"That is only because the Goblin King found your 'garden' more pleasant than his own," Fate growls like a disapproving mother.

"I wish you would quit referring to my wife as-," Saint grumbles and is cut off by Fate.

"Wish. Wish. Wish. All you ever do is wish. Really. Just what are you good for?" Fate's cruel gaze levels on Saint with a malicious glee about it. "You know as well as I that wish-granting is reserved for only those who earn it. Wishes come true, not free, dear brother. If you have nothing useful to say other than wishing, you should keep your mouth shut. Perhaps your pretty face will allure one of the witches of Oz, or the new child they put on the throne. Ozma, they call her."

Fate's revelation of a new ruler of Oz is enough to send Law up out of his chair. With a roar, he sweeps his arm over the maps and scrolls before him, sending the papers into the air and the other items to the ground with a loud crash. With a donkey kick, his chair skids back. He comes around the table, stalking toward his wife, Fate, like a wolf about to devour the rabbit. Taking her forcefully by the arm, he pulls her close enough she can feel his hot breath on her skin. "And just how do you know there is a new ruler in Oz?" He hisses through his teeth. "Dear wife, is there something you would like to share with the rest of us?"

A Woman's Touch

In the entryway is a man eavesdropping on the Emperor and his family. His robes are shabby and singed and mud stains cover a fair amount of the hemline. His beard is tied into a neat cylinder of shapes down his chest, and his silver hair is spiky and short. His eyes dart between the six of them as the argument devolves into screaming and shouting at each other. Fate's revelation of being in contact with the Ozians surprises even him. It is also troubling. She is likely working to stage a coup with one of the witches. The four witches of Oz are the true power of the nation and his time with the "Good" Witches has taught him not to underestimate the newly founded nation. "I come with great tidings, my lords and ladies," his voice rings out over the chaos in the room.

All six of them stop in their bickering to turn and face the interloper.

With a wave of his hand, Law rights the items that have been strewn about, leaving everything in pristine order. "This is not over." He lets go of his wife's forearm with a murmured threat before he gracefully settles at the head of the table and the others follow suit. "Ah, Merlin, what news do you bring us from Ozrail?" His tone changes immediately to pleasant and regal.

"It would appear news travels faster than I can. The Ozians have crowned an Empress, and it is no longer Ozrail, your grace. It is just Oz. Ozrail, according to old wives' tales, refers to some mythical place where they banish convicts to." He purposely points out Law's error in a quick jab. While Merlin was revered as the most powerful person in Nodd and Emperor once, he does not seem to be able to end the Six's rule. He allows them to rule with their petty laws and twisted plots. Some say he is biding his time until the return of Aesop and the Grimms. Others believe he might be Aesop in disguise. His actions are often a mystery, even to the Six.

Law's eyes narrow as he watches the elderly man approach. He would like nothing better than to send Merlin to oblivion as well. If it were not for his meddling, they would have been able to complete the rituals the night of their creation.

"She is a child, only twelve years in age. Her magic is

strong, but her confidence lacks." He takes his seat at the opposite end of the table of Law and assess the temperament of the others. He sees so much of his three daughters in them. "The witches chose her because she is malleable. They would prefer to rule Oz, but the people there do not trust the witches. Thanks to the Wizard, they are skittish of magic and rely more on intellect, ingenuity, and technology. You should see the wondrous things they have built." Merlin removes his spectacles and rubs them casually with his robe. As he does so, both the tiny lenses and his robes lose all hints of grime and dirt. They shift into more regal attire, and he looks more like an Emperor than the man sitting across from him.

The Six are spellbound, watching, and listening to him. A faint smile forms on his lips as he continues to assert his dominance, proving to himself that he can control them. He can feel the tug on his cheeks reminding him of how his face still holds remnants of the stoning spell he nearly fell prey to that fateful night. He releases them and continues, "I am sure you are eager to know how my meeting with the witches went." He pauses for dramatic effect as he seats the small lenses upon the bridge of his nose. "It went well. There are two witches to contend with. While they have apprentices, and followers, they are the only ones with true power. There is Glinda of the South, and Locasta of the North. The sisters the locals claim as 'Wicked', the Witches of East and West, were vanquished by the outlander Dorothy. There are rumors that Delphine, the Witch of the West, survived, though, and is in hiding. I could not confirm this." He lies smoothly to them. While Dorothy did indeed land on the Witch of the East, the rumors of water melting Delphine had been exaggerated. Merlin spoke with all three witches in secrecy to help them secure the most beneficial position they could against the Six.

"If you want to control the land of Oz, you will need to eliminate the witches and place your own adviser to the empress. Ozma relies heavily on Locasta and Glinda for how to rule Oz and has yet to demonstrate any magic of her own."

"And of the Wizard? Where is he," Fate asks.

"He left with Dorothy. Returning to a place called Kansas from what I understand, and in a balloon, of all things." Merlin's response is matter of fact and his face neutral.

"We should go after him and bring him back to account for his crimes," Order chimes in.

"How well did that go for you the last time you ventured into the other world?" Merlin looks pointedly at Order and Chaos, as if he knows exactly of their failure in Lloegyr.

The two wilt into their chairs. They had been hoping to avoid Law's wrath for their failure to capture the Grimm on the island.

"What are you suggesting old man?" Law cuts in.

"I am suggesting that you somehow subdue the two witches and take their places at the Empress' side. Shape her decrees to fall in line with your laws, allowing you to graciously step in which will allow the child to focus on healing her people from the disruption of Dorothy while we take over the more tedious tasks of protecting their borders and trade with the other parts of Nodd. Brute force and dominance will not work with these people. They are far too cunning for that. You will have another bloody uprising, and the people of Oz will turn back to their own power before they ever submit to yours."

"And of the Grimm? What if he returns?" Law is not taking any chances. Grimms are far too dangerous to their cause to allow them to roam free in Nodd.

"I will go to this Kansas and track him down to deal with it." Merlin refrains from sighing at the petty near-sightedness of the man across from him.

Law narrows his eyes and watches Merlin for long enough that the others feel the awkward silence like a roaring lion in their face. "Very well. I expect proof of his demise."

"Of course, your Grace," Merlin stiffly pushes up out of his seat and begins toward the door. "Oh, and I thought you should know," pausing at the doorway before he vanishes. "They have named a new Lady of the Lake. You should send an ambassador. This would be an opportune time to discuss her bringing her magic to Nodd." With that, he vanishes.

Law drums his fingers gently on the table. He wants to send Desire and Fate to Oz to secure the nation, but does not want to lose the opportunity to acquire Avalonian magic. The mystical powers of Avalonian women have intrigued him greatly over the past twenty years. The previous ruler shunned him, claiming some stupidity about men not being allowed on her island. His gaze settles on Chaos. She is too unpredictable to trust with this delicate mission. Her dark gaze meets his with a daring defiance and he cannot help but smile at his sister's spark.

"Fate and Desire will go to Oz. Chaos to Lloegyr." He gets up and motions to dismiss everyone. The men start to protest, and he holds his hand up to silence them. "Avalon, if the Grimmerie is true, is sacrosanct and only tread upon by women. They do not allow men on the island, and the two of you are not ready for such a task as talking two witches into submission. I would prefer to handle this without bloodshed."

Defeated, everyone leaves except Fate. Her demeanor is light and amused as she comes closer to Law. "I do love when you are worked up." She trails her fingers along his shoulder.

"Hrmph," is his response, but he pulls her close to him. He brushes her hair back and leans in to kiss against her skin just below her earlobe. He murmurs, "If you fail me in this, I will send you back to where Merlin found you." Then he eases away from her and follows the others.

Her eyes narrow as she watches him go, and she retorts to the empty room, "I would like to see you try it."

Pixie Dust

"You are insane, Jakob. Insane! Father specifically wanted us to leave. Why would we go back?" Wilhelm runs his fingers through his hair. After much discussion, sleep, and food, the two brothers feel confident the other is not an impostor.

With a heavy sigh, Jakob watches his brother's animated pacing and flapping of his arms. It reminds him of a bird angrily flitting about the room. "Tell me what you named the infant," he finally chimes in.

Wilhelm halts in his tracks, opens his mouth to speak, then closes it, furrows his brow, and starts again. "What infant? We should be finding our brothers, not chasing after some infant."

"I see," Jakob frowns, "Then what did you carry

through the stones? Where did you go for all those years? I turned over every nook and cranny of Lloegyr and you were not there. You took the infant and jumped through the stones without thought."

"There is no infant! I just came from Lloegyr where *you* and *William* tried to detain me over..." He stammers again and sputters, the words he wants on the tip of his tongue.

"They wanted to know the whereabouts of the infant as well, did they not? Do you not find it odd that everyone except you knows about this infant?" Jakob's voice is soft, trying not to rattle his brother, but needing him to accept that something is not right.

Wilhelm hates to admit his concern at the fact he is missing memories. The witch at the stones did this to him. Her faceless shape haunts his dreams. The fog obscures her features from his mind. He snorts in response, making Jakob miss their father even more.

"Frank is one of the most brilliant mind manipulators I have ever seen, and he is in Ozrail. Ozrail is in Nodd. We have no way of communicating with Frank without being in Nodd." Jakob's tone shifts as he becomes the condescending big brother. That tone had always irritated Wilhelm.

"All I know is that I need to find William and Hans. That every bone in my body tells me that is the path to walk. Going back into Nodd without knowing the state of the world is illogical and risky. Father would not approve." Wilhelm bucks up stubbornly.

"By the stars, man! Frank is your brother. Would you

abandon him to be alone in Nodd?" Jakob shifts gears to manipulate Wilhelm into thinking this is part of his quest.

"Do not you try that with me," he points a finger at Jakob. "I am finding William and Hans before I do anything else. If you are not going to help me, then I will go alone." Even as he finishes his ultimatum, he knows he sounds like an ass. "What if I made myself forget, on purpose? Apparently, this mysterious infant is important, and I must not have wanted her found."

Jakob pauses and stares at his brother in shock. It had never crossed his mind that Wilhelm would be so brilliant as to erase his own memories to protect the child. That means he may have permanently damaged his mind, which explains this laser focus on a single task. He is not fully convinced of Wilhelm's brilliance, but he does not want to make an enemy of his brother. "Fine," he says with reluctance. "I will return to Nodd to fetch Frank, and you will set out to find William, or Hans."

Wilhelm exhales relieved his brother is not going to continue to fight him on this. "Do you have any idea where they are?" He asks, revealing his lack of knowledge sheepishly.

Jakob has a hearty laugh at his brother's expense. He wipes the tears from his eyes while he pours them both a drink. "I know William travels. I believe he is currently in Italy, posing as a playwright. As to the year, I cannot place him. When we passed through the stones, none of us landed in the same place, nor time."

"I know how to navigate the stones. That is not a problem." He waves a hand dismissively.

"Oh, you are an expert now, are you? Just how did you learn to navigate the stones?"

"I learned," he starts to say from where, but then he stops. It is on the tip of his tongue but the harder he tries to say it, the more he cannot. "I just know, alright!"

"I see. Well, we should prepare before we go. In case something happens to one of us." Jakob moves around the room, gathering up a few odds and ends. He watches Wilhelm as he works, deliberately touching his brother's things to get a rise out of him, and failing. Jakob grows more concerned. He comes close and clamps a hand on his brother's shoulder, looking him straight in the eyes. Jakob holds his gaze, his grip firming as Wilhelm jerks under the surge of power. He searches into his brother's soul, trying to break the fog free of his mind, only to find it growing thicker. The more he pushes the more Wilhelm's mind fights. Minute after minute, Jakob tries to press through the fog, until he realizes that if he presses any further, he may become bewitched himself. He is breathing hard, and both men are covered in sweat from the effort. Jakob does not release Wilhelm, but he does relent on the assault on his mind. Instead, he cheats. "I am sorry, brother. This is for your own good." Jakob blows a handful of pixie dust into his brother's face. The glittering dust fills the air and Jakob releases Wilhelm, stepping back to avoid getting caught in his own trap.

Wilhelm gasps and sputters before he tries to cover his mouth. It is too late. The substance fills his lungs and makes his eyes water. The room warps and shifts while Jakob appears to fly away several miles. He coughs and shakes his head. As much as he does not want to succumb to the addictive powder, he knows that he cannot will it out of his chest. "Why?" he looks angrily at Jakob.

"Your mind has been altered, Wilhelm. I need you to follow me back to Nodd. We will find William and Hans after, but we must restore your mind first." Jakob issues the command and knows Wilhelm will comply. His guilt weighs heavy on him, but he has convinced himself he has no choice.

Wilhelm doubles over and shakes his head, trying to force himself to walk away from Jakob. Even as he knows that is what he wants, he feels his head nodding yes in agreement to his brother's demands. His body calms as the dust takes hold. He discovered pixie dust quite some time ago. Fairies produce it as a defense mechanism from predators, causing the threat to become compliant and placid. Their wings are worth a pretty coin on the black market. He and his brothers created Neverland to protect them. The island was intended to be a haven for the fairies. To prevent Noddians from adventuring to the island, the exact location was wiped from their minds by their father. Never, in all his years, did he think his own brother would use their addictive dust on him. Now, he follows his brother around the manor until Jakob is satisfied they have everything they need.

The grimace on Wilhelm's face is enough to tell Jakob he may never forgive him.

Then the pair are out the door and back on the road to the village where Jakob found Wilhelm. Wilhelm walks stiffly and his gait becomes staggard, telling Jakob that the pixie dust is starting to fade.

Jakob picks up the pace and the two of them are breathless as they come upon the stone circle Wilhelm popped out of a fortnight prior. Giving Wilhelm a side glance, he clears his throat. "It works better if we focus on the same person."

"I know that!" Wilhelm's tone is bitter and sharp. "I have never met Frank," he snaps.

Jakob frowns, as he had not considered that. Ozrail had been newly added to Nodd before they left, but Wilhelm had been so completely enraptured with the Silver Court that he had not bothered to meet the new Grimm. "Well, then think of me and take my hand."

Wilhelm tries to not take the hand. His entire arm trembles in resistance.

Jakob moves forward to step through the center stone, his hand still extended.

Wilhelm continues to resist.

Jakob's form disappears into the stone, only his hand left extended.

At the last possible moment, Wilhelm reaches out and takes the hand. He is yanked into the stones and feels as though his entire body is on fire, being ripped apart. He twists and turns, unable to see Jakob, but can feel him. His screams are muted in the deafening silence of the in between. The stars swirl around him. The air is ripped right from his lungs. The ground roils up like waves in the ocean. Fear grips him as he feels himself being torn apart.

27

Cat & Mouse

Just as quick as the universe contorts with the invasion of the two men, it relents and the torture ends. The two brothers are on the ground, coughing and gasping. The stone circle they are sitting in is nothing like the circle they left Nodd in. This has intricate carvings and markings that remind Wilhelm of another place, but try as he might the place eludes him. His face feels warm against the moss-covered stones.

Not far from him is Jakob. His face is marred and bleeding, and he is breathing shallowly.

While furious with the man, he is still his brother. Wilhelm pushes up and comes to him, rolling Jakob onto his back, he sees the man has been skewered by a large stone fragment.

"Oh brother," he breathes out. He stares at the damage and carnage, not sure how to help him.

He looks about, trying to discern where they are in Nodd, but this place looks foreign to him. Once upon a time, he had known exactly how to help Jakob. Now, all he feels is fear and displacement as the fog eats away at what once was.

"Wilhelm," Jakob's voice finally breaks through the panic. "Wilhelm, look at me."

Wilhelm looks down with tears in his eyes.

"Heal me." His voice rings true, and as much as Wilhelm had been trying to resist him earlier, he snaps to attention. "The stardust..." Jakob struggles to point at his bag.

He lets go of his brother to rummage through Jakob's bag until he finds a bottle of stardust. When he returns to Jakob, he pops the cork and pours it over the chest wound first. His hands tremble with fear, but he is careful not to spill one drop as he pours it over Jakob's face, and then corks the bottle.

The pixie dust works its magic, burning through the fog as Wilhelm gently pushes Jakob's wounds closed. He does not have to think, or second guess himself. The magic of the addictive dust makes him comply with Jakob's commands without fail. Even if he wanted to let his brother suffer, he could not. It is agonizing how long this process takes. He sits back, his body propped against the stone, and watches his brother. "I hate you." He whines like a child. "I will hate you more if you leave me here alone." Closing his eyes, Wilhelm breathes slow, deep breaths. He can feel the last of the pixie dust burning out of his system, leaving him in control of his faculties once more. He contemplates abandoning Jakob here, but he fears the fact that his mind is slipping. He cannot even remember who did this to him any longer. Rage at his helplessness fills him.

"Good thing for you, I will survive," his brother's voice is weak, but full of mirth. Jakob is still lying where Wilhelm left him. The wounds that were gaping and severe are now jagged red lines across his body and face. His breathing is steady and strong. Jakob does not want to admit it, but those wounds had nothing to do with the stones rejecting their travel. Someone had attacked them in transit. He had not heard of such an ability before, but now he is convinced the stones are being watched. "We should not linger here."

"Where *is* here?" Wilhelm sounds calm, but Jakob can hear the bubbling fury barely contained in his brother's voice.

"We are in the Labyrinth of the Goblin King. He is not friendly to Grimms." Jakob rolls up onto his hands and knees, testing his strength. Then he looks up to meet the angry face of Wilhelm, who is already standing and offering his hand to help him up. "I had no other choice," he offers as an apology.

"You always have a choice, Jakob," Wilhelm snaps back. "I cannot remember the path out."

"That is because it has changed. The Goblin King alters the Labyrinth to keep the creatures from escaping. After the incident with the girl from the other world, he has been more cautious." He shifts uncomfortably as he walks from the circle.

"I cannot remember where, but I have seen a circle like this before. I am sure of it." Eager to be out of the circle, he nearly collides into Jakob.

"I find that hard to believe, Wilhelm. That circle has been hidden from most of Nodd for more than a millennium. I recently found it by sheer luck." It also helped that the Goblin Queen, a prisoner of the Labyrinth, summoned him to her, but Wilhelm does not need to know all of Jakob's secrets. The two of them make their way through the maze, which is as alive as they are.

Wilhelm cannot help but to look over his shoulder often. The feeling that they are being watched, or followed, will not leave him.

"Eyes front, brother, or you might get lost. We do not have time to play out the riddles of the Goblin King."

"We are being followed," Wilhelm grumbles.

"I know," Jakob replies. "It is the Labyrinth's guardian. She is trying to determine if we are invading or lost." Jakob pauses at a wall with vines of dead leaves. It is unassuming and tall, much too tall for anyone to scale it. "This way."

"Jakob, that is a wall. There is nothing to see—."

Jakob walks right through the wall.

"By Merlin!" Wilhelm quickly chases after him, not

wanting to encounter the approaching guardian. On the other side of the wall are open fields. The sun is shining bright and there are two horses tethered to the signpost. It is as if Jakob knew this was the path and planned all of this out. Wilhelm still feels uneasy about this and cannot remember why he does not like things to play out so easily, but he does not trust it.

"A lot has happened since we left. We are in the southern-most part of Wonderland. The Red Queen's spies are all about, trust no one here. Not even those you called friends once." Jakob saddles up and waits for Wilhelm to follow suit before they start at a breakneck pace to the West.

Wilhelm's eyes are drawn to the burning plumes in the distance. The feeling of it having been a prominent place to him nags him mercilessly. He does not linger on the thoughts and pushes his horse to keep pace with Jakob.

Over the next few hours, they do not say one word to each other as they race along the dirt road leading to Oz. However, as was true hundreds of years ago, Grimm magic is still tracked. In pursuit of the two is an army of men dressed in black and white, their rank identified by a number and symbol. "Halt! In the name of the Red Queen!" The order carries to them as the vanguard gains upon them.

"Blast," Jakob growls and urges his horse on further, looking back only to guarantee Wilhelm follows suit. Their horses snort and push faster, already exhausted at having run for hours at a hard pace. Jakob fishes into his pocket and throws a small pack over his shoulder behind him. An explosion of brilliant light flares to life behind them, leaving a crater and a cloud of debris in their wake. It only slows their pursuers momentarily. "We have to get to the border. They have no authority beyond the border of Wonderland!"

"Why are they chasing us?" Wilhelm shouts in fear.

"Because we are Grimms," Jakob shouts back as he spurs his horse on faster.

In the distance is a figure, massive and dark against the scorched plains of Wonderland. His ear twitches at the sounds of the stampede of horses in the distance. He picks at his nails and casually waits for the Grimms to get too close to outrun him, even on horses. Beyond him, it is only a few miles to the Ozian Wall. If the Grimms make it into Oz, he will have to answer to the Queen. The last thing he wants is to receive her ire. Another ear twitch tells him that there are two of them ahead of the others.

"Jakob! Look!" as they round the curve of the road, Wilhelm points out the Cheshire Cat.

"Fiddlesticks!" Jakob fumbles around in his saddle to produce a metal stick.

Wilhelm has never seen such a contraption before.

Jakob tucks his reigns under the saddle, primes the stick, and cocks it. He takes aim at the figure in the distance.

"What are you doing? We have to turn!" Wilhelm continues to follow Jakob, but looking back he can see the armed men closing in. Their horses cannot outrun all of them. There is a loud crack in the air, and Wilhelm's horse rears up in surprise, nearly throwing him as it stomps in place, refusing to run any further.

Jakob's horse snorts his displeasure, but otherwise keeps running.

The figure in the distance jerks, then vanishes from sight.

"Do not stop!" Jakob roars as he tucks the pistol back into its place. "Wilhelm!"

The soldiers are upon Wilhelm as he tries to calm his horse.

"Do not stop!" Wilhelm yells as he is lost in a sea of soldiers.

Jakob turns from Wilhelm to face forward again and out of nowhere a massive man of a cat leaps through the air, tackling Jakob off his horse. As the pair of them hit the ground, they tumble into the tall grass.

The cat digs his fingers into Jakob's arm, piercing his skin with sharpened nails. Jakob throws a right hook, and it sails through the Cat as he flickers from sight momentarily.

"Stop struggling, Jakob. I do not want to hurt you further." His growling purr is low and feral. He does not believe in turning over the Grimms to the Red Queen, but his duty is to Aesop, not to his reckless sons.

"Rot in Neverland," Jakob spits back.

The Cat easily rolls the other man into a sleeper hold, choking him until he stops struggling. He tosses his prey up over his shoulder like he weighs nothing, then moves toward the group subduing the other Grimm.

"Bind them and bring them quietly. The last thing we need is for an upstart Huntsman to take them to the Six." The cat settles the unconscious Jakob over his agitated horse.

The others repeat the process with Wilhelm, who glares at them as he is treated like luggage.

The Cat vanishes from sight again and leaves the soldiers to begin their trek North to the heart of Wonderland.

Wicked Is as Wicked Does

The hours pass as they march along the path, eventually making camp at sunset. It will be at least three days ride back to the heart of Wonderland. Jakob and Wilhelm are bound to a post driven into the ground by the lower grade soldiers. While others start a fire and prepare to feed the camp. These lands are desolate and dreary. The once lush gardens of Wonderland have not survived the blood kiss of war.

The orderly bustle of the camp is slowly overpowered by the dull roar of large wings flapping. Wilhelm furrows his brow as he looks up, seeking the source of the cacophony. To the South, the otherwise bright sky is dark with a blackish blue cloud quickly rolling towards them. A few of the soldiers notice and they nudge each other, pointing to the sky in awe, Unsure of what they are looking at, they laugh as they try to decipher what could be flying toward them.

"Secure the prisoners!" The commander barks, having taken one glance at the incoming cloud. "To arms!"

"Jakob, wake up," Wilhelm harshly whispers as he kicks his brother awkwardly from his sitting position, but gets no response. The massive cloud grows closer and he can hear the screeching and skittering of creatures communicating. He squints, trying to pick out details as the swarm splits and swirls around the soldiers. He has never seen such creatures before, not even in the Aesop Nation.

They look malicious and terrifying, sporting massive raven-black wings and wicked claw-tipped hands. The beasts swoop down, lifting poor card-men into the air before shredding them to pieces with their front and back claws. To little avail, unfortunately, as the soldiers are the Suits of Wonderland. As they hit the ground, their pieces instantly begin to slither and twist, reforming the soldier. The Suits are a mixture of flesh and living paper and one of the greatest creations that Lewis ever imagined. They are not the smartest creations, but they are loyal to a fault and nigh impossible to kill. The winged beasts appear to never end. The entire sky is black and blue with them.

Wilhelm shrinks down as low as possible, trying to cover his brother to keep him from being mauled to death beside him.

The soldiers are running everywhere, their weapons flailing wildly at the beasts.

Wilhelm is face to face with one of them, his gaze affixed by the intelligent eyes staring darkly at him from an ape-like face. Massive leathery wings flare out behind the creature, causing shadows to dance along its fur mixed with scales, and the dark blue diamonds tattooed across its face.

"What is the name of thou father?" The beast growls in a heavily accented dialect.

Wilhelm blinks in disbelief, and as he goes to respond he finds the name is gone. Horror washes over his face, and he looks like a codfish as he opens and closes his mouth, trying to force the name of his father off the tip of his tongue.

"Aesop," Jakob croaks, but it catches the beast's attention.

The creature screeches and another beast lands in front of Jakob. They say something in a language that Wilhelm does not understand, then the two men are roughly hoisted up off the post, and buffeted with harsh winds as the beasts fling themselves into the air, absconding with their prizes. As they soar above the brutal massacre of soldiers, there is a screech from the beast carrying him, and the others soon follow taunting their victory over the regenerating card soldiers below.

The brothers gasp and grimace in pain as the claws of the winged beasts dig into them, carrying the brothers far above the ground.

Not wanting to fall to his death, Wilhelm hopes they have not been rescued only to be eaten by these monsters. His arms go numb as they pass from war-scorched fields to poppy fields. In the distance, a massive wall made of copper and stone looms along the border. The creatures fly higher and higher until the ground looks like a map itself.

"Ozrail," Wilhelm murmurs.

As they pass over the wall, the world changes vastly. There are lush fields, tall snow-covered mountains, and a glittering emerald-colored city off in the distance. The creatures veer to the west and swoop down low, close to the top of the forests. The sun gives way to the moon when the beasts touch down at the foot of what looks like a mountain. The fortress's stone steps behind the wrought-iron gates wrap around the building like a snake around its prey. The two men are gently set upon their feet as the cloud of winged monkeys disperses, leaving them with a mere guard contingency.

"This way," the guttural accent is hard to understand, but when the beast opens the gate with an echoing squeak it is obvious what is expected of them.

The Grimm brothers are ushered through it and wind their way through long corridors and curving stairs until they are deep inside the tower. The brothers are out of breath and covered in sweat by the time they reach the top and left in an attic. Bedding is thrown about and the roof is missing in places. There are scrapes along one wall, and a scorch mark with green splatters on the floor. The beasts shut the door with a loud thud behind them.

Jakob stumbles over to Wilhelm and the two of them work to get their hands free. Each of them are careful to not use magic, just in case it could be tracked here. The air whistles through the room like a howl of revenge. Wilhelm moves to a window the size of two men and looks out over the horizon. From here, he can see the Emerald city glitter in the distance. This place is nothing like he thought it would be.

Jakob settles into a chair and peels his shirt and vest from his right arm. "Wilhelm, come. Help me."

He takes in Jakob. His brother is pale and clammy and fumbles to peel the shirt away with a shaking hand. Worry gnaws at him as he eases closer to assist.

"The Cheshire Cat's warning," Jakob answers Wilhelm's unasked question. "His claws have poison that subdues his prey, allowing him to catch them with great ease."

"What can I do to help you, brother?" All the anger and fury from the day's events ebb away in the face of Jakob's condition. Wilhelm is sure he was right in not wanting to come back to Nodd. This is the second time since arriving that Jakob has been gravely wounded. "The stardust?"

"No. The Cat's poison cannot be countered with magic. I need the antidote, or something to pull the poison from my blood." Jakob's voice is light and thready as he leans back.

"And what happens if we get neither?" Wilhelm, try as he might, fails to recall anything about Cheshire

Cats, poisons, or antidotes.

"He will die," a stern, feminine voice fills the room.

Wilhelm, startled, whirls around and puts himself between Jakob and their new visitor. When he sees nothing, he shifts closer to Jakob, eyes scanning all the dark corners for the unseen threat. A crystalline laugh echoes through the ruined attic before a slender young woman, wearing an all-black gown, comes into view. The dress is fitted to her waist, then flairs into a full skirt, which swishes gently as she moves closer to them. Her hair is pulled back in a simple braid down her back, but what holds Wilhelm's gaze is the tone of her skin. The vibrant green contrasts the room in such a stunningly beautiful way that he cannot look away. His heart races and his chest feels tight as he is mesmerized by the beauty before him.

Wilhelm watches in fascination as she shoves him aside, rips the tattered remnants clean from Jakob's shoulder, and places her hands over the wound. Her green fingers quickly stain with the starry blood of his brother.

"He did not give you a full dose," she states with confidence.

"Is that good?" Wilhelm asks.

"If you consider a slow, painful death good, then yes. The Cat's poison causes your muscles to stop working, your blood to slow. You lie there paralyzed while he slowly stalks toward you. After which, he disembowels you. Unable to scream. Unable to move. You just lie there while you are murdered." She fishes out a small vial from somewhere within her skirts before taking the cork between her teeth and gently releasing it from the vial full of silver dust.

"Just how do you know all this?" Wilhelm is bewildered by her gruesome recount of the Cheshire Cat's abilities.

"Because he told me when I sought his help in appearing dead." She does not look at Wilhelm as she begins to dab the liquid into the puncture wounds. She rubs her fingers over the wounds roughly and Jakob inhales sharply in pain as silvery veins spider out from the wound.

Wilhelm crosses his arms and rubs his eyebrow, watching her manhandle Jakob. After the vial is empty, the silvery veins fade, the wounds close, and Jakob's arm begins to move. He looks like death warmed over as his head lolls against the cold stone wall.

"You should sleep, Jakob Grimm, you will need your strength if the Six find you here."

Jakob nods and tries to tug what remains of his sleeve into place. The mysterious woman stands and comes face to face with Wilhelm again, studying him, and he catches her scent. She smells as sweet as honey with a tinge of metal, as if she has come from a workshop. He cannot help but stare at her, quite taken aback when their eyes meet. Her eyes are filled with stars. While she is much smaller than he, she is terrifying and menacing. "Why, beautiful lady, would you want to appear dead?"

"Because the Six are coming to take my home, and I

want to be able to fight them without being enslaved to them." She tries to shove by him, and he blocks her path with purpose.

"The Six?" He knew of all the Numbers in Nodd, and it was always Three, never Six.

"Are you daft? The Council of Six? Law, Fate, Order, Chaos, Saint, and Desire. The rulers of Nodd who have been destroying this world for nearly a few hundred years?! Who are you, anyway?" Her eyes narrow darkly as she judges whether this intruder is a threat.

"Delphi, be nice," Jakob chastises her.

"Who am I? Now who is the daft one? I am—." Wilhelm puffs up before he is abruptly cut off by Jakob.

"No one of import. He is just an outlander that needs your help." Jakob glares at his brother.

Wilhelm takes the hint and does not say his name. For whatever reason, Jakob does not want this green menace to know him. This only makes her more intriguing to Wilhelm.

Who is she? How does she know Jakob and not me? Why does Jakob not trust her?

Dark thoughts swirl through the fog in Wilhelm's mind, trying to piece together this puzzle and failing.

So, instead of trying to work his brain too hard, he gives her a lopsided grin. This rewards him with her grunting and shoving him out of her way a second time. She flits past him with unnatural speed, a sure sign of someone with natural magic which cannot be contained.

"You are an Ozrailian Witch," the words fall from his

lips in shock.

This brings her to a full stop, and she turns to face him again. "There is no such place as Ozrail. You are in Oz. And yes, I am a witch. The *Wicked* Witch of the West, at your service," she gives him a mock bow before losing all pretenses at pleasantries. "I would watch who you call a witch in Oz, good sir. You might find yourself cursed worse than you already are." With that, she slams the door closed behind her and locks the two men in the small room again.

"Wait! You cannot leave us here! Do you know who we are?!" Wilhelm shouts at the door, pulling futilely against the rough iron ring, then gasping as it singes his hand.

"It is of no use. She cannot hear you. This place is hidden from prying eyes. Come, help me find a comfortable place to sleep." Jakob pushes himself up and starts moving debris aside to find the palate he slept on the last time he snuck into Nodd.

"Why did you not want her to know who I am?" Wilhelm positively glows as he bounces over to help his brother.

"Because there are bounties on all the Grimms, especially you. You are wanted by the Six for kidnapping the Heir." Jakob collapses down on the bedding and begins to relax. "While she is willing to harbor one criminal, I am not sure she will harbor two."

"Kidnap who? I did no such thing! What kind of prank is this? I am not a criminal. I... I—." His voice peters out as he twists his face in consternation, trying to recall that which his brother was referring to.

"You cannot remember half of what you ate yesterday, let alone what you did hundreds of years ago."

"Hundreds of years? Jakob, it has been a mere decade or two, at most. Do not try to feed me nonsense. What is her story? Why does she need to be dead to fight off this mysterious Six? How can we help her?"

Jakob rolls his eyes and thumps his brother. "She is one of the four witches of Oz. The others turned on her. They destroyed her sister, murdered her lover, and sent a child to assassinate her. She is the most powerful of the four. She has the gift of foresight, but her green skin makes the Ozians hate her. The only person who knows her origin is Frank. Remember him? Our brother, a Grimm, and self-proclaimed Wizard of this land?"

"How terrible," he sits down next to Jakob. "Why does she think I am cursed?" He ignores all the rest of Jakob's explanation.

"Wilhelm, your memory is disappearing." Jakob studies his brother with worry. "The longer we wait, the worse it gets. If she comes back while I am asleep, do not be rude. She is an ally."

"Rude?" Wilhelm asks in an incredulous tone. "I'm never rude. You just lay there and go to sleep. I will keep watch."

29

A Mother's Duty

Three years have passed since that fateful day in the clearing. Arthur has continued to push his claim for the throne, but the other lords have dug in and resorted to guerrilla tactics to thwart him. Long have they parted from the shores where the mysterious nymphs played, but he has not forgotten the alabaster skin and raven hair. This war has become drawn out and bloody. Women and children have become as much the targets of those who fight against him as the men who wear his heraldry. It is barbaric, and he would weep if he could ever bring this war to a close.

Priestesses claiming peace and guidance from the Mother have become more common through the lands under his control. It is an old religion, and one which he puts little faith in. The healers tending to his wounded embrace it, which gives him pause from just banishing the strange women proselytizing in his camps. That, and the lilting accent upon their tongues tickles memories he thought long lost.

"Maybe we should just step back. Concede our claim and go back to our farms." Arthur stands with his war council huddled around the strategy table. Winter still holds her claim on this part of the country, and the frigid air blows through their tents, reminding them that if the war does not kill them, freezing to death in their armor is still a possibility.

"Do not say such foolish things, boy. You are the rightful heir. There is no question about it. Uther should have named you heir publicly before he passed, keeping this from ever being an issue. This war is on *his* soul, not yours," Merlin snaps at Arthur with all the fatherly wisdom he feels is needed. "The rest of you should not let him talk like this. He is your king, support him! Do not let him wallow in self-pity because this road is difficult." He thumps his staff on the table for effect. "Now, I must go. I am to meet with an ally to arrange a bride for you."

"I do not see how a wedding could solve my problem of war, Wizard." Arthur grumbles at him. "I need you here to help with the next battle."

Merlin thumps him on the head. "Think boy! A strategic marriage to a powerful ally gives you more leverage against your enemies than a sword, or spell, ever would. Wars are not won with bloodshed, but with amnesty. You must be smarter than your enemies." Merlin thumps him on the head again and leaves the council.

The others watch him with as much contempt as they have for this weather.

"Do you smell that?" Gawain asks.

"It is just the fire. Likely young Galahad grabbed the wrong kind of wood again," one of the other men chimes in and they have a good laugh.

"No. That smells like-," his words are cut off by blood-curdling screams tearing through the night air.

They rush from the tent, drawing their swords, becoming engulfed in smoke and fire. Women are screaming and men are running to put out the fires. Arrows whistle through the air, screaming their promises of fiery death from above. Horses screech and whine, pulling against their tethers, trying to escape the fire closing in on them.

"Ambush," Arthur breathes out, stunned for a single heartbeat as he takes in the chaos.

"To arms! To arms!" His forceful shout spurs his men into action.

"Gawain, the horses. Tristan, the armory. Galahad, sound the alarm. Rowan, you tend to the healers. Get them and the children to safety." Arthur wheels his sword in hand and begins moving towards the screaming with all the ferocity of the dragon that is his house symbol. From the mists, men painted like Druids flow forth, but they are no more Druid than Arthur. Their armor and swords say otherwise. Without fear, he swings and slashes, felling men left and right.

His men disobey his command and instead fall in, fierce and strong by his side.

The screams of the women and cries of the children overpower even the clash of steel as the camp is overrun. The flickering inferno of burning tents cast wicked shadows over the men protecting the healers' tent as they fail to stave off this assault. The shadows curl around the very fabric of the tent, twisting and clawing at the invaders as the last of the men fall. Merlin stands firm, hidden from view, staff planted in the mud as he tries vainly to protect that which is most precious.

"Come sisters, pray with me." The woman dressed in simple robes kneels in the center of the tent, pulling in those who are terrified, regardless of the terrible chaos of the world around them. "Mother, hear our plea. Our faithful hearts beg for your mercy and protection." She repeats herself, growing louder, offering comforting arms to those around her.

The other girls quake with fright and follow her lead, chanting the cry for help.

Hundreds of miles away, Morgan's head snaps up and pulls her from the bowed position she is in. The isle is in full festive swing, welcoming forth the blossoming embrace of Spring. She does not see the bright colors, nor the joyous music. Rather, her eyes stare off into the distance, the blessing of fertility lost in the sudden onslaught of the prayers from her daughters. A tidal wave of primal fear washes over her as the banshee cries ring in her ears. The scent of death fills her nostrils. Quickly, Elaine and Isolder are at her side as her eyes narrow. Overhead, a single clap of thunder is all the warning the revelers have of the impending promise of violence. The sudden downpour of rain smothers the smaller fires, reducing them to a smolder. Ice cold winds whip across the plateau, forcing the priestesses to run for shelter. Morgan's eyes flood with inky darkness as malice blooms in her heart. She drags Elaine and Isolder with her, their three forms turning into the menacing leaders of Avalon. The roar of the dragons in their pens echo the rage in her heart, and their riders mount up without being told. The healers rush back to the circle with their herbs and salves braced against the wicked gale.

Morgan moves as if she is the very water in the air, fluid and fast. The louder the pleas fill her ears, the more her temper rises. Seconds later, behind the invading army, the water of the channel to the sea rises like a tidal wave, and out from it steps Morgan alone.

Merlin stops dead in his tracks, letting the protective spell he had been casting, slip. He blinks and rubs the rain from his eyes as time seems to extend to eternity. "Maab?" the one word comes as a strangled whisper from his lips and the moment is shattered.

The ethereal figure of Morgan steps forward and men perish at her whim, falling to the ground and writhing in pain. Lightning strikes the ground and sets men ablaze. Soon, the night sky is pierced by the ear-splitting roar of dragons appearing overhead, women atop them. They guide them to swoop down and pick off the enemy warriors with a hawk's precision. From the water basins in the tents, the healers appear. Their blue and silver robes stand in stark contrast to the earthy colors of the healers of Arthur's camp and their sisters. Isolder steps forth from the basin and with a casual flick of her hand the air reverberates, pushing back those that would seek to do harm, leaving only the women, children, and those needing healing in the tent. Her soothing presence calms the praying women, and those unable to defend themselves.

Elaine guides her winged warriors to encircle the camp, using the water dragons to put out fires while using the fire dragons to push back the invaders. She trusts Morgan's sense of whom to destroy. The fearsome creatures deftly dodge arrows and swords while taking out warriors like they are nothing more than flies. Her rage builds as she takes in the senseless loss of life, but not to the extent of Morgan's rage.

Morgan stands firm in the middle of the chaos, holding one man by the temples. His eyes roll into the back of his head and his body twitches violently as she rips through his mind without care of her destruction. There is nothing human, or gentle, about the furious wrath of the Lady of the Lake. The storm grows more violent with wind and hail. She strips from the man any knowledge about who is friend or foe, until there is nothing left. Once she has what she seeks, her fury is unleashed. Hail, precise and deadly, tears through all who would bring harm against her children, and the chaos of the battlefield falls quiet as the storm subsides. Men stand in awe and horror, watching those next to them get slaughtered by the falling ice while they are left untouched.

The men not destroyed by the dragons, or by Morgan, are rounded up by Arthur's men.

The healers emerge to tend to the wounded. The dragon riders once the battle has subsided are dismissed. Elaine sends her dragon back to the island as well. As much as they would love more glorious battles like this, their existence is not accepted by the lords of Lloegyr.

Isolder finds a young boy, Galahad, gurgling and begging for help, an axe embedded deep into his mid-section. She frowns, kneeling next to him. "Oh, sweet boy," she coos softly, trying to calm him, but sure she cannot heal him.

Elaine comes to Isolder's side and takes up the boy's other hand. "Be brave, young warrior. It will all be alright. You did well and will be honored." She looks to Isolder who simply shakes her head no.

Arthur, covered in blood and half dead from exhaustion, comes upon them. "Galahad!" he drops his sword and muscles the women away from the boy. "Oh, you stupid boy, why did you not listen to me?" He pulls him close and tears well in his eyes. He does not care that the two magical women, one of scales, and one of vines, stand there watching this terrible goodbye.

"Help! Someone, help him!" Arthur's tender heart

shows as he cries bitter tears of remorse over the young squire. He promised his sister Galahad would return home safe. She will never forgive him if his nephew dies. "Please, do not just stand there. Do something!" He begs of the women watching. Hoping beyond hope they will save him.

The storm fully subsides and the people encircling them part like the seas for Moses as Morgan approaches. No one wants to be caught in her path. She looks more like a violent, beautiful, spirit than a woman. She says nothing as she kneels in the mud opposite of Arthur and the boy.

"Milady, he is too far gone," Isolder murmurs.

Morgan says nothing and cants her head as she stares at the boy. She gently takes the boy from Arthur, lying him flat on the ground. With little effort, she pulls the axe from his chest and tosses it aside.

Blood flows freely as the boy weakly cries in protest, growing pale. Galahad's hands fall limp and all Arthur can do is watch.

A single, silent, desperate prayer to the Mother shines in his heart, pleading for her to give this raven haired angel the power to heal the boy. The haunting words that come from Morgan's lips echo the words burned in his memory three years prior. He watches in awe as a faint glow grows over Galahad's body.

The entire camp stands silent.

The longer Morgan chants, the more the boy glows. The wound slowly rewinds itself, flesh weaving back together like an elegant tapestry. Her hands stain with his blood as she rubs the crescent moon on his forehead with her chant. Her breathing becomes more difficult, and she finally pulls away from the boy, leaving his unconscious body on the ground. His wound is sealed. Where his body was still with death before, his chest now rises and falls gently with life.

She stands and Elaine steps to her right while Isolder to her left. The two say nothing as they support their drained leader.

Arthur stares at Morgan, awestruck.

The rest of the camp remains silent as the miracle performed is even beyond the old wizard's ken.

Merlin keeps himself hidden from Morgan's sight. The fact she used Avalonian magic on the boy makes her a danger he was not ready to face yet.

Arthur's men finally come to stand alongside their king, their weapons still drawn.

"Lady, I am in your debt," Arthur kneels with his sword, much to the astonishment of his men. There is hesitation, then they follow suit.

"Rise, Arthur Pendragon. I am not here to receive your allegiance. My daughters begged for my protection, and I granted it. Nothing more." She stands tall, the endless night dancing dark in her eyes, never betraying the bone-crushing weariness she feels.

Arthur rises and his men follow suit again. He cannot take his eyes off Morgan. He would know this beautiful creature anywhere. She has haunted his dreams nearly every night since the day they first met. "Please, wondrous lady, grace us with your name."

"I am all that is the beginning and the end. I am the life in your soul, the heart in your chest. I flow through you. What name would you have me give?"

"I would have the name you call yourself. So that I may give you thanks properly in my prayers."

That brings a faint smile to her lips. "I am the Lady of the Lake, High Priestess of Avalon. But you, Arthur Pendragon, may call me Morgan."

30

Star-Crossed Freedom

Delphine returns and looms over the sleeping Wilhelm. She studies him, head slightly cocked to the side, one finger tapping gently against her lower lip. She looks tired and frail from the years of hardship she has suffered. Could he really be the Grimm she saw in her glass? Jakob is being careful to conceal this man's identity. Fate keeps harassing the Ozians about outlanders and then they appear out of the Labyrinth's stones. He must be a Grimm. But to see the curse upon him, makes her question Jakob's sanity. Grimms cannot be cursed, and yet here one lies, cursed. The Animals are getting restless and want to attack, but she is certain that path only ends in death. The path to life lies with an unknown. A figure locked away in the mind of this buffoon. She leaves him to sleep and silently moves to Jakob. She checks his skin, and that he is still breathing. There is nothing more terrifying than a Grimm being injured. The Cheshire Cat was supposed to make it look convincing, not actually hurt him.

Delicate fingers trail along his wounds and he gives a half-cocked grin, cracking one eye open to gaze up at her. "You know, if you wanted to see me naked, all you had to do was ask."

She rolls her eyes and lets her nails dig in. It does the trick, and he hisses in pain. "You are lucky to be alive, Jakob. What happened?"

"Someone attacked us in the stars," he lowers his voice to not disturb Wilhelm. "I could feel Wilhelm there, then another figure, unseen. Who would be powerful enough to wait in the stars and then to attack another being traveling through it?" He pushes himself up more.

"The Six have been pawing over all the lore of Nodd. They raided the Labyrinth's archives some time ago. They claimed all the lore must be kept safe from the rebellious Aesopi. They have created a citadel in Silver City, claiming it unrivaled in splendor of all the lands." She retrieves another small vial from her skirts and a cloth from another pocket.

The stinging pain radiates through his arm and down his body when she gingerly dabs it against his wounds. "By Merlin, what is that?" He recoils from her touch, and she uses well-manicured nails to force him back into place.

"It is called rubbing alcohol. The Wizard told me about it. In a place called Cansass. It is for cleaning wounds, such as the one on your arm." She continues to dab at his chest and arm, then leans down to blow against the places she dabbed.

The color in his cheeks rises and he coughs uncomfortably, shifting her off. "I am fine, woman. You keep your odd Ozian tortures to yourself."

She rolls her eyes and gets up. "What do you intend to do with him? His mind is as broken as all the Wonderland mirrors." She resumes her looming vigil over Wilhelm. Her visions have warned her that something which cannot be undone happens between them if they touch. Be it fear, or spite, she refuses to let the glass dictate her fate to her.

"I was hoping Frank could help him. He has a knack for this sort of thing." Jakob's voice is tinged with hope.

"Frank is gone." Her voice is sad in the revelation. "He fled with the wretched brat from Cansass. He abandoned us to the Six." Bitterness filters through despite her efforts to hide it.

"Fiddlesticks," Jakob grumbles. "I tried to heal his mind, but nearly lost my own."

"You Grimms are all alike. Thinking you can solve every problem with your brutish magic." She snorts in irritation and looks back at Wilhelm's sleeping face. She gently waves her fingers over it, revealing the small rune tattoos enchanting his skin. She cants her head and for all of a thought he looks like the man she lost fighting the Six. With a hard swallow, she tries to focus and decipher the runes, banishing those memories back to the abyss they had crawled out of.

"He did not do it to himself," she states after minutes of silent inspection. "Whoever did this did not want him to remember where he has been, or who he was with."

"I know that, but he is forgetting everything else as well. His stars are dimming." Jakob reveals more about Wilhelm than he means to.

"That is the problem with mind magic. Everything is connected, one way or another." She sighs and resigns herself to having to touch him after all. She had already guessed he is a Grimm, but Jakob's slip of the tongue confirms it for her. She takes a deep breath and settles on her knees, hoping that the glass was wrong, just this once.

"Sun in the East, Moon in the West, Water in the North, Earth in the South," her voice lilts and cants in the Ozian tongue. "Guide me to the path I need to lead the lost home." Her fingers splay out and each touch a rune on Wilhelm's forehead, leaving her thumbs to cover over his eyes.

Jakob watches, mouth agape as she glows with the light of Aesop. The entire room fills with the brilliance, projecting around them Wilhelm's fog of memories. Jakob is awash with the memories of Wilhelm's fear of being hunted, the smell of blood and wood smoke in the air. The figures projected are clouded by the mists and moving in reverse. There are so many figures that

Jakob cannot count them.

Delphine's hair starts to float with the static electricity filling the room. Ozone fills his nostrils as overhead thunder roars like a freight train. The entire building shakes in fear.

Wilhelm yells in furious pain as the fog darkens and swarms menacingly around them.

Jakob loses sight of the two. All he can make out is an emerald glow in the center of a swirling fog of stars and shades.

"Where are you?" she breathes out to Wilhelm, lowering her head in concentration. Their faces are so close it looks as though they will kiss. Her brow furrows in concentration and his wrinkles in pain as the runes blaze to life on his skin, searing at her fingertips. Try as they might, the Lady of the Lake's runes cannot resist the demand of Delphine's ability to see all.

Then the pair stand in the stone circle, dressed in rags, and smelling of the morning dew.

Wilhelm looks angry and near death. "Witch!" he roars at her.

She barely has enough time to side-step the large sword he manifests. The violent fog dances around the circle, and the stars are all muddled. She looks to the heavens and then back at him in time to throw her hands in the air. The sword dissipates into water, leaving him standing there with his fists clenched.

"Filthy witch! Give it back!" The man roars at her, shaking the vision with the need of his demand.

"I am not the thief, Grimm. Do you not recognize me?" She lowers her hands and realizes they are no longer green. She is astonished by this discovery and does not see him bull rush her and they thud to the ground with him on top of her. The man may look small and wiry, but his strength is overwhelming.

She is no wilting violet, though, and makes him earn his victory over her. She arches and bucks under him to throw him off her. "I am not her! I am trying to help you!"

"Liar," he roars at her and rears back to strike her.

Her eyes lock with his and he hesitates.

The Lady of the Lake has blue eyes, like the waters of Avalon. This witch's eyes are as green as a dragon's newly hoarded gem. While she is dressed like the Lady, she is not that vile witch. He snags the hand she darts up to claw him with and struggles with her again to pin her back down. "Who are you?" His breathing is hard, and he dare not look away for fear she might steal something other than his mind. "Let me out of this prison. You have no right to hold me."

"I," she hesitates. Her heart pounds and she cannot catch her breath. Desperation wells in her and she realizes that there are only two ways out of this prison; love or death. That is when she truly sees him, Wilhelm Grimm, inventor of 'True Love's Kiss'. The man had always boasted that it was the second most powerful thing in existence, rivaling even the power of a wish. She gazes up at him and she can see the stars in his eyes, though they are full of rage and hate at the moment. Her heart hammers in her chest as she loses herself in those stars.

He frowns down at her. "No. Do not do... It is not... You will--,"

She kisses him. It is hot like fire and sweet like wine the way her lips taste.

Struggle as he might, he cannot pull away from her kiss.

Her fingers lace into his hair and she presses up to him, surrendering to the weight of him on top of her.

The illusion of the Lady fades and beneath him is the emerald witch of Oz. Her ebony hair splays on the ground, and her green skin makes the grass look as pale as the moon. He knew the moment her lips touched his, they were bound forever. Once the kiss is broken, he looks down at her sternly.

"You have no idea what you have done." A loud crack fills the air, and the rain pours down like a monsoon into the stone circle.

She shrieks in pain. The water droplets blister her skin and burn through her clothes like acid. The vision shatters. Delphine is thrown from Wilhelm and hits the ground unconscious.

The foggy shades disappear, and the attic is dark once more, allowing Jakob to see Wilhelm and Delphine. "Delphine," Jakob pushes up and struggles to get to her.

Wilhelm is wide awake now, staring at the young woman on the floor, guilt and anger filling him. While her kiss was true, they were not destined for each other. It is his father's check on the trickery of "true love".

Love, even true and honest, is easy for a heart to house, and many a woman have found a place in his heart over the years. That is where his father intervened. Lovers never meant to be become star-crossed, and their lives together will never truly find happily ever after, always resulting in a tragic end for one of them. Sorrow fills him as he recalls how often it is not him that suffers in those tragedies.

"What happened? Why is she unconscious? What did you do, Wilhelm?" Jakob struggles to get her upright, his limbs not fully usable yet.

Wilhelm slowly gets up and easily scoops her up, cradling her to him as he runs a gentle finger down the side of her face.

"Oh no! Did you kiss her? You know what happens to them when you interfere." Jakob inhales sharply as he realizes Wilhelm may not actually remember his previous indiscretions, or the consequences of his loosely given 'love'.

"This is different. She kissed me. It does not matter, now, for we are bound all the same." He does not sound overjoyed about this fate, but the change in his persona, and the recognition of Aesop's binding makes Jakob breathe a sigh of relief. "Now, if you would get the door, brother, she is not the lightest of witches."

It is Always Three

Rumors of the defeat swarm through the other war
camps like bees. One after another, they learn of the
women rising out of the water and dragons appearing
in the air to squash Arthur's foes. With each telling, the
story takes on a life of its own until the tale of warriors
and fantastical weapons is no longer the truth at all.
The current version making the rounds has Arthur
returning from bathing at the lake with a new sword of
jewels and the strength of a dragon. The recounting is
that he cut through man after man, until none resisted,
and the miracle of Galahad is attributed to the devout
love Arthur holds for the Christian God. Any trace of
the witch he now keeps with him, or the wizard,
Merlin, are long gone from the tale. As the Pendragon

camp moves along the countryside, people submit to Arthur with little resistance. He is met with fear and awe.

Morgan sent Elaine and Isolder back to Avalon with instructions for keeping the island moving in her absence. In spite of their pleas to not linger among the men of Lloegyr, she dismissed them and remained at Arthur's side.

The months pass until Winter returns once more. Trees droop with the weight of snow on their branches. Soldiers huddle around fires or find the warmth of a woman's tent for the night. Life is starting to feel normal among the war-worn camp. In the massive tent for the king, Arthur sits sullen and moody at his war table. His back is to the bath steaming behind him where the delicate figure of Morgan enjoys its warmth.

"I am the leader of all Lloegyr, and yet you deny me the one thing I want," he growls like a petulant child.

"And what is that *your majesty*?" mocking his title.

"You," he grunts. "It has always been you. From the moment I saw you in the forest."

Morgan steps out of the bath, her pale skin shimmering in the light of the fire as it catches the small beads of water cascading down her. The shadow she casts on the wall taunts him without mercy.

He takes another heavy gulp of his mead and shifts in his seat. "You are torturing me."

"I am doing no such thing. You are torturing yourself," she pulls on her shift and comes to comfort him. These months have been a dream. She feels the need to be near him, as if their fates are intertwined. She does not want her sisters' influence on the matter. The winds howl outside and the tent ripples around them. Her control of the winter storm has kept all foes at bay, guaranteeing peace for a short while. It also helps to buffer them from that meddlesome wizard. Merlin always lectures the two of them every time he gets near, chastising Arthur for falling for her wiles. He has even threatened her with curses and imprisonment. Then he vanished without warning. Wherever he went, he used the stone circle, and she has not felt him return.

She reaches up and pulls the silver comb from her precariously pinned hair, allowing it to cascade down her shoulders and to her waist like ink spilling from the bottle.

Arthur looks up at her and swears he can see the night sky in her eyes. "You are such a beautiful creature," he murmurs. He dares to touch her, wanting to feel her supple curves.

"Tut, tut, what would Merlin say," she coos to him and eases even closer, sapping the warmth from him as she trails her fingers along his cheek.

"Mhmm, I do not want to talk about old, smelly wizards with you," his hands firmly pull her to him until they are touching. "I do not want to talk at all, witch," he teases.

Her eyes narrow, and she pushes against him. "What makes you think I will give you more than you have earned?"

"By the Gods, woman. Tell me how to earn it. I will do anything." His hands tighten on her hips with the promise of not allowing her to slip away from him.

"Anything? Careful, your majesty, you might give away more than you have." She smells of berries and the rain. Her shift clings to her form only to taunt him more.

"Anything," he re-affirms as he moves to his feet and puts his arm around her waist, the deft movements of a young man pressing his advantage to the girl before him. A few steps more and the back of her knees press to his makeshift bedding.

She clings to him to keep her balance and frowns up at him. "Make me your Queen and allow Avalonian magic back into Lloegyr." Her voice is a whisper against his ear and his eyes close.

His hands slide from her hips to down around her buttocks, only separated by his britches and her shift.

She wriggles against him in mild protest, "No. Not without the union of our kingdoms."

He sighs in frustration and tries to push her against the bedding, only he finds her immovable. The icy wind of winter howls louder, sending frigid air through the tent, stealing any warmth that was between them.

"I am not one of your peasants that you can just bed and make empty promises to, Arthur." She puts her hand to his chest and pushes him back with an ease that unsettles him, though not as much as the abyss dancing at the edges of the stars in her eyes. "You will be mine, and mine alone."

"Is that so?" He gives her a rueful grin and then he takes hold of her wrist and spins her around, pulling her arm up roughly behind her. It forces her onto her toes and causes her to cry out in pain. Before she can react, she is pushed forward. He bends her over the bedding until his weight is behind her, shoving her face down into the furs.

"No," she jerks and then winces when she feels his fingers fumbling with the hem of her shift. She kicks back, hard, and gets a grunted yelp in response, followed by a growl.

"Arthur, stop!" Panic laces her voice as she struggles.

"I am the king here. You will submit to me." His voice is different and graveled. "I will not be dictated to by a whoring witch." He thrusts his knee between her legs and pulls her arm up, threatening to dislocate her shoulder.

The furs smother her, and she is sure that he is about to snap her arm right in two. Tears well in her eyes and the winds scream with her frustration. The rain pelts down on the camp with daggers of ice. fires threaten to blow out as the snow grows heavier. She rears back against him, arching up off the bed, not caring what was to happen to her arm. Her head butts into his nose, forcing him to let go of her, and she grunts as she hits the furs again.

"Filthy bitch," he growls as he wipes futilely at his bleeding nose and climbs onto the bedding after her.

Morgan's eyes shift to a murderous black. Fury consumes her. How dare this man betray her this way.

She moves like lightning and grabs hold of the fire stoker. Her ivory fingers curl around the iron, burning her skin, and the red tip arcs through the air with the grace of a skilled swordsman. The eerie line of fire that scorches Arthur's face is enough to send him reeling back. The way she leaps from the bed makes her look like a feral monster more than a young girl. "I curse you, filthy mortal." The words come, dark and heavy with the promise of revenge. "Arthur Pendragon your days will be numbered by your own sword. Forever will you be bound to that which you covet. All that you love will be lost." The laughter in response is not what she expects to hear.

His hideous laughter booms in the tent. The man before her is not Arthur at all, but a tall, slender man with dark hair slicked back and his marred skin is as pale as hers. He backs away from her, once again taking the form of Arthur, and slips from the tent.

She sinks onto the bedding, dropping the stoker, her hand marred and gruesome. Tears well in her eyes and she longs to be back in Avalon with her sisters and her daughters, where life is simple and men rule nothing. The snow and ice fall heavy, like the tears on her cheeks.

Outside, with his men, Arthur looks to the heavens as the blizzard becomes insufferable. He frowns, then glances back at his tent. He does not fully understand how it works, but he knows the weather dances at her whim. The worse her emotions get, the more the weather mirrors them. "Get settled men. Keep the fires going. It is going to be cold tonight." He dismisses them and moves away, leaving his pint with young Galahad. With a tug, he pulls his furs tighter around his shoulders. The sudden change in weather makes him approach his tent with caution. When he comes near, he frowns at the sign of boots in the snow. Rage and fear well within him. With his heart is in his throat, he draws his blade as he pushes the tent flap back. "My Lady?" his voice breaks midway, still caught between child and adult. He squints with the fire blazing behind her, casting her in shadow. Her hair is loose and wild about her with hands upheld and palms open, trembling. It is startling to see her so vulnerable. "Oh, Morgan," he drops his sword and comes to her.

She recoils in fear, crossing her arms over herself, and he stops dead.

"Morgan, look at me. It is Arthur." He holds his gloved hands up like he would when approaching a wild horse. "Shh, shh. It is me. It is all right. I am here." Cautiously, he moves forward until he is kneeling before her. He takes her wrists and guides her hands closer to him. "Who did this to you?" his voice is soft, and try as he might to be calm, anger seethes within him. He is careful to not touch her hands where they are burned, but he inspects her otherwise. She is only in a shift that is damp and clings to her. The smell of sex does not fill the air, and his bedding shows no signs of innocence lost.

Morgan mewls and tries to pull her wrists from his grasp. She will not look at him.

He allows her, realizing he is gripping them tight. "Do not move. I will get a healer." He leans up and kisses her forehead before parting. He pauses to pick up his sword, then steps outside of the tent flap. "Galahad!" he bellows.

Within moments, Galahad and two others are waiting outside the tent. Morgan can see their silhouettes on the tent flaps. Whatever Arthur is saying, she cannot make out the words, but the others are quickly gone. His figure disappears and she shivers, bringing her knees up. She does not understand what is happening to her, or why she cannot shake this terrified feeling. The sense of hopeless dread fills her.

An older woman enters a few moments later, her bony and crooked fingers curled around a small basket. "Sweet Lady, what have you done?" She accuses Morgan as much as shows concern for her. She comes forward and beckons for Morgan to join her at the war table. "Now let ol' Fanny have a look. Tsk," she inhales at the sight of Morgan's palms. "You must have touched iron, wee faerie." Morgan is convinced the woman is not speaking in any language heard around here.

"I... He tried to hurt me," Morgan replies in the same tongue. Her body feels heavy, and she is starting to regain her composure. "I can heal it," she murmurs as she watches the old woman work.

"Of course you can, but let ol' Fanny help you. You tell her what happened and she will make it all better." She rummages in her basket to bring out a small glass jar, jade in color. Her other hand reaches up to brush back the ebony curls that are blanketing Morgan's face. "Poor thing. You look as though you have seen a demon." In a few easy strokes, she has cleared Morgan's hair from her face, and wipes away the tears. "There, sweet girl," she coos.

Morgan watches Fanny in fascination. The way she turns her hands and how she rubs the salve in just the right places reminds her of her mother and causes her heart to ache for the woman she had been raised by. She is sure she sees the hint of starlight in the other woman's eyes. The old, withered face investigates the youthful doll of a girl, their faces so similar they are opposite sides of the same coin.

"I know you," Morgan says, unsure of how she knows the old woman. "What are you putting on my hands?" Morgan watches as the wounds bubble and ooze in her palms, mending the threads of her skin whole.

Fanny takes cotton strips and wraps Morgan's hands firmly. "Three midnights, deary. Keep them bound and keep them dry."

"Why three?" Morgan's brow furrows, and she turns her hands over in the wraps. There is no pain where there had been burning before. "Why could I not heal these wounds with my magic? And what is that salve?" She bubbles with curiosity at the odd woman's work.

"It is always three. Just like the beginning, middle, and end. The Maid, the Lady, the Crone. Three is lucky, and three is right. Do not forget. Three midnights," Fanny explains, yet does not explain, as she packs up and moves away from Morgan. She stops and looks back when Morgan stands to demand she come back and answer her questions.

Ol' Fanny's tone changes and, for a blink of an eye, she is the majestic ruler she once was. "You would do well to remember that not every answer is solved with magic, Morgan le Fey." Onyx eyes speckled with silver sparkles lock with inky black eyes. Then the flap flutters and the withered old crone is walking away in the snow.

"And put some clothes on! You will catch your death in this cold!" She cackles at the thought that someone would believe that poppycock.

Morgan moves to the bathing area of the tent and pulls her robes on to tie them closed. She then loosely braids her hair or tries to with her hands bandaged. Sleepy and heavy, it feels like all the energy in the world has been sucked from her. Her temper subsides, allowing the raging blizzard to calm to a quiet winter night. She flexes her hands again and looks back to the front of the tent. Arthur is taking a long time to return.

What if the fake one returns? How will I tell who is real? Am I going mad? Did I imagine the whole thing and just grab a hot poker without reason?

Arthur re-appears at the entrance of his tent, his cheeks flush with the cold, or excitement, and with him is a very sour looking elderly gentleman. The man is dressed in white, and his hair is disheveled, like he had been sleeping and was dragged by the whirlwind king from his comfortable, warm bed.

"Come here, Morgan," he motions emphatically.

From her drowsing perch on the bed she reluctantly leaves the warmth of the furs.

Her approach gives Author the distinct impression of a curious cat. "Do not be afraid. I am going to do what I should have done months ago."

The elderly man's eyes open wide in surprise. He sputters, fumbling for the book already in his hand.

"What is that? Go home to your farms?" She teases, but comes close enough to stand by him. Her shoulders are tense and legs are ready to bolt at any sudden movement.

"No," he rolls his eyes, and he pulls out a small cloth with the seal of the dragon on it. "Giving you the only thing I can. Now, if you would be so kind," he gently takes her bandaged hand in his and the priest mutters his mumbo jumbo in the crude Latin language he knows.

She watches Arthur the entire time, taking in his anxious posture mixed with vibrant excitement. She understands what this ceremony is, and his willful disobedience of Merlin begins to infect her emotions. A smile forms on her lips and her fingers curl around his, joining their hands together. This is all she has ever wanted, and before long the excitement banishes all thoughts about the imposter or the curse she had flung from her head.

"And with this binding, your houses become one under the House of Pendragon. I mark thee Morgan le Fey, Lady of the Lake, as the betrothed of Arthur Pendragon, rightful King of Lloegyr."

32

Do As I Say

"It was glorious!" Chaos cackles with malicious delight. "She actually believed I was that filthy boy." The raven-haired menace plops down into her cushioned chair and pops a berry into her mouth.

"Have you looked in a mirror, darling," the pompous man at the desk not far from her looks at her gleeful display with disdain. With a wave of his hand, a mirror appears before the young woman, and the gaping wound across her face is still evident. She shrugs and dismisses the mirror.

"Does not matter. It will heal. I do not see what Merlin has his staff in a twist over. She is just a powerful witch from an island with strange magic. It is not like she can actually hurt us." Her berry shifts to an apple, and she savors the snap of the firm flesh as her ruby lips curl in glee. The irritation on her husband's face is as delightful as hearing someone scream in pain.

"Wait, this is the girl Merlin was ranting about?" He stops what he is doing and gets up from his desk. The distance between Chaos and Order disappears, and he has her by the chin, lifting her out of the seat. There is fear in her gaze now, the bite of apple held in her mouth. His eyes narrow and he stares at her long and hard. "What were you doing on the other side of the stones?"

"I do not have to answer to you, husband," she wrenches her jaw free and tries to wriggle away from him over the chair. He is the faster of the two and catches her by the forearm. With a jerk, she is off balance and falling towards him. They are face to face again and his fingers dig into her arm to keep her steady.

"You will answer me, wife." His nose gently rubs against her. It would look tender if the two of them did not hate each other more than all of Nodd. Tricked into their union, they quickly learned Merlin is not to be trusted. He then murmurs against her lips, "Or I will remind you what happens when you do not follow the rules."

Silence fills the air between them, and if she had a heart, it would be racing. The slow grin that forms on Chaos's ruby red lips infuriates him more. He can no more hurt her than she can him, but he would have it his way, or there will be hell to pay.

"I was curious," she finally answers. "How can a young girl, who has never been here, be the savior of Aesop? She does not even talk to animals. She *is* an animal. Filthy and stinky, just like the rest of them on the other side. Merlin is wrong. I even tricked her into cursing that wretched... Wart they call him?"

"How did she know to use iron against you?" His other hand comes up and with a deft brush of his finger strands of starlight weave her cheek back to near flawless perfection. He takes intense pleasure in making the pain heightened for her, without releasing her. He knows she will attack him or flee, and he wants his questions answered first.

"She did not. She just grabbed the first thing she could." She purposely leaves out that she then made herself look just like Order. Or that it also hurts the girl to touch iron. He had not said please. To further kill his joy, she leans into his grasp as if she is enjoying his touch. "You would like her. She follows the rules. We should go to see her again."

"I would advise against that," the older woman's voice muses as she enters the room, causing Order and Chaos to part. "That *girl*," the intruder emphasizes the label, "Commands the weather, can resurrect the dead, and has been gifted all the power of the stars. You would do well to remember that the next time you try to rape her." Fate takes a seat at Order's desk and drums her fingers on the cherry-stained wood. "We have more pressing matters to attend to than taunting the outlanders." Her gaze is far beyond the Silver City, looking to the lands of Oz.

"Just because you have the gift of sight, sister, does not mean you know everything," Chaos pouts as she shrinks from Order to sulk in her chair again. "What could be more pressing than the toys of Merlin?"

"Ozian witches harboring Grimms," Fate still sounds far off and dreamy, using the gifts granted to her to spy on the witches of Oz. Glinda, the Uplander in the South is the easiest to control. So eager to please, no matter the cost. She murdered the witch of the East, though it only strengthened the witch in the West, who, by all accounts, should be dead. Yet Fate could see the threads of her story still being weaved. It troubles her that she cannot see the witch, but she can see the imprints her void leaves on those around her.

That leaves Ozma, the child empress, and her advisor Locasta of the North. That one is truly troublesome. The child has declared herself ruler of Oz in place of that buffoon, Frank, or the Wizard, as they all called him. She continues to resist the tempting tithes of Fate and Law. Together, they would be a powerful nation. Apart, they have too many vulnerabilities, especially from the rebellious Aesopi. It is all the Six can do to keep them under control.

Lost in her seeing, she ignores Chaos's glee at getting to go torture Ozians.

Order even finds some delight in the prospect as well. "Fate," his voice cuts through the fog. "What would you have us do?"

When she turns her gaze to him, her eyes blink back to vibrant gold, and she smiles. "I would have you bring our guests to the Silver City, so we can show them a proper welcome back to Nodd."

Chaos and Order vanish from the room. Their desire to hunt down the Grimms is far greater than any petty feud. Like shadows in the night sky, they streak to the Ozian walls, stopping only outside the range of the Tick Tock armies.

"What are we waiting for?" Chaos asks when Order places a hand on her shoulder.

"Patience, my love. There is a proper way to do this. One that does not involve leveling all of Ozrail." His fingers gently squeeze as he watches the massive wall before them.

They would need to get in undetected, and then confirm the Grimms are being harbored by the witches. Fate had not given them much to go on, and he felt like they are being set up for something far more sinister than a simple capture of fugitives. While he can admire his wife's gusto in such matters, her well-being brings him just as much concern.

She may brush off the gaping wound from iron, but he can still see the angry red scar faintly shines, which pricks his anger. She must have burned all her energy returning home, keeping him from properly fixing what was broken.

"Let us seek the Uplander Witch, see what she knows, and enjoy the frivolity of her court for one evening," he gently requests, which elicits a narrow-eyed gaze from the younger immortal.

Her eyes are dark and violent as she tries to gauge him. She is met with firm and calm ambivalence, causing Chaos to snort at him. "Fine. One night. Then we do it my way."

He almost yearns for her to create chaos just so he can right the world again, but, alas, it is not to be. His smile is genuine. As he leads her from their hiding place, their clothes and appearances transform into the Ozrailian style of clothing. His suit, complete with top hat and tails, fits precisely. Her gown is shimmering and soft satins complete with bustle and corset to accent her petite frame. They glide past the guards at the main gate, then turn south.

After they are far enough away from the gates of Oz, they move at the speed of thought again. Their shadows flicker over the yellow brick road until they can see her estate in the distance. Glinda, the Good Witch, lives in the most ornate, opulent estate in all of Ozrail, rivaling even the opulence of the Emerald City itself. When they shift back into their forms, they walk quietly side by side. After a few exchanged words with the well-oiled guard, they are granted access to the grounds. Inside the gate there are cherry blossom trees, full of pink and soft leaves. The wind flutters through them to make them appear to dance. The grass is vibrant green, and not even the stone holds moss. It is all perfect, in every way. Order approves of the perfection this witch demands of her domain.

Chaos, though, would make vomiting motions at the

ostentatious abuse of magic if they were not being prim and proper. They are guided up the grand steps into the shiny gold and white building. The alabaster stone looks as though it has been scrubbed clean just moments prior. Around the estate, Munchkins bustle about, happily bopping to whatever their little minds think on. The pair are ushered in and the marble floor with Grecian columns put this palace over the top in decor. A few more steps and they find themselves in a parlor that looks like the Wonderland Queen vomited her red hearts everywhere.

"Miss Glinda, will be with you momentarily. Please, sit, enjoy some sweet berry wine," the servant, an Uplander himself, bows formally, and then exits, leaving them to their devices. Meanwhile, in the other room, standing in a shimmery blue chiffon dress, with a prim little hat, white gloves, and heels to match, Glinda looks positively radiant. Her strawberry blond curls bounce with every movement and her sweetheart face is absolute perfection.

The winged Beast before her paces anxiously back and forth. If he is caught here, they will both be in trouble. A small frown pulls down her lips, but not a wrinkle mars her face. They had been making plans to meet with Delphine in secret, especially with the news he brought her today.

"Well, you cannot leave looking like that," her voice sweetly fills the air. A spark sprawls forth from her fingertips and the winged Beast transforms into a Munchkin with a soft pop. "It will wear off in a few hours. You will just have to walk until then. Tell her I will meet her at the old Oz dust place at midnight." Glinda watches as he toddles off in silence. She rubs her fingers against her temples, stressing about all this cumbersome work to hide Grimms, perplexed that her life has become so complicated since she helped murder her best friend. This is not how this was supposed to go. She checks herself over in the mirror and pulls the frown upside down before going to meet her guests. "To what do I owe the—,"

Chaos is out of her seat and her fingers curl around Glinda's throat. She leans in close to smell the sticky sweet perfume of the pretty little witch, then flicks her tongue along Glinda's cheek.

"Enough," Order's voice growls with stern resolve from his seat. "Do not be rude, my love. Allow her to sit down first."

Chaos gives Order the dirtiest of looks.

While his tone is cordial, he is commanding her and expects compliance without question. There is a tense moment between the two where Glinda dares to think the possibility of throwing them both in a bubble and fleeing. That they are here together is bad, so unbelievably bad. Instead, she gingerly sits in the chair Chaos guides her to. "There, pet, that is not so bad. We just want to chat. No need to be afraid. Unless you have been... *wicked*." His eyes flash, showing her the sadistic pleasure he will take at disciplining such a vibrant young thing until she complies in every way.

The Good, The Wicked, & The Naughty

Glinda knows she is in trouble and that there is nothing she can do to get out of this. She looks from Order to Chaos, one with a dashing grin, the other with a wicked stare. Her heart pounds in her chest, and all she can do is hope that she can live through this long enough to warn her best friend that the Six are on to all of them.

"Now, my sweet witch, what tasty little secrets are you hiding?" Order's long and slender fingers trail along her temple before he begins to pluck the thoughts from her skull. She tries to resist but finds his command impossible to deny. Into the ether little bubbles of motion pictures dance and hover. One by one he pulls everything he wishes to see, and more.

With each tug of her mind, she whimpers and tears stain her perfect cheeks as yet another memory is ripped from her. She opens her mouth to scream for help, only to find Chaos clapping in glee as her voice is muted and echoes in her mind only. Glinda watches in horror as all her knowledge and wisdom is drawn from her skull and displayed for the world to see. Moments of her life flit about the room in opalescent globes, showing her learning spells, making friends, living, loving, and heartache. All of her is put on display. Order strips her psyche back, layer by layer, until all he leaves is the innocence of childhood, where the ability to discern friend and foe has not yet been developed.

The drawback of this magic is that anything Order permanently removes from Glinda must be incorporated into his own psyche, or they will return to her. It is a pain-staking process that leaves them both breathing hard as Order sifts through all her life, finding that which he requires.

Glinda slumps in the chair, her eyes glassing over as her psyche adjusts and changes itself to that which Order left, her vapid tendencies only. With great care, he orders and draws the bubbles to him, popping them one at a time into his mouth like candy, grunting from the effort to swallow them whole, until he has all the important thoughts consumed. He now knows them as if they are his own.

Chaos leans over Glinda and coos, "Now, my pretty, was that so terrible?"

"I. Oh! Dear me, I must have dozed off. What were

we discussing my friends? Do you intend to go to the Wizard's ball?" Glinda's girlish giggle chimes like bells in the parlor, her tear-streaked make-up forgotten.

"Alas, my dear, we cannot stay much longer. We must get back before nightfall, and I believe you were getting ready for a meeting?" Order stays Chaos with a gentle touch when she tries to correct him.

"Oh! Fiddlesticks! I completely forgot about the meeting. Silly me," she giggles again. "Yes! I must get ready. I am in no state for a meeting! Please excuse me!" She is out of her chair and flounces her way from the parlor.

"Did she just... Flounce?" Chaos snorts a laugh.

"I believe she did, dearie." Order's off-hand change of her pet name draws a side-glare from Chaos. She always hates his adjustment period when he does this.

"Why in Tartarus did you let her go? We had her where we wanted her."

"What makes you think we still do not have her there? That," he pauses to find the right word, "child with a wand, is going to be a threat to us no longer." He looks smug.

"I think you might be as dense as she, dear husband. What could you have possibly gained from those little bubbles? How to torment a Munchkin? Oh, I know! How to flounce?" Chaos deftly steps back when Order attempts to take her by the throat.

"I know that her meeting is with the Wicked Witch of the West." He growls.

"Then you are daft. Delphine is dead."

"Is she? Where is the girl that supposedly murdered her? Where is Frank? The thoughts I took from Glinda all indicate the witches are working in league against us with the Grimms, and that Delphine is very much their leader. Her meeting tonight is to trade intel about the Grimms they smuggled into Oz recently. It would seem we will need to add shooting down any flying monkeys we see outside of Ozrail to the list of duties for the cards."

"And you are going to trust her to just off and go straight to Delphine?"

"I do. She is a child with shiny baubles at this point. We follow her, confirm Delphine is alive, and take the traitor back to the castle for Fate to deal with."

"And Glinda?"

"Well, I am sure she is going to be reckless and get herself killed in the dark streets of Emerald City. Such a shame, two witches lost in one evening."

"Oh," Chaos lights up with malicious glee. She flounces into Order's arms. "Husband, you are irresistible when you are devious like this."

"Hmm," he graces her with a gentle kiss. "Your flattery will not get you out of punishment for going to the other side alone."

✶✶✶✶✶✶

Under the starry night sky, Glinda shines like a beacon of stardust amongst the grime. Emerald City's underbelly is as dark and dangerous as the Neverland prison. She looks about, obviously trying to not appear suspicious, and failing miserably. She waves to every passerby, giggles, and engages with those that stop and talk with her. Glinda of the South in this part of Emerald City has more than one person curious. Her high-pitched giggle as the latest couple walks away stands out in stark contrast to her surroundings. Her gloved hand darts into the little purse dangling from her shoulder and pulls a compact from it. Turning this way and that to get the best angle in the tiny mirror, she fluffs her curly blond hair and pops her cherry red lips. She is the perfect doll, waiting on the steps of the Oz Dust Theater.

From a shadowy alcove across the painted brick road, Delphine frowns at this spectacle. She watches as Glinda flirts and waves, primps, paces, and primps some more. It reminds Delphine of when they were young, and Frank would encourage them to try new things. Glinda has always been beloved, and Delphine has always felt isolated. Her vertigree deters a lot of Ozians from seeing beyond her skin. As she watches Glinda, she decides that this is not an impostor, but that there is something terribly wrong with Glinda. She will need to tread lightly, but she cannot abandon her friend. Delphine steps from the shadows after a quick glance to guarantee they are alone, the hood of her ebony cloak pulled high to keep her face from sight. Black boots click against the aging bricks, their yellow long worn away and chipped to give them a gnarly gray and grimy look. Another few steps and she is trotting up the stairs. "Glinda, what are you doing out here?"

"Ooooh!" Glinda squeals in delight, then looks quite distressed. "You are not supposed to be here," she waggles her gloved hand at Delphine. "I came here to tell you to not meet me tonight. You are in danger! At least, I think you are in danger. Maybe I am in danger? Oh! No, I might be the danger to you! Oh dear!" Glinda goes from bubbly, to distressed, to tearing up in two seconds.

Delphine's eyes widen in surprise at this gibberish outburst.

"Do not be afraid of me, Delphi!" She then grabs Delphine's forearms and gives her a firm shake, knocking Delphine's hood from her head. "Oh! You know better than to furrow your brow! Look at those wrinkles!" Glinda then promptly reaches up and brushes her thumbs against Delphine's forehead.

"Glinda," Delphine's voice barks at her friend. "Stop."

"Oh," Glinda whimpers. "I do not want to make you mad. Do not be mad. Do you not like me anymore?" Her lower lip juts out and quivers in the promise to cry if Delphine says she does not like her.

"Do not be daft. What is the matter with you?"

"Matter? Nothing! Nothing at all now that I know you do not hate me!"

Delphine sighs and gently removes Glinda's massaging hands from her forehead. "Why are you acting like this? What has happened? Did someone do this to you?"

From the shadows, Chaos and Order watch the two women interacting. It takes all of Chaos's resolve to not laugh aloud at the circus that is now Glinda of the South. Order frowns as he watches Delphine, feeling the echoes of the emotions he took from Glinda welling in his heart. He blinks and the frown smooths out. He has work to do and could not afford to let Glinda's emotions to weaken his resolve. With a glance to Chaos and a small flick of his head, they agree to flank Delphine in the efforts to capture her. Fate has made it clear, that Delphine is not to be killed.

Chaos slithers through the shadows to re-appear behind Delphine.

Order waits until his wife is in place before he strolls forward, the shadows parting from him like a veil being lifted. He enjoys the shock and surprise on Delphine's face.

"Oh! You are here! Delphine. This is my new friend." She pauses then and pouts. "Oh, phooey. He is who I came here to warn you about. He is nice and likes it when things are neatly--."

"Glinda, run." Delphine cuts her off as she puts herself between Order and Glinda.

"Run? Why would I run? We are all friends here, right?" Glinda's eyes are the size of saucers as she struggles to understand why Delphi would be so upset.

"Of course, my dear. Now, Delphine, you have been very wicked, and Fate would like to talk with you." Order chastises Delphine with a fatherly tone.

Without warning, a glittering star-shaped wand is thrust into his face. "Are you going to do naughty things to my friend," the still bubbly tone demands of the man.

Shock flits across his face for a heartbeat before he gets it under control and his stoic visage returns.

Delphine's head whips around as Chaos, unable to contain her cackle, bowls over laughing only a few steps away from the witches.

"Hah! You *are*!" Glinda sounds quite incensed at the idea of her friends wanting to hurt her other friend.

Delphine struggles to back them away from Order and Chaos, finding her feet are already entangled by shadows. "For the love of Ozma, run Glinda!"

"Why? He is my friend! He will not do anything naughty to me, and he is very much," as she shakes her wand in Order's direction again, "not going to do anything naughty to you!" The wand is now being brandished at Delphine. "Because you," she boops Delphine's green nose with the wand, "have stars in your eyes! And only the boy that put them there can do naughty things to you!" She giggles and boops Delphine again with the wand.

Glinda makes zero sense and is brandishing a child's toy in her face. Then, before she can break them free of Chaos's hold, she is booped a third time with the wand.

"Bibbidi. Bobbidi. Love is for you!" Then an iridescent soap bubble encircles Delphine, ripping her free from the shadows.

Delphine watches in horror as she literally floats into the air, unable to stop whatever strange magic Glinda is using.

Order and Chaos watch dumbfounded, as she rises further. Then the bubble pops and Delphine is gone.

"Now you will not be naughty!" Glinda nods decisively to the two members of the Six and turns to skip down the steps, flouncing away.

Order, still in shock, murmurs. "What. Just. Happened?"

"I believe the child with a wand just got the better of you," Chaos mimics Order's voice to perfection as she parrots his dismissal of the power of Glinda.

"Of us," Order corrects.

"You are in so much trouble," Chaos giggles.

"Oh, am I, dear wife? Whose shadows failed to stop the glittering heart soap bubble?"

"Killjoy. At least we know Delphine is still alive."

In the distance, the sound of Tick Tock soldiers echo off the brick.

Chaos and Order frown, looking in the direction that Glinda went. There are faint traces of glitter, but it is obvious she bubbled herself away as well. With a growl, Order yanks his wife to him and they flee the city, defeated.

hearts & Stars

Jakob and Wilhelm sit on the crates, hunched in thought about their next step. Both men are anxious about this clandestine meeting that Delphine had to go to. Wilhelm does not like all the risks she takes for a place that barely tolerates her existence. The faint sound of a bubble popping rouses them from their silent ruminations. They look up to see little heart-shaped soap bubbles fluttering down at them, popping mid-air. As they stare at the strange trail of hearts, a massive iridescent globe appears above Wilhelm. Both men can clearly see Delphine trapped within. She twists and turns but cannot pop it. It gently floats from the middle of the room, and once over Wilhelm, it pops. This showers the trio in tiny little hearts and causes

Delphine to free fall into Wilhelm's lap. Her vibrant green skin shimmers from the glittering stardust kissing it.

"Why are--?"

"No," Delphine brandishes a finger at Wilhelm, cutting off this line of interrogation.

"But I just want to--." Wilhelm grins.

"Not a chance." Delphine grouses.

"Why are you covered in glitter?" Jakob rolls his eyes at their lovey-dovey exchange.

"Because Glinda has been compromised by the Six." Delphine settles into Wilhelm's arms.

Jakob frowns and plops back down on his crate.

Wilhelm leans back against the wall, petting his hand down Delphine's back. "What do you mean, compromised?"

"I mean the woman booped me on the nose with a child's toy and told me only the boy who put the stars in my eyes could do naughty things to me compromised." Delphine crosses her arms and sulks, enjoying the warmth of the arms around her.

"Fiddlesticks," Jakob snorts.

"Well, why is that such a terrible thing?" Wilhelm's voice is low and sultry as he stares into Delphine's eyes.

In spite of her normally rough attitude, giggles at Wilhelm.

This makes Jakob frown, and he trails a finger along her glittered skin before bringing it to his nose. With a heavy sigh, he shakes his head, and can do nothing to stop the stardust from taking hold of the young lovers.

"It was Chaos and Order," Delphine finally says as she watches Jakob.

"And you are still alive how?" Jakob narrows his eyes.

"Fate wants me alive and taken to the Silver Citadel." She narrows her eyes back at him.

"Good, let us go then. We put these Six back to bed, find father, and then hit the pub by dinner." Wilhelm beams with all his knight-in-shining-armor gusto.

"Do not be daft," Delphine chastises, and this makes Wilhelm pout. "You can pout at me all you like, Grimm, but storming the citadel only wins you death. No Grimm who enters has been seen again. Not for two hundred years now has a Grimm dared to show his face outside of Oz. Frank was the last, and he is gone."

"What do you mean, gone?" Wilhelm asks in fear.

"What do you mean, last?" Jakob asks at the same time.

"I mean what I said. The Six have hunted all the Grimms of Nodd to find Aesop. None remain." Delphine's rough tone grows quiet, killing the playful mood.

The silence between the three is palpable as Jakob and Wilhelm realize just how dire the situation truly is.

"Then we must find William and Hans, to bring them back."

"I agree. What about you, Delphine?" Jakob frowns at her.

"I have been getting along just fine without you two. In fact, my life will get that much easier with you gone." She can see the hurt in Wilhelm's eyes but does not waiver in her assertion that they are trouble. "I have allies throughout Nodd, and you two are putting us all in danger. If you cannot defeat the Six, we are in for a far worse fate than your sulking pout, Wilhelm." She eases out of his lap with great reluctance and moves to a grimy canvas tarp on the other side of the room. With all the flourish of a magician, she yanks the tarp free, revealing a fully intact Ozian glass mirror.

"These are legend," Jakob murmurs as he comes forward.

"No! Do not touch it. You will alert them to your presence."

This causes him to recoil from the mirror. She rolls her eyes at the legendary Grimm dramatics. She motions the Grimm brothers to stand to the side, and she steps to the mirror. Her fingers delicately slide into place in the grooves of the ornate wood frame and the glass begins to shimmer as green as her skin with sprinkles of stardust showering over it. "This is Fair Verona."

In the glass, the men look upon what was once a bustling city of vast merchants, nobles, and fairies. Now, before their eyes lie smoldering ruins and poverty-stricken people. All the color has been drained from the world as if a painter had thrown black paint across the canvas.

"This is Wonderland." Her voice is haunting in the silence.

She shifts her fingers, and the green ripples fade from the ruins to a new scene. It is far more gruesome and violent. Cards fighting cards. Animals being enslaved. The once stunning rose gardens are nothing but thorns and burned shrubbery.

"Now, the Forbidden Forest." Sadness tinges her voice.

"Wait. There is no such place," Jakob counters.

"Really, Grimm? You know this land so well for having been missing for two hundred years?" She cuts the man a dark look. "Why would I make something like that up?"

"Because you want to scare us," Wilhelm mutters.

"You should be scared. This forest stands where Nimh's garden once stood."

She shifts the mirror. Where a thriving and lush forest once stood with the Aesop Nation at its center now stands a tangled mess of vines and twisted trees that would make nightmares look pleasant.

"Show me the Silver City," Wilhelm demands.

"No. As it is, they will be aware I used the mirror." She pulls her hands from the frame and the mirror goes still. Before Wilhelm can touch it, she throws the tarp back over it. The brothers frown at each other, and she crosses her arms. "Well, where are William and Hans?"

"We do not know," Wilhelm confesses.

"I swear. You Grimms are useless." Delphine mutters as she moves by them to the scrying pool next to the green smear that is supposed to be her. "Do you two not know how to do anything?"

"Delphi," Jakob grumbles.

"Jakob," she retorts.

"Just help us, please." Wilhelm requests gently.

She gives him a look as if to say she would always help him, then eases the stone away from the scrying pool.

He recognizes the Avalonian tool and smirks at the idea that Avalonians are hiding in Oz. His gaze transfixes on Delphine as she works, memorizing the curve of her jaw, the cute little ebony wisps of hair that escape her braid. A sinking, dreadful feeling in the pit of his stomach makes him think this might be the last time he ever gets to gaze upon her.

"Stop staring. It is rude." Delphine grouses, but her cheeks flush purple under his scrutiny. "I can see William's thread."

"And Hans?" Jakob asks.

She furrows her brow and focuses on the pool. The minutes tick by and when she breaks the scrying pool's connection, she sighs. "Nothing. I cannot find his thread."

"He is dead then," Wilhelm shoots Jakob a steely glare.

"No. It means he is not anywhere I can reach. If he were dead, I would have found him in Erebus. He was not there."

"One problem to solve at a time. Let us go to William first, and maybe he has a clue about Hans." Jakob offers. "We cannot use the Labyrinth again. They are watching the borders."

"There is another way. Gather your things and come with me."

The men exchange a look and gather what few things they have. The three slip from her tower and through the castle. The only movements are from the Winkie guards who pay them no mind. She does not bother with explaining as she leads the two men from her castle and out into the fields beyond.

"There are no gates in Oz. You know this." Jakob grumbles at her.

"I did not say I was taking you to a gate. Stand here," she motions to a spot in the middle of the open field they now stand in, just west of the castle.

The two men stand shoulder to shoulder. She looks them over and she lingers at Wilhelm before she leans up and kisses him softly.

His arm slides around her waist, and he pulls her close.

Jakob clears his throat, and she steps back, blushing again. "Now, it is critical you focus on William and only William. You must both concentrate."

"What happens if we do not?" Wilhelm asks.

"Then you die. Do not move from this spot and focus on William only. Do you understand me?"

"Yes," both men say.

"Good." She turns on heel and walks away.

Wilhelm and Jakob look at each other and furrow their brows.

"I said to focus on William only!" She shouts across the distance she has put between them, and it makes the brothers grin. They watch the silhouette of Delphine grow smaller and smaller until she is lost to the shadows of night.

The two stand in silence, trying to focus on William. They conjure images of what he looks like to them, what he sounds like, and what he might be doing right this moment. That is when they hear the first whistle and Jakob notices the tall grass rustle around them. He closes his eyes to keep his focus.

Wilhelm turns his head to look over his shoulder, and his eyes grow wide. The starry sky is blighted out by a slim cyclone tearing itself from the heavens, whipping down to devour them. The closer it gets, the louder it is, until it is roaring with wicked intent. Wilhelm and Jakob open their mouths to scream and are engulfed by the cyclone.

Just as quick as it appears, it disappears back into the now dissipating clouds above. Delphine drops to her knees and pants from the efforts of summoning the cyclone. The Wizard had taught Ozians to travel by weather, not by stone. It is not without its own perils and her hands clutch over her heart, hoping against hope the Grimm brother will be alright.

35

The Calm Before The Storm

Morgan stays with Arthur in his war camp until the promise of Spring requires her to return to Avalon. Arthur had protested and wanted to send guards to accompany her. It was then she informed him that no man is allowed on the island. Now she walks quietly to the edge of the lake. The homecoming is bittersweet. She will have to figure out how to allow for men on the island while preserving all that is her home if she is to become his queen. The little canoe teeters as it comes to her. Stepping into the well-worn boat she motions gently, and it pushes back off from the shore, sending her into the ever-present mists clinging to the water. Once safely into the mists, she parts the rest to allow her clear sight of the island as she contemplates what is required of her. By the time she reaches the shore, Elaine and Isolder are waiting for her, arms crossed.

"What?" She asks innocently, eyeing the other two women.

"Uh-uh. We thought you had forsaken us *great mother*." Elaine teases.

"You, maybe, but I could never forsake Isolder." Humor tinges her tone as she teases back.

The three women erupt into laughter and hug each other. Morgan listens quietly to the voices calling to her, praying for her attention as they meander up the path. Elaine talks about something happening with the dragons where their scales are becoming brittle and flaking off. Isolder talks about the harvests waning and how the war in Lloegyr is starting to affect their crops as well.

"Is he truly going to end the war?" Isolder asks with a hopeful look.

"Do not be daft. He is a man. He thrives on war." Elaine grumbles.

"Morgan trusts him. She has been blessing his camp all winter."

"Enough. I have come to perform the Rites of Spring and to give him time to move toward our union." Morgan interjects.

"Your what?" Elaine growls.

"Oh, Morgan. You cannot be in a union with him. You are the Lady of the Lake. Your duty is to Avalon. No mother takes a husband. They are more trouble than happiness. How would you even handle that? He is forbidden from here." Isolder chastises gently.

"I am the Lady of the Lake. I make the rules."

There is a distant rumble of thunder, which causes Elaine and Isolder to look at each other. Silence falls upon the trio as they approach the temple. The discussion of Morgan and Arthur's union left for another time.

******

"Wart, listen to me," Merlin shouts across the field as Arthur walks away. "You cannot wed the girl. No matter how much you both want it. You are not meant to be with her."

Arthur stops and turns to look back at Merlin. "Do not presume to tell me what to do, *wizard*. That girl, whose name is Morgan, has done more for the kingdom of Lloegyr than you have. She has healed the sick, inspired the men to protect her, and wants to merge our kingdoms. She brought Galahad back from death. She is even more powerful than you."

Merlin's eyes narrow as he watches the young king. No one is a more powerful Noddian than he, not even that ass of a man, Aesop. The only person who has the potential to be such is the Lost Heir. If this girl is that infant, he would know it. She is a powerful Avalonian witch, yes, but as for being a Noddian princess, not even a hint in the stars. He did not have time to run a fool's errand and confront her. He needs Arthur to take the throne. In the Ozian witch's prophecy, he saw the boy on the throne to get what he wants.

"Boy. You know not what you talk about." With a

loud pop, he appears before the young man and jabs his finger in his chest. "The only reason you have a kingdom at all is because of me. Did you really think all those people would go out of their way to rally behind the bastard child of Uther Pendragon if it were not for me? *I* am the one who negotiated with the lords. *I* am the one who convinced them you had a righteous spirit. *I* am the one who showed them glimpses of power they could barely comprehend, so they would follow you. Do not underestimate me, boy. For it is much easier to tear something down than it is to build it up."

The men stop to watch the interchange. Merlin's tone promises malice and more than one knight casually draws their weapon while watching the pair.

"No. You rallied *some* lords. You frightened others. Then you vanish for months on end without a word. You were not there when we needed you and in one fell swoop she turned the tide of war. *She* unified each camp as we approached without bloodshed. *She* blessed their children. *She* removed sickness and blight from the land. *She* listened to their woes and soothed them. What more could I ask for in a queen? You are the one who is always thumping me to think!" Arthur thumps his own temple. "Then the one time I do you are suddenly here threatening me with your sorcery! I will not have it!"

"That witch makes a great ally, yes. But mother of your children? Honestly think that through, boy. You would put a Druid on the throne? For that is what any son she gives you would be. Is that any kind of king your precious lords will follow? They do not follow her. They follow *you*. She has beguiled you. Clouded your judgment. All you are doing is chasing a good lay, not a queen. She is the only one who gains from this union. Start thinking like the king you say you are. Now, *your majesty,* I must go attend to the final lords seeking recompense to stand behind you." Merlin vanishes from sight and Arthur roars in frustration.

"He is not wrong, Arthur," Gawain offers. "She stands to gain far more than you. Have you seen what is on her hidden island? They may have nothing of value and become our burden after your union."

"It does not matter if her island is not but barren ground and drowned shrubbery. She is the gem of that island, and I would be a fool to cast it aside."

"Agreed. She is a jewel. Perhaps you could sway those who doubt her with a gift from her island?" Gawain tries to bridge the gap of Merlin's wisdom and Arthur's heart, but can sympathize with the frustration in the young man.

******

Spring flourishes into Summer. Arthur's army, massive in size, lays siege upon Uther Pendragon's keep. His cousin holds the keep and as much as Arthur would like to run him through with his sword, he refuses to murder his own people being held. Frustration grows as he has not seen hide nor tale of Merlin, and Morgan is not due for another three days. His men have kept Arthur preoccupied with war plans and strategy to prepare for taking the keep and finally unifying the lands. Arthur's cousin has made it quite clear that no bastard son of Uther will be his king. As the sun sets, warning whistles from hidden scouts around Arthur's camp chitter and the men spring to arms. From the foggy mists of the forest emerges a single cloaked woman.

She eases her hood back to reveal her identity, and when Gawain comes to greet her, he smiles. "Milady, Morgan," he bows formally.

"Sir Gawain. I would have thought you to be inside the gates by now," she frowns as she looks up the hill to the keep.

"It is much harder to open the door when one cannot reach the heart of the people hidden behind it."

"Where is the charlatan? Could he not worm his way into Arthur's home?"

"It would seem they have had a mild falling out, milady. The wizard has left this task to Arthur alone. I believe he is attempting to teach him a lesson. I give you fair warning, my sweet lady, the king is in a mood." The elder knight offers his arm to escort her.

When she enters the tent, Arthur is pacing in frustration. She gives Gawain a nod and turns to face her betrothed.

"My love," Arthur exclaims in excitement. "You are days early."

"I am. I came to discuss our union, son of Pendragon. Please, sit."

"Son of Pendragon? We are so formal again? Have you decided to forgo that which I have offered?"

Arthur's anxious gaze searches Morgan's face for a clue of what she means by discussing their union.

"My duty is to Avalon first, my love. I cannot forsake the promises made before my heart promised me to you." She clasps her hands in front of her.

"You say that like I do not have duties and promises of my own. Why is it such a terrible thing to bring forth a union of our two lands?" His expression darkens as he jumps to the conclusion that Merlin has meddled here.

"That is not what I meant. I know you have duties and promises as well. Your people look to you as a beacon of hope and peace. Would they follow the Avalonian ways as well?" She struggles to keep her voice calm.

"There is no harm in trying to teach them your ways. I cannot speak for the hearts of other men, but I am willing to learn."

"Arthur," she sighs in frustration and comes closer, brushing his curly golden hair from his face. "A will to learn does not make a believer. Your people fear me as much as they do Merlin. The only reason they accept me is due to your might."

Arthur huffs and takes Morgan's hands. "Morgan, you are the strongest, most beautiful woman I have ever seen. You have a place in their hearts because you are radiant and divine. You are the heart of my heart. You are the stars in my night. I have loved you from the moment my eyes first fell upon the nymph in the woods. You are my everything, and habberdash it all, if

I were not king, I would have wed you on the spot. Therefore, if no one would protest marrying you as a peasant, then why should I hear their protests to marrying you as a king?" As he finishes his profession of his love, he stands. His piercing green eyes gaze deep into hers and his voice rumbles deep as he brings smolder to his argument.

It takes Morgan's breath away, and any argument she had has fallen silent. She is swept into the chaotic sweetness of Arthur's true love. "Well, good king, you make an extraordinarily compelling case for love... And hope. How could I refuse such a noble demand?"

"Good. Then we shall be wed as soon as I claim my home and unify Lloegyr." He kisses her forehead to seal the promise.

"I had come to gift you your father's sword in consolation of breaking our betrothal."

Arthur gets a roguish grin on his face. "I guess that means you get to keep his sword as I get to keep you."

Morgan giggles and swats him. "Do not be daft. The sword is mine to give, and I choose to give it to you."

"If that is your wish, my lady. I will never turn down your favor, but I must ask how you have my father's sword if it is in the hands of my cousin." He studies her, worry tinging his voice.

From beneath her cloak, she retrieves the blade still bound in its scabbard. "The blade your cousin holds is but a mere replica, meant to convince men your father still held the blade after returning it to the Lake. This is the true sword, Excalibur. Kneel my sweet king and receive the blessing of Avalon."

Arthur raises a brow but takes a knee before Morgan.

"Arthur Pendragon, may this blade ever sing true, for it is the reflection of your soul. While you wield it with pure intentions in your heart, you are the true king of Lloegyr." She offers the sheathed blade down to him. When he takes the sword and lowers it, she leans down and kisses his forehead.

Arthur gasps as the sword forges a bond with his soul. The Avalonian magic courses through his veins, healing his wounds, chasing away his doubts, and sealing his claim to Lloegyr.

happily Ever After

Arthur rises with an air of confidence that had not been there before. His shoulders appear broader, and his head is held higher. He pulls Morgan to him and rests his forehead against hers. "I will unite all Lloegyr and you will be my queen. Promise me, Morgan, that you will be here when I return." His voice is deep and quiet, filled with anxiety that she will vanish while he is fighting.

Morgan closes her eyes and tunes out the masses for a moment of peace with Arthur. She had considered giving him hope and then departing. Elaine and Isolder would encourage this wisdom. She knows Merlin would enjoy winning the battle of her vanishing from Arthur's life, but here, in Arthur's arms, she wants nothing more than to be his. The way he looks at her and how he clings to her clouds her judgment. "I promise." The words release the breath she had been holding, and she nestles into his arms. The fear and excitement bubble through her emotions. The faint whistle of the wind picking up causes Arthur to chuckle.

"I must win this battle on my own, my love. If I am to be king, I must be strong enough to stand for all. Let me do this for us." He kisses her forehead gently and then parts, ready to settle this matter once and for all.

Morgan's shoulders slump as the visions the sword conjured swim in her head. What roots her to the spot is a single vision, burning bright in her mind. The vibrant blue eyes of an infant stare back at her, bringing hope. When she finally moves from the spot where Arthur left her, she can hear the thunder of the army moving. The camp itself is eerie in it silence. The mass of soldiers looks like a black fog creeping up the hill. The war drums beat in thunderous warning.

Arthur sits atop his horse staring at the wall before him. "Kay! I have come to claim my father's home"

"You? A mere bastard child, come to claim Uther Pendragon's home? Never!" His cousin crows back from the crenelations above. "You can amass your armies as much as you want, but these walls have held for generations. They will hold still even after I am gone of old age!"

Arthur can hear the grumbling of the men behind him as they shift in anticipation of finishing this siege. He stills them by drawing his sword. The blade rings true and shimmers in the sun. The murmurs and hushed awe of the word, "Excalibur," whistle around the battlefield like a whistling wind.

"I come wielding the true blade of Pendragon." He holds the blade aloft, like a beacon to the heavens. The jewels and steel shine bright compared to the darkness of the soldiers' attire.

"Heresy!" Kay shouts back. "For I am the true wielder of the blade. I do not know where you found that bauble, but if you ask for forgiveness, I will be lenient in my judgment of you."

"Leniency? I do not need your leniency. I have come to challenge you for my home, *cousin*. A duel, for all the lords of Lloegyr to witness. Let us not shed the blood of our people any further over this squabble. For an honorable king would fight to protect his people as much to claim them. Prove your sword is true and fight me like the honorable man I once knew."

Kay's face turns purple with rage. He cannot publicly back down from such a challenge. Even if he can hold the keep, he would lose face among the lords that backed him. No man wants to stand behind a coward, and Arthur has beguiled the people with a sense of equality and fairness. He storms down to the courtyard as the massive iron gates are lifted and the lone rider, Arthur, passes through.

A clergyman steps forward and shouts for all to hear, "May God have witness upon this duel for rightful claim of the Keep of Pendragon. He who yields first, loses. Once blood is drawn, the victor will be he with blood on his sword. To slay your opponent will be to bring damnation upon your head from both God and man alike. Fight fairly and fight justly. May God have mercy upon your souls."

Morgan frowns up at the keep from the camp, as no sounds of war echo down the valley. No men cry out in pain. No healer prays for guidance. There are no whistling arrows, no metal clanks of shield and sword, just the deafening silence. Fear bubbles inside of Morgan again as she struggles with the desire to rush to Arthur's side, or even to flee forever. A gentle hand rests on her shoulder and draws her attention from the keep.

"Patience, milady. We would know if Arthur were dead." Gawain offers a gentle smile.

"I should be fighting alongside him." Her hand covers his, and she leans into the friendly gesture, drawing what comfort she can.

"You would only be a distraction. That distraction would cause him to lose you to Kay. If all you seek is a kingdom, then go. If it is Arthur you seek, then stay. For a sword will always return to its scabbard." He holds a twinkle in his eye as he talks in such a forward fashion to her.

Morgan's cheeks flush hot and she sulks, reminding Gawain that while she may be a powerful witch, she is a child just like Arthur. He is pleasantly surprised when all she does is curl her fingers into her skirts and remains rooted in place to stare at the battlefield. Gawain had volunteered to remain with her at the war council, knowing that it was him or young Galahad. Galahad stood no chance against Kay's men should it come to that.

Back at the keep, Arthur stands firm. He can feel her emotions via the bond he has forged with her through the sword. He draws deeply upon them to firm his resolve as he squares off against his cousin. This war has taken a large toll upon them both. The last time he had seen his cousin, Kay had been full of vim and vigor. Now, Kay is aged, and his face is lined from the pressures of ruling. While his face shows the wear and tear of the war, the sword never waivers in his hold, showing his resolve and strength.

As the two men circle each other, Arthur takes in Kay with his false sword. Once upon a time, Arthur had worshiped Kay for possessing the weapon and believed him to have the power to wield Excalibur. While Kay holds the weapon firmly pointed at Arthur, Arthur now knows the truth of the matter. His own blade is firm in his grip. His cloak flares around his mud-stained boots as he takes step after step, judging, and waiting to see how his cousin will react to this challenge. He does not have to wait long before Kay's blade flicks out at him, like the darting tongue of a snake. The sword from his Lady glimmers in the fading light of day as he handily parries, keeping his opponent from landing a blow. The sword is light as a feather in his hands, despite being a massive weapon, and moves like an extension of his arms. He feels more alive in this battle than he has in all the war.

It is all Kay can do to keep the enchanted steel from connecting against his flesh when Arthur counters. The men are in lockstep with each other as they continue to circle in this dance of death. The courtyard is filled with the ringing blows of the expert swordsmen. It is not until the final beam of sun paints the ground a dark reddish color that Arthur gets the opening he needs. Kay overextends in desperation, and the crowd gasps as the steel in his hand is sundered in twain by Arthur's forceful swing of Excalibur.

Arthur stands over his cousin, showing great precision in lightly nicking Kay's throat, causing a small trickle of blood to seep down it.

"Yield, cousin, this war is over." Arthur's voice is as hard as granite and booms across the courtyard. He holds his breath as his cousin contemplates his next move.

"As you say, *my King*, this war is over." Kay takes a knee.

Arthur, surprised his cousin yields, releases the breath he was holding. The war is finally over.

Once Arthur secures the victory and the lords take to their knees in fealty as well, he turns to Galahad. "Ride as the wind and fetch Lady Morgan." He watches as the young boy scurries onto his stallion and beats out of the keep like he is being chased by the wind itself.

Morgan watches as darkness clings to the hillside. The shifting of the soldiers can be seen, but making out any true actions is impossible. Her heart pounds in her chest, and she clenches her jaw.

Why has Arthur not sent for me? Or returned? I should go to him. What if he is too hurt to call for me?

Gawain has not left her side, standing like a stone statue beside her. Then the clop of hooves can be heard. The women in the camp stir. Closer and closer the boy rides until he pulls the reins, causing his horse to rear before Arthur's tent. "Milady, the King summons you post haste. The war is over!" He is jubilant and breathless in delivering the king's message as he struggles to get Arthur's horse under control.

When Morgan turns, Gawain is already walking to where the horses are kept. She moves forward and reaches out to steady Arthur's horse for Galahad. The stallion calms under her touch until he stamps at the ground and his muscles twitch in irritation. She is assisted onto a horse and the three ride up the hillside. The sea of soldiers part for them, giving the trio a grand entrance into Pendragon's keep.

Arthur stops mid-sentence with the lords when he sees Morgan, abandoning his discussions to her. Instead of turning back to the lords, he walks her straight to the clergyman who had just officiated their duel. "You are a man of the cloth and can officiate a noble union, yes?"

"Yes, my King?" The clergyman stammers in confusion.

"Good! Then you are to wed us here and now."

"Sire?" Panic paints across the holy man's face.

"I did not stammer and it would be wise to do as your king commands."

"But... But... Sire. She is a witch and does not follow our ways." He looks to the surrounding lords for support.

Arthur snaps his fingers in the clergyman's face when he looks away. "I am your king and you have sworn fealty to me. Do you value my divine right to rule so little that you would seek counsel with my lords?"

"No, Sire," he whimpers.

"Good. Then you will wed us without hesitation." Arthur's voice holds a sharp suggestion to not question his command again.

"Good lords and ladies," the clergyman stammers out as he performs his duty. Several minutes later he timidly announces, "What God has brought together, let no man tear asunder. I pronounce you man and wife. May God have mercy on our souls."

Arthur's look darkens as he stares down the clergyman before Morgan gently clears her throat. When he turns his gaze to her, she is grinning like the cat who caught the canary. He sweeps her into his arms and draws her into a passionate kiss, sealing their union.

37

The Price of Rebellion

Delphine pants from the efforts of conjuring the storm and guaranteeing it safely takes the Grimm brothers to their destination. Her body trembles from the effort and fatigue settles in as she struggles to push herself to her feet. Tears cling to her eyes and the walk back to the castle feels as though her boots are sunk in mud. The Winkie guard who sees her first scoops her up and carries her to her chambers.

"Be vigilant. The Six know." Her words are soft as the guard lays her on the bed.

"I will send for Locasta, Mistress."

"No. It is too late for that. Send word to protect the Empress and to trust no one. Glinda is lost."

He frowns at the emerald witch he has come to

respect and cherish. While she has been labeled *Wicked* by the rest of Oz, he knows she has done more for the Ozians than they will ever know. She may not be as fancy, or frivolous, as her counterparts, but her heart is pure gold.

******

The first hints of sunlight dare to brush across the floor, and Delphine's eyes open. She is aware she is not alone. For a split second, she is trapped in the tower again with that girl, Dorothy Gale, and having to suffer the burns from the water to fake her own death. As she rolls to her side, she stares at the pinks and oranges of the sunrise, creeping ever closer to her. She forces her breathing to slow and takes stock of the room, assuring herself she is no longer in that tower, or being hunted by the girl from Cansass.

Delphine sits and ignores the figures in the shadow. She knew her days were numbered. The downside of being a prophet. Try as she might to stop the events that led her to this moment, she still is held at sword point. "Delphine, The Wicked Witch of the West, you are under arrest, accused of treason, and are to be taken to Silver City where you will stand trial before the Six."

The Winkie guards burst through the door and raise their spears to defend her. "No. Stand down. Do not let your men shed blood for me. You know what you must do." Delphine stands and rights her clothing. Then steps toward the guards brandishing swords at her. Once within arm's reach, the captain snatches her and binds her hands behind her. He blindfolds her and gags her as well. His firm grip on her forearm guides her to what she can only surmise is the stairwell.

When she hears the splash of boots on water, she begins to panic. "No," she whimpers against the gag and balks.

"Silence, prisoner."

"No. No. I am allergic to... NO!" her voice is muffled and blocked by the gag. Her screams reverberate off the stone walls as another officer takes her other arm and the men hoist her from the floor. They then leap into the puddle to water walk. She is still screaming when they re-appear in the Silver Castle.

With a grunt, they throw her to the floor. Then they watch in horror as her skin bubbles and burns.

She writhes on the floor, screaming and struggling. Pain fills her and all she can think about is that she needs to get out of these clothes before they burn her to death.

"You fools! Fate explicitly said to retrieve her unharmed. There is a reason we told you to use the stones."

"But... But Sir. Mistress Chaos informed us the stones are compromised and she would escape." The poor guard stammers, trying to recover from this mistake, afraid for his own life.

"I will deal with that later. Be gone!" He shouts at the guards, who flee in terror. He kneels and rests a hand on her to still her. "Shh, it will be alright little one." As his fingers brush over her clothes, the water pools out and trickles along the alabaster floor. He continues to pet her until no water remains, the pain subsides, and her burns are healed.

Delphine trembles on the floor, unsure of what to do. She had expected to be taken by stone travel and intercepted, but now she is terrified that they have confirmed her allergy and could use it against her. When the blindfold and gag are removed, she blinks at the brightness of the Silver Palace. Her eyes focus on her would-be savior to see a man approaching his mid-thirties with dusty blond hair and the palest blue eyes. Saint's expression is soft, and the full beard with mustache gives him a fatherly look.

He eases her to a sitting position and unties her hands. "Come with me, my dear. Fate is most eager to speak with you."

"I bet she is," Delphine grumbles and refuses the hand offered to help her stand.

"You misunderstand me child, that was not a request. Now, come along, before I am forced to make you comply."

Delphine's emerald green eyes focus on Saint for several moments. While his visage is gentle and trustworthy, she can see the darkness within. The swirl of malevolence at being defied floats to the surface the longer she hesitates. "And no harm will come to me?"

"If you are innocent, then why would harm ever fall upon your head?" True confusion paints its way across the strange man's face.

Her shoulders slump and she nods, falling in line

with him as he guides her out of the room.

The castle is massive, with twists and turns throughout. It is enough to make a person dizzy if they are not careful. Over-sized doors are pressed open and Saint leads Delphine into a grand dining hall with opulent drapery and gaudy furniture, far too ornate to be of any real use. At the head of the table sits Law, an old man, spindly and sour of expression. His silver hair is slicked back and tied neatly at the base of his skull. His clothes are pristine and regal in appearance. To his right sits Fate, an older woman with a dark copper mane of hair. Her eyes glint with mischief, and her gown is no less regal than the older man. To his left is Desire, a young woman, with strawberry blond hair, and a gossamer gown that leaves little to the imagination. To the right of the copper-haired woman, is Chaos, a young woman with hair as black as ink and wild as the wind, and eyes to match. At the other end of the table sits Order, a man with slicked back mahogany brown hair. His clothing is reminiscent to that of a puffed-up military general. The five of them turn to look at who dares to disturb their meal.

"Ah, I see you have succeeded in your efforts," Fate chirps with glee before she cuts Chaos and Order a dirty look. "Come, Delphine. Join us for breakfast." With the wave of her hand, Chaos is shunted closer to Order and an empty chair is placed between her and Fate.

Saint guides Delphine to the chair before taking the empty seat on the other side of the table, next to his wife.

This is the first time Delphine has seen all the Six together in one place. What she would not give for one of those glorious, stunning bombs filled with the Cat's venom to be hidden among her skirts. She rests her hands in her lap and clenches her jaw to keep from blurting out an insult. The food has been forgotten by all but Law, who casually continues his meal with little regard for their guest of honor.

"Come now. You must be starved after that little storm you whipped up," Fate coos as she fills a plate for Delphine. "Tell us all about who you sent to the other side and why they would want to travel by storm in the first place. I hear it is tricky business, riding a tornado."

"You are too kind, Fate. I do not wish to be a burden," Delphine's voice sounds timid to her, and she is struggling to not throw this food in Fate's face. To confess any part of the tornado could lead to much more dire consequences.

"Oh, I insist. You look famished. Your skin is pale, and your eyes show shadows of exhaustion. Besides, you will need your strength to fulfill your duties to your Empress before your trial."

"My Empress? What have you done to Ozma? Where is she?" Delphine loses any control of her expression and her panic shines through.

Fate's eyes darken with rage and frustration. "*I* am your Empress, Delphine. Not some child you witches play at ruling with."

Chaos leans over and mockingly stage-whispers into Delphine's ear, "Empress!" She knows it will get a rise out of Fate.

Order gives her a stern look and shakes his head no.

"My duty is to Oz first, and Nodd second. I will only serve the rightful ruler of Nodd, the Heir." Delphine chokes down the terror she feels and stiffens her back, sitting as prim and powerful as she can pretend to be in the ornate chair.

Law looks up from his meal then, "Well, we are the current rulers of Nodd, not the heir that is missing. You *will* respect our authority." His voice booms through the room.

Delphine's eyes widen as she feels the crushing weight of his command upon her. Horror fills her face as her free will is smashed under a ton of bricks. "Yes, Emperor Law," she stammers obediently.

"Good. Fate. She is all yours." He turns back to his meal as if he had not just usurped Delphine's free will.

"Now, as I was saying, eat your fill. You will need your strength."

Silence fills the table as all seven of them eat breakfast. Delphine's cheeks are again stained with tears. Even Chaos remains quiet. There is a reason they defer to Law.

Once breakfast finishes, Fate guides Delphine to her parlor.

Delphine frowns at the Ozian glass mirror Fate has sitting in the room. With that mirror, Fate can see all the threads and outcomes of what is to be through

Delphine.

"Be a good girl and put your hands on the mirror. I desire to see what you know."

38

Trials & Tribulations

Delphine lies on the cold stone, staring at the moss growing on the far side of the cell. There are no windows or doors. She has no idea if it is day or night. The draining power of fighting the control Law placed on her as she did Fate's bidding has left her without energy and feeling ill. She showed her what she knows to be, and *only* what she knows to be. She did not show her what had come to pass, or what might wait in the future. Delphine's clouded visions had left Fate angry and frustrated. It also filled the "Empress" with arrogance. Delphine's poor showing of her gift of sight left Fate believing she was the stronger of the two prophets. Being who she is, and the magic she holds, allowed her to interpret Fate's vague commands as she saw fit while remaining obedient.

Her taxing day spent under Law's command had been so long ago she guesses it has been three days. Everything in Nodd revolves around three. Delphine lies on her back and stares at the stones above. Her thoughts drift to Wilhelm. She can only hope he and Jakob arrived safely in the other world. Curse her for her recklessness in sending them off by storm. She only hopes the Winkies gave Locasta access to her grimoire. Only another Ozian witch will be able to open the tome and it contains all her notes, all her secrets, and how to return the memories she deliberately had Frank hide from her mind before he left. Jakob had not been joking when he said Frank was a master manipulator of the mind. She misses Frank too. His carefree, gregarious nature often lifted her spirits when all seemed lost. They had seen, together, what was to come for the Grimms. The only way to prevent that was to leave Nodd. While they can all still be hunted, the ability to locate and contain a Grimm in the other world grows exponential in difficulty. She and Frank had been on the trail of what happened to Lewis when he was cast into the stones of judgment. As the years passed, she became less confident in ever finding the missing Grimm. She knows that he is pivotal to what is happening in Nodd, just not how. She closes her eyes and listens to the sounds of the dungeon. There are faint groans, from other prisoners. The sound of water can be heard, and it terrifies her. Silver Castle is surrounded by the clear waters that lead out to the

Neverland Sea. One large leak and the entire dungeon would be flooded. Blinding light floods the cell as a door appears on the far side, silhouetting Order as he stands in the entry gazing down at her.

"It is time, young witch, for you to meet your just end." The chimes of the clock tower ring twelve for high noon.

Delphine rolls her eyes and stands. There is no point in fighting at this stage of the game. She is marched through the castle and brought into the main ballroom where the Fairy Godmother used to grant wishes. The room is pristine and divine in appearance. Opalesque crystals dangle from chandeliers, radiating inviting warmth and acceptance to all who enter these hallowed halls. The windows shimmer in the sunlight with all the colors of the rainbow stained into the glass. The only specs of dirt are those that cling to Delphine's plain black dress, and even those wash away as she is escorted further in. Everyone who is anyone in Nodd is present. There is the Red Queen of Wonderland and her pet Cat. There are the dreary lords of what remains of Fair Verona. Her step hitches when her eyes lock with Ozma, the young Empress of Oz, who is flanked by Glinda and Locasta, as well as protected by a small cadre of Winkie soldiers. Even the last of the Hunter's Guild is present, his grim expression offering little comfort to Delphine. She is paraded to a small dais in the middle of the room for all to see. The Six sit on high in their thrones where the Fairy Godmother once stood. She cares little for them. What

297

makes her take pause are the three shining glass coffins hovering above them. Encased like trophies are Titania, Maab, and Nimh. For hundreds of years, it has been believed they are dead. Yet their forms look peaceful in slumber without a hint of decay. Her wrists are bound in a fine silver chain, latching her to the spot.

Order then proudly struts to his throne on the stage. The murmurs grow to a deafening roar before Law stands and silences the room.

"Delphine of Ozrail, you are being charged of high treason to Nodd. For you have harbored, aided, and abetted Grimms." The loud gasps from all the fanciful onlookers of the silver court make his charge even more dramatic. "How do you plead?"

"It is Oz, not Ozrail, you dolt. Not guilty!" Delphine retorts and lifts her chin in defiance.

"Since you have entered a plea of not guilty, it is by decree of the Six, that you shall stand trial." Law's voice is even and shows no reaction to her taunts.

Delphine rolls her eyes as he sits on his throne, believing himself so high and mighty. She goes to make another crack about them being usurpers when she feels a furry hand cover her mouth. She turns her gaze to the slender albino Rabbit standing next to her in a dark pin-striped suit. His long, beautiful ears are gently bound by a tie behind him.

"Do not say another word. You make them angry, you will lose. It is simple as that. If I need you to make commentary, I will ask. Plus, their side goes first."

Another round of gasps draws Delphine's gaze away from the Rabbit to see what the commotion is. Her heart skips a beat at the hope it might be Wilhelm to save her. The hope is dashed as the figure eases the hood of his robe back, revealing the half-stone visage of the old, fallen emperor, Merlin.

"Oh, dear me! What is he doing here? This just became more complicated." The Rabbit simpers.

"Lords and ladies," Merlin begins. "I present you irrefutable proof that the Wicked Witch of the West has been harboring a Grimm. I will also reveal to you her collusion with the Grimms to stoke the flames of rebellion against our rightful and honorable rulers." Merlin stutters his steps, milking the stoning he had received from the Grimms, even though Delphine knows he has already reversed any damage done by the spell. Merlin, upon reaching the center of the room, raises his staff and conjures the mirage for all to see. In the air, plain as they are today, the visage of Jakob Grimm and Delphine argue fiercely. There is no sound to go with the animated figures. It becomes a collage of her bringing him food, turning away search patrols, and finally it shows her giving him the Labyrinth's map. "As the lords and ladies of the court know. I can only conjure visions of that which has transpired. It is with a heavy heart that I must show that such a lovely young woman has fallen so far." He dramatically turns to the Six. "I understand this proof is irrefutable of her harboring and aiding a Grimm, but I so humbly request leniency and mercy for her sake. For she is young and beguiled by the Grimms. We all are aware of the tales of them seducing young women to meet their ends."

Delphine snorts as Law rises once more from his throne. "Rabbit, does your defendant have a rebuttal."

"Oh, you bet I do!" Delphine cracks.

"I told you not to speak," the Rabbit whispers frantically. "You are going to get yourself killed. Let me handle this."

Delphine gives him a pointed look, then motions dramatically toward the Six.

"I," he starts in hesitation, "do have a rebuttal, Emperor." He bows formally.

"Then get on with it," Law growls in irritation as he takes his seat again.

"It is truly as Lord Merlin says. She is but a young, fair damsel who was powerless to resist the charm and enchantment of a Grimm. She was beside herself with grief from her true love being cruelly ripped away from her." The Rabbit pauses as the Silver Court gasps again, this time in sympathy.

It is all Delphine can do to keep from rolling her eyes to the ceiling. She bites against her cheek to hold her tongue. This trial is a farce, but she commends Merlin and the Rabbit for finding the only possible narrative that may stay her execution. Grimms are as much a fairytale to the court as the other world is.

The Rabbit spends the next hour droning on about how all the troubles of Nodd stem from a Grimm. From the moment that monster, Aesop, stole the heir, no one was safe from a Grimm's whim. If you were to believe the Rabbit, Delphine is nothing more than a young girl bewitched by wicked Grimms. He even dribbles stardust before her to have it reflect the stars in her eyes, claiming it proof of her beguiling. If she survives this, she will make sure Wilhelm pays for that.

"And that, Emperor, is why we seek to have all charges dismissed."

Fate is watching with great interest, her grin never leaving her face. Law is as stoic and unreadable as ever. Order sits stoically, but his malicious grin tugs at the corners of his mouth, as if he is enjoying Delphine's suffering. Chaos drapes over her chair, like a toddler being forced to sit still in church. The only thing keeping her awake is the occasional nudge from Order. Desire sits on the edge of her seat, scrunching her dress in her hands with anxiety, as if she does not already know the outcome of this trial. Saint, sits proper in his chair and dabs at his eyes with a white handkerchief, complete with gold filigree embroidery.

"Brother," Saint's voice quivers with emotion. "This poor girl has suffered so much at the hands of a Grimm."

Delphine's eyebrows raise to her hairline in surprise. She realizes one exceptionally important quality about the Six today. She can only hope her allies see it as well. The Six are not infallible, perfect creatures, and can be swayed.

Law stands for a third time, giving Saint a murderous look, he then turns to the court and says, "Having heard the testimony of the defendant and having seen the arguments of the prosecution, the law is clear. While my heart goes out to young Delphine, for having been so abused by the Grimms, it is not a valid mitigating factor for the actions she has taken. Your sentence will be," he pauses for dramatic flair.

"Execution at midnight."

Delphine is not surprised by the outcome. She is surprised by the chaos that ensues throughout the court.

"Off with her head!" The Red Queen cackles maniacally.

"Clemency!" Ozma screams from her box.

"Traitor!" Another voice in the crowd shouts.

"Harlot!" Yet another voice cries from the anonymity of the crowd.

Cards swarm Delphine as the court presses in to protect her as well as to keep her from escaping in the madness. The Silver Court is anything but civil in these chaotic times.

Delphine's eyes catch Merlin's and she sees nothing but sadness. She snorts, unforgiving in her anger, and continues searching the crowd for any ally other than the wizard. The silver tether around her hands is yanked, and she is forced forward through the crowd.

The Cards march her straight out of the castle and into the ruins of Nimh's garden. The charred and mangled branches are all that stand in stark contrast to the bright and sunny day around them. Nothing grows here anymore. The edge of the Forbidden Forest threatens to consume the remains of the once lush gardens.

Delphine stumbles along, debating the wisdom of conjuring a storm to escape, but she can feel it. Her magic is bound as much as she is by the silver chain, and under the watchful gaze of the Six and Merlin, it would be a futile gesture.

It takes hours to march to the stones, and it is well after dark when they stake her chain into the center of the stone circle. The loud clang of the hammer reminds her of the clock tower chimes. She looks to the stars and silently prays that Wilhelm and Jakob are swift in their endeavors. She has done all she can, the rest is up to them. Nodd's existence depends on it.

39

Off With her head

Left alone in the center of the circle, Delphine looks to the sky. She bites against the inside of her mouth hard enough to taste blood, refusing to be the bait the Six are hoping for. She will meet her end and never once cry out her wish to be saved by Wilhelm. While they know her wish is to be rescued, the magic only works if she says the words. To the rest of the Silver Court, Law's sentence is a warning to not rebel. There are those sympathetic to Delphine that feel her punishment is unjust, but fear silences their voices. No one wants to be passed into the stones of judgment alongside her. The grove is terrifying in appearance. Stone soldiers from Maab's court are frozen reminders of the betrayal of Aesop. Their deaths hundreds of years ago live on in an eternal memorial, only altered by the lush moss and ivy spiraling up their figures, Nimh's last gift to cradle them forever. The mix of horror and rage in their expressions are enough to deter any faint-of-heart souls who wander too near the stones.

The lords and ladies gather for the spectacle of execution with fascination and fear. To murder a Noddian is no small feat, and Delphine is not only Noddian, but she is also Ozian. The Silver Court is not welcome beyond the copper gates as the Ozians have not accepted their fates and the Ozian witches defy the Six at every turn.

Locasta and Glinda stand with Ozma. Glinda is blubbering and sniffling. Her friend, Delphi, is in so much trouble and all she wants to do is make everyone love the green witch as much as she does. Locasta stands stoic, her expression blank. Delphine never listened and always went into battle headstrong and willful. Had she just played along, she would not be in this predicament. Even Frank had warned them that they needed to think before they acted. She could not understand why Delphine does not just use their own magic against them and wish herself free of this situation. Staring at her friend, she mourns the loss of greatness. Delphine had foretold this very moment, and it is critical that Ozma see just what kind of rulers the Six are before she signs the treaties to give away her control of Oz.

The Red Queen cackles as she takes her place front

and center. Her shadow, the Cheshire Cat, stands behind her and to the right, his arms crossed. A mix of disdain and fear is what he sees from the Silver Court. All Aesopi have been branded with the stigma of rebels. It was all he, and the rest who were not affected by the curse of Aesop, could do to not be executed on sight. The Rabbit and he agreed that Wonderland was the safest place to infiltrate society. Most of the other Animals fled to Oz. His friend would be furious to see what these golems have done with his vision. The poor girl being made an example of has more compassion than one witch should hold. From the moment he saw her defend Animals from enslavement in Oz he knew he would fight alongside her. His part must be played and while the Rabbit had concocted this hare-brain defense, the wizard went along with it. None of them expected Law to sentence her to execution regardless of the proof. His whiskers twitch in irritation as he believes either the Rabbit, or Merlin, has betrayed them. The Rabbit is far too honest to pull off such treachery, which means the Cat will have to keep his guard up with the wizard.

The Huntsman positions himself at the far end of the circle. He has marked out the path he will need to run to avoid the Cat and the Cards. These arrogant rulers did not even think to prevent weapons from entering the grove. While he understands how powerful they are, they still must catch him. He has faced down the Wolf and lived to tell the tale. Besides, who would save all their damsels in distress in the woods? He gives his head a shake to not think about all the glorious ways young women pay for heroics. Tonight, he has one prey to hunt, and provided she does not do anything stupid he will see her to safety. He would have liked to have the three days of planning normal trials have between sentencing and execution, but beggars cannot be choosers. His wish was granted long before these rulers appeared, and he paid his price for his skills.

"Lords and ladies," Law's voice booms throughout the grove. "Delphine, The Wicked Witch of the West, has been found guilty of treason and sentenced to death. Let this be a lesson to all of you, that traitors do not win. The wicked will always fall to the just." He then turns to Delphine, taking her by the chin to force her gaze to meet his. "This vile creature held her Empress under her spell while she smuggled in criminals to the Emerald City. She tricked and tortured souls with her false prophecies. She dared to control the weather, claiming to travel to the mystical other world. What did you call it? Cansass?"

Delphine's eyes burn with helpless rage as she stares at Law in defiance. She will not buckle under his lies. "I will not be a puppet to usurpers. The Heir will return. She will free us from this oppression. Stand together and fight. Do what is right!"

Law snarls and imposes his will upon her. "Silence. You will no longer spout your vile words."

Her teeth clack as her mouth snaps shut. She narrows her eyes as she squares her shoulders, not daring to give him the satisfaction of seeing her defeated.

The first chime of the clock tower can be heard in the distance and the grove remains silent as they watch. Law steps from the circle as he and the others begin to use their magic to open the stones' power. The second chime rings and the ground quakes with power as the runes on the stones light up with an eerie blue color. The third chime brings a howling wind that is enough to force those present to cling to each other. That is when it happens, the surge of magic flooding like a beacon in the starry sky. The fourth chime rings, followed by the fifth and the six.

"The Heir," Delphine murmurs, and her eyes widen, revealing that his command only held for a moment. The amount of magic coursing through her is making her sick to her stomach. The stones are not capable of amplifying magic, they are merely the gateway to other worlds. She shifts her weight and struggles to pull the spike loose of the stone.

The Huntsman springs into action as the Six look to the heavens. The seventh chime, followed by the eighth, bring an ominous finality to the situation. The buzzing of magic grows louder and stronger around the grove. The stars burn brighter in the night sky, transforming it to a pale imitation of day and every Noddian in existence, other than the Huntsman, is transfixed on the sky. He jams his hunting knife under the head of the pin holding her chain and gives it a great stomp, forcing the iron spike to release from its hold. Without her permission, he throws Delphine over his shoulder and pushes forward in a bull rush to get to the Forbidden Forest.

Saint and Desire look to Law and he nods, forgetting all about his little game with the Ozian witch. They vanish. Another look makes Chaos and Order vanish. He offers his hand to Fate and the pair climb the steps to the stone circle, facing each other. The Noddians look on in horror as the two of them clasp hands, causing a thunderous crack and beacons of light to shoot from the stones. It is horrifying watching the elder man and his fiery-haired wife whip around in a gruesome dance of magic and malice. The ninth and tenth chimes ring ominously throughout Nodd.

"After her! Do not let her escape!" The Red Queen's voice finally rips through the grove. This sends the Cheshire Cat into action as he leaps in pursuit of the Huntsman and Delphine. Her hideous shriek is enough to stir the otherwise transfixed masses, who run and scream, fleeing in fear of what is happening to Law and Fate.

Order and Chaos re-appear in the tower of the Silver Castle.

The man bound to the chair looks up at them in fear. His eyes are wide and full of stars. "No. You cannot do this. This is madness! Ah!" As they each place a hand to his temple and then a hand to the stars above. He convulses and screams in torturous pain. The very stardust that makes up his existence floats from his fair temples, around Chaos and Order, and out like a shooting star in the direction of the grove where Fate and Law continue in their hurricane of magic.

Saint and Desire appear in the stone circle in Lloegyr. While holding each other's hand, they throw their free hands to the sky, anchoring their circle to the starlight. The magic flows from the circle of stones up through their persons and into the night sky, where the shooting stars are falling to meet them. All Lloegyr, Avalon included, quake as the very fabrics of existence are ripped apart in the powerful conduit the Six have created, forever pulling the magical group of islands into Nodd, and removing it from the other world.

The Big Bad Wolf

Delphine watches in horror as she can see the brilliant tears in the starry sky. Her body jostles and bounces on the Huntsman's shoulder as he storms toward the forest. Her gaze rips from the horrific vision to see the glint of the Cat's eyes. "Run faster," she whines. "Faster! He is gaining on us. Faster! By the stars, run faster!"

The Huntsman grunts as he trips over a root and sends Delphine tumbling into the edge of the forest. The trees appear to swallow her whole, causing her to vanish from sight. He rolls just in time to miss the Cheshire Cat leaping to tackle him and scrambles to his feet to run without looking back. A battle with the Cheshire Cat is a fool's errand. He can only hope he can outrun him in the forest.

The smirk on the Cat's face looks as sinister as ever and he does not pursue into the Forbidden Forest. The smirk grows until it is a feral smile full of sharp teeth. Slowly, his visage fades, allowing him to disappear. He continues in the direction that would make more sense to run if a person feared the forest, like most Noddians do. It will result in punishment by the Red Queen, but she would not harm him permanently. He is her favorite, after all.

Delphine whimpers and groans as she is confident one of her arms is broken. The silver chain that bound her hands has dissipated into stardust. At least she is alive to make her way back to Oz. She pushes herself carefully to her feet and cradles her injured arm to her chest before she begins to press deeper into the forest. The tales of this forest fill her mind. Every tree looks angry. Every root appears to slither on the ground. The path veers around as though it changes its mind on a whim. There is no rhyme, or reason, to this forest, other than to cause frustration and fear. The third time she passes the bit of cloth torn from her dress she drops to her knees and cries. Her body trembles in fear and she cannot even see the night sky through the canopy to find her way home.

A forlorn howl in the nearby distance makes her heart pound faster. When the Animals first retreated to Oz hundreds of years ago, they came with frightful tales of a monster so vicious, so cruel, that not even the Grimms could save them. Those who dared to enter the Forbidden Forest in search of their beloved nation became lost. With each telling, the monster grew in size. There were a rare few that claimed to know the Wolf before Aesop's betrayal. He was cunning and vicious, but with a heart of gold. He was the best Captain of the Aesopi guard. Over the years, the hunters of the Huntsman's Guild dared to venture into the dark and menacing forest. Only for their bodies to be recovered at the forest's edge, if they were ever seen again. It is believed that if he catches you, he will impose his will upon you and hold you down with fear just before he strikes. The Pigs had lamented their tale of trying to build their homes in the forest to hide. In the end, they found themselves fleeing for their lives as the beast demolished them.

With visions of monsters dancing in her head, Delphine struggles to get back to her feet. This struggle is compounded by her trying to look all around her for the source of that howl. Unsure of its source she picks a direction and flees. Running as fast as her feet will carry her to escape the Big Bad Wolf, she does not dare look back for fear he is closing in on her. Her senses are tingling with the urge to keep running. Hysteria sets in as she trips over a root and lands on her injured arm again, skidding across the mossy grove. Her only comfort is that the bright moonlight shines here. Her eyes dart around the edge of the grove to see the massive stones protruding through the vines and underbrush, but no monster. "The Aesopi Stones," she gasps.

Her elation at finding the long-lost stone circle is short-lived as the massive beast steps into the grove. With fur as black as ink, eyes burning red with rage, and shoulders easily dwarf that of the Cheshire Cat he is every bit the monster he has been described as. His arms are as massive as tree trunks with razor-sharp claws at his fingertips. He no longer sports the pristine uniform of a soldier. Instead, his pants are well torn and the only strip of clothing he sports. With a cock of his head, he focuses on Delphine.

She can feel the oppressive blanket of terror draping over her. His claws spark against the stones as he slowly circles Delphine, forcing her to cower in the center of the grove. Fear and exhaustion keep her from fighting back. He stalks toward her with murder in his eyes and she knows there is no pleading for her life. She raises her good arm above her head and balls up, preparing to be shredded to death. Darkness shrouds her, and strong hands hold her still. There is a loud snarl mere inches from her and then a snort as the beast growls at whatever is holding her in place. Another heaving inhale from the monster, and then she can feel the ground reverberate as he bounds away, as if he can no longer see her at all. Delphine dares to open her eyes and comes face to face with the Huntsman, who is holding his finger to her lips to indicate silence. Her eyes are wide with a mix of fear and surprise. What magic had this hunter used to ward off such a beast? She watches as he gently eases the cloak away from his head and cranes his neck around to inspect the grove.

Satisfied the Wolf is gone, he stands and helps her to stand as well. With an easy flourish, he twirls the cape around and clasps it at his neck. Upon inspection, the cloak is a vibrant red color, lined with a silk ribbon. He grimaces at Delphine as she cradles her arm to her and he reaches into his belt pouch to retrieve a small vial of glittering liquid. "Here, drink this," he brings it to her lips after removing the cork. His hand is strong against the small of her back as he guides her to drink the stardust potion. "There, that should do the trick." He brushes a stray ebony lock from her face. "Better?"

She nods as the warmth of the liquid fans through her system, mending the wounds from the day's affairs. Her arm aches and will take a full night's rest before it fully heals, but stardust is as powerful as pixie dust, without the side effects. "H-h-how did you do that?"

He offers her a gentle smile. "I have lots of tricks up my sleeve, little witch. We do not have long before he circles back. Neither of us should be here when that happens." He eases his glove from his hand to reveal tanned and calloused skin. With a grunt of effort, he removes a ring from his finger. He then reaches for her hand, turning it palm up. He hesitates, staring at the ring. It is one of the many gifts his beloved gave him and to give it to this girl now meant he would have no way to reach his beloved should she return.

Delphine watches as the Huntsman struggles in decision. She is unsure what a ring would do for her, but this man has saved her life twice today, the least she can do is silently wait for his decision regarding the jewelry.

"You will put this ring on and go through the stones." He nods in affirmation, as if his decision on the matter is final. He pulls her hand closer and hovers the ring over it. Holding his breath, his grip tightens on her wrist. Then he releases the ring and watches with fear in his eyes as it drops into her emerald palm.

Delphine looks from the ring to his face and fear begins to bubble back to the surface with his behavior. When he finally drops the ring, she closes her fingers around it, holding perfectly still, feeling the intricate carvings of scarab beetles shifting in her palm.

The Huntsman exhales. "Good, you are worthy."

"What is that supposed to mean? What would have happened had I not been?"

"You would have been devoured by the ring."

"Devoured?!" Delphine croaks. "Just what do you mean by devoured?"

"We do not have time for that, little witch. Now, into the stones you go." He turns her to face one of the stones.

"Are you mad? I am not going into the stones! I will be murdered!" She tries to resist his direction, but in her weakened state she is like a newborn babe to the man.

"Do not be foolish. The stones are gateways to other realms. You navigate them by thinking of who you wish to find. But you do not need to worry about that. That ring is your guide. Put it on your finger." He waits until she complies. "Now, enter the stone. Do not be afraid, nothing will harm you."

"I'm not going into--," her scream cuts off mid-sentence as the Huntsman shoves her into the stone.

A Curse Revealed

Morgan's eyes fly open. Something is wrong, terribly wrong. Panic and fear course through her in tidal waves. It is as if all her people are terrified at the same time. She cannot move, and it makes the fear grow. The initial panic filling her causes her to struggle and squirm, forgetting she lays in bed next to her husband.

Arthur groans in his sleep and he moves to pull Morgan closer to him, shifting his weight to spoon against her. His brow furrows as his efforts to snuggle to his wife are being thwarted by the squirming woman next to him.

Morgan breaks free of his grip and sits up. The room is wrong. The ground is shaking. She barely gets out of the bed in time to vomit in the chamber pot. The drapery is finer and thicker than what she remembers from before falling asleep. Turning back to the bed, it is an ornate, wood-carved monstrosity, not the bed they found themselves in hours prior. "Arthur, wake up. Something is wrong."

"Nothing is wrong, my nymph. Come back to bed." Arthur grumbles and cracks an eye open at the naked woman standing at his bed.

"No, no, no," her voice sounds frantic as she tears through the room. "Where is it? I knew I should not have taken it off."

Arthur sighs and sits up. "Woman, your things were put away. Now come back to bed. We have much to do in the morning." He glances to where he left his sword and narrows his eyes. "Where is my sword?" He comes out of the bed.

"That is what I am trying to tell you. There is something wrong. I need to go to Avalon. Something is happening."

He grabs her wrist. A dark look crosses his face. "No. You are staying with me. Your place is here now. We will travel to Avalon together to merge our kingdoms, but you will not disappear like that old wizard does."

Morgan snatches her wrist from Arthur and thunder booms loud enough overhead the entire castle shakes. "You dare dictate to me when and where I can go to my home, *husband*. I am not your slave. We are equals. My people need me. Where are our clothes?"

Arthur presses into her personal space and his hand takes her forearm this time, as if his firm grip could keep her in place. Morgan's eyes widen in fear as she believes, for a fleeting moment, this might be the impostor Arthur again. Her scream wins them guards bursting into the room.

These armored guards bear a crest that is not that of a dragon, but of a lion. "Halt! Thieves! How dare you desecrate the king's bedchamber."

"I *am* the king!" Arthur roars at the men. He immediately pulls Morgan behind him to hide her naked body from their prying eyes and stands firm, even though he is naked himself.

The men look at each other, then to the pair before them. "Right, boy. You are barely a man and you expect me to believe you are King Richard? Now. Come along quietly you love birds, and we will pretend this never happened."

"Boy? King Richard! I am your king! I am Arthur Pendragon, son of Uther Pendragon, the rightful ruler of Lloegyr!" Arthur stands firm, righteous indignation burning deep in his eyes.

The men burst into laughter. "Oh, we have ourselves a live one with a pretty little dove that he has tricked. Seize them." The men surge forward, and Arthur is ready to fight them off when Morgan smashes the washbasin on the floor. All the men pause to turn and look at her. Before they can regain their composure and act, she takes Arthur's momentum to shield her again and drags them into the puddle on the floor.

Water fills his lungs as he shouts and struggles. Her fingers cling to him and they appear on the other side on a dirt road, leading to a nearby forest. The castle in the distance looks nothing like Pendragon Keep. They are both still naked and now soaked. The skies above open and rain pours down in heavy blankets. The night sky is no longer starry and bright, but full of storm clouds. Arthur coughs, sending the water he inhaled sputtering like a fountain from his mouth. They both get to their feet and Arthur covers himself where Morgan looks at their surroundings. Everything is wrong. The magic here is angry and violent. Her people are still screaming in fear. She sways with the dizziness of so much power coursing through her. A small step to Arthur to seek comfort in his embrace and she is held at bay by his strong hands.

"What have you done to me, witch?" He roars at her, giving her a firm shake.

"Witch? What do you mean done to you?" Morgan blinks in disbelief and whimpers as his hands tighten on her forearms.

"You did this! You stole the sword back and made me nothing!"

"Arthur, have you gone mad? Something is wrong. Can you not feel that? We are no longer in Lloegyr. All our things are gone. Where are your men?"

"What have you done with them?" He shakes her again and then casts her aside to pace in front of her. "I am nothing without that sword. Nothing!"

Morgan hiccups as the rain grows heavier from her heart breaking. Elaine and Isolder were right, man cannot be trusted. With a gentle motion, she conjures their clothing from last night, though it offers little comfort. She notes that his sword is still missing, and her amulet is gone. "Arthur, come with me to Avalon. We will figure this out. Please. I would never hurt you. I love you."

He scoffs and shoves her from him. "Love me? You love me?" He turns to face her and stalks toward her, forcing her to back away in fear. It makes Arthur stop in his tracks. While rage fills him, he would never strike her, but he can see the panic and fear in her expression as she believes he will. "If you love me, then why you would take the sword from me? I need it to be king" His words are low and full of malice.

"I did not do anything with your sword. You do not need the sword. We have each other. It will be enough. Please, come with me. Help me undo whatever has been done."

"From the moment I met you there has been nothing but trouble. Your meddlesome magic has hurt my men, thwarted my attempts to reclaim my throne, and now, now you taunt me with your beguiling farce of a wedding only to strip it all away from me. Why, witch? Why would you be so cruel to me? I have done nothing but love you. Or is that a lie too? All part of your spell to steal my kingdom from me."

Morgan stares at Arthur, wide-eyed in shock. Not but twelve hours prior he had told her he loved her no matter their titles. That he would love her no matter what. The vile and hateful things he spews at her cause her to rock as if he had physically struck her. She is beside herself and unable to respond.

"I suspected as much. I wish I had never laid eyes upon you, you vile seductress. This is all your fault," he snarls. He cannot see the tears rolling down her cheeks, for the rain that is falling has soaked them both through. The words are coming out of his mouth, and he is as horrified as Morgan. That is not truly what he feels or believes, but it is too late. The words have already left his mouth, and the damage done. His beautiful, courageous, and carefree wood nymph now stands before him a girl, broken by his cruelty. He takes another step forward, trying to draw her in and apologize, to tell her his outburst is out of line.

Morgan's lower lip trembles as she watches Arthur. Every moment of their relationship playing in her mind. Was this a cruel trick of Merlin? Has he cast his spell on Arthur to drive them apart? Then the memory surfaces of that winter night. The night the impostor tried to rape her. The night she touched iron to save herself. The words sear through her mind like the pain of the iron burning her skin. *She* did do this to him. It *is* all her fault.

Arthur Pendragon your days will be numbered by your own sword. Forever will you be bound to that which you covet. All that you love will be lost.

She stares up at him, her mouth agape to explain and to apologize. She cannot think straight and feels the bile rising in her throat at the idea that all this is her curse and that he no longer loves her.

I cannot stay here. He will destroy us both. I must fix

this. I will save them all and make everything right.

He takes a step toward her, and she does the only thing she can think to do.

She vanishes.

42

The heir Returns

Elaine and Isolder look to the sky. The stars burn as bright as the sun, then they are blanketed by storm clouds. Rain pours down on them, and the two women know they are in danger. Their stoic faces give away nothing of the fear threatening to spill from their souls.

"She will come." Isolder affirms as she looks to the east, silently calling to Morgan.

"Of course she will. That is not what I am worried about. I am worried she will bring *him* with her." Elaine snorts.

The minutes tick by and the thunder rumbles in violent anger, causing both women to startle. They look to the sky again and both frown. Then they feel it, the sudden wave of grief and rejection. It takes Isolder's breath away while Elaine snarls, "I will murder him."

Seconds later, they feel the comforting essence of the Lady. She does not appear at the circle, as they expected. The two women look at each other again and Elaine turns to rush into the temple.

The young girls who serve in the temple are fearful as they motion to the Lady's quarters.

Elaine picks up the pace and bursts into the room. She expects to find Arthur sprawled on Morgan's bed, or worse, finding the Lady in battle with unknown foes. At first, nothing appears out of place. The room is immaculately kept, with a few old tomes on a table. The bed is untouched, the shrine to the Mother is lit. Then her eyes fall upon the fountain, or at least where the fountain used to be. The wall is spun open, revealing the vault. Elaine eases closer, drawing her sword, ready for a fight. She can hear sobbing coming from within the vault.

Isolder lingers at the circle, watching the mists. She had never seen the mists shift and move as they do now. Their damp blanket had been protecting the island for eons. Everything about the earth below her is wrong. It weeps as if it has been fatally wounded. It pleads with Isolder to make it stop, to have the Lady right the wrong done to it. It feels both old and young all at once, forcing Isolder to lean against the stone wall to keep from swooning. As she blinks away the tears, she can see the veil fading. The mists over the lake dissipate like a cosmic broom is sweeping in to brush them away. "Oh no," she whimpers. Whatever is happening to them, this is not good. They will no longer be safe. She can hear the dragons roaring in their pens in confusion, followed by the shouting calls of their riders. Even the magic Isolder taps into to soothe the earth under her is off kilter. It struggles to heal and unadulterated hate flows through the ley lines.

"Morgan," Elaine calls as she proceeds slowly. Her eyes land on Morgan's back. Her friend is soaked to the bone, and she is openly crying as she rips tome after tome from the shelves, frantically flipping the pages as she mutters in dismay, followed by tossing the book away. Elaine takes pause, watching her friend grieve. The vault, once orderly in its clutter is now in complete chaos. Elaine's gaze pulls from Morgan's back to the trinkets and baubles strewn about. The tomes now piled on the floor, some open, some closed, some being bent and mangled. It all adds to the destroyed organization of this vault. She sheathes her sword and steps close enough to rest her scaled hand on Morgan's shoulder. "Morgan, what happened?" Her voice is quiet enough that she is not even sure she spoke the words aloud.

"Curse. Curse. Curse. No. Break curse. There must be something. Anything." Morgan's words are breathy and frantic. Tears are rolling down her cheeks. She ignores Elaine and continues moving through book after book. It does not matter that she retains the knowledge of every Lady of the Lake before her and knows well enough there is no answer in these old tomes. She defies the truth and will find a way to save her Arthur.

"Morgan, stop," Elaine spins Morgan to face her and holds her shoulders. "Look at me. You need to calm down. You are going to drown the island." From this vantage point, she can see the broken soul that is her best friend. She has seen Morgan rage, fear, laugh, but never broken. She instantly pulls her into a tight hug, refusing to let Morgan continue this maddening pursuit.

******

"It worked!" Chaos's far too chipper voice grates on Law's nerves.

"Of course it worked. It was my plan." Law preens like a peacock.

"Careful, husband, we still do not control said island." Fate's smooth voice taunts him.

"Then what are we waiting for?"

"What we are waiting for is our power to recover. Saint and Desire have yet to return as well." Order frowns, as he hates to admit he is feeling drained.

All of them stiffen as the Red Queen saunters into the audience chamber. "Emperor," she coos as she bows gracefully. "Good news. My Cat confirmed the little green mouse fled into the Forbidden Forest. It is not but a matter of time before she is no more. We all know what happens if you dare to enter that forest." She looks quite pleased with herself.

Fate rolls her eyes and shakes her head. "You are a fool, woman. Send your Cat in after her. I want the body."

The Red Queen's eyes narrow, and she gives a grunt in response. She is about to retort some pithy comment when Law cuts her off.

"That is going to have to wait. First, amass your soldiers. We have a task for you."

"Oh? Is it invading? I do so love to invade places! Please tell me I get to keep it for my own!" The Red Queen's eyes light up.

"Yes, it is an invasion, my dear. The small island is ours, but you may do as you wish with the rest." He dismisses her. No sooner than she is dismissed, he has Ozma summoned before him.

'We have need of your armies, young lady. You will hand over control of the Tick Tock and Winkie armies immediately."

The young girl standing at the end of their war table is precious in sight. Her golden curls neatly pinned atop her head give way to a slender doll-like face. Her gown is emerald in color and shimmers with each step. Her baby blue eyes narrow to slits as she stares at the old man commanding her army be relinquished.

Locasta, of the North, stands regally in deep purples. Her ebony skin is smooth and sleek. Her hair is short to her scalp, uncommon against the long flowing manes of the other witches. She remains stoic and tall next to the child empress.

"I do not answer to you, Emperor Law. I too, am an Empress and I decide where my armies go." Ozma says.

"You are not but an upstart, child. You *will* do as I

say," he snarls in response. He puts what little power he has left behind imposing his will upon her.

Silence falls from Fate, Chaos, and Order as they watch this interchange. All believe Law will simply get what he wants. He always does. Then the strangest thing happens.

Ozma blanches and looks at Law in confusion. The silence beats on for several moments as she looks as though she is struggling with her response. Then she crosses her arms, stomps her foot, and shouts at him. "I am EMPRESS of Oz. Not you. They. Are. Mine! Locasta, I want to go home. Now." She juts out her lip in a pout as she looks up to the witch.

"As you wish, Empress." The two vanish in a whirl of air and flower petals, leaving the four rulers of Nodd to stare in bewilderment where they once stood.

Law is the first one to recover. "That is unfortunate," he sighs. "We will have to make do with the cards." He turns to leave the room, expecting the other three to follow as if nothing had happened.

Fate falls in silently behind her husband with Order at his side, in step with Chaos. The two share a look. Both had seen that Law was not, in fact, omnipotent. Slowly, a malicious grin forms on each woman's face before they look forward again and obediently follow behind their men.

******

Elaine moves Morgan from the vault, pulling the lever to close it before guiding her friend to her bed. She has not said a word to Morgan since she embraced her, but rage fills Elaine. She has half a mind to take her dragon across all Lloegyr and burn Arthur Pendragon to a crisp wherever she finds him. Instead, she sits in silence, running her fingers down Morgan's back to soothe her. Morgan cries herself to sleep against Elaine and the dragon keeper gently tucks her further into the bed. They need Morgan as the Lady, not this blubbering mess.

"She is not to be disturbed by anyone other than Isolder and myself," she commands to the young women lingering to tend to the Lady when she exits Morgan's chambers. Her steps carry her back to the stone circle at the top of the temple where she finds Isolder. "Have you been out here in the rain this entire time?"

"I have. Look." Her slender finger points out to the lake.

Elaine's eyes narrow, and she tilts her head, looking at the mists. With a gasp, "They are almost gone."

As if Elaine's gasp pushed the last of the mists away, the rain trickles to a stop.

Across the clear waters, far as the eye can see, stands an unfamiliar shore lined with what appears to be men dressed in uniforms. Their paper-thin skin is unaccustomed to such deluges and wrinkles on their forms.

As Elaine takes them in, she sees no end to the soldiers in red and black uniforms. That is not the part that truly worries her. The part that worries her are those paper-thin men boarding the small flotilla of ships. Without the mists to protect them, the entire island is in danger. "To the dragons!" She shouts and sends her commands to the other riders. She pulls Isolder from the edge, "You wake Morgan. If ever there was a time we needed the Lady, it is now. I will hold them off as long as possible." The women part, one transporting down to the dragon pens, the other running into the temple.

"Morgan! Morgan, we need you!" Isolder bursts into the Lady's chambers and looks around frantically for her friend.

It causes Morgan to jolt awake, gasping. Panic setting in again as she assesses where she is. "What? Isolder?"

"Come quick! We need you. The mists. They stole the mists."

"What? Calm down. What are you talking about? The mists are—." She is cut off by the screech of dragons in the distance, followed by the whoosh of them spitting fire and ice. This is followed by eerie screams as the ejections connect with their targets.

Morgan follows Isolder, trying to gain control of her faculties and push down her emotional nightmare that is the curse she laid on Arthur. Bare feet slap against the stone until the two women are standing at the edge of the circle, looking out over the lake. Before them is mass chaos. Dragons fill the sky like death clouds of flames and ice. Boats are filled with impaled and burning men. On the shoreline a raven-haired woman dressed in vibrant red is barking commands. There are no mists to be seen. Morgan does nothing at first, as Elaine appears to have this easily under control. She will wait her return to replace the mists.

"Look there. Who is that?" Isolder points.

Morgan follows her direction and casually strolling to the shoreline is a man who haunts her nightmares, the impostor Arthur. She gasps and recoils, swallowing hard to force herself to not run and hide. Everything feels as though it is moving in slow motion as she watches him stretch his hands to the sky. The scent of ozone fills her nostrils as her hair lifts from her shoulders. Try as she might, fear paralyzes her from dissipating the storm and from screaming in warning. Bolts of lightning rip through the clouds in a blinding display of destruction. She and Isolder are forced to shield their gazes as the terrified screeches of the dragons fill their ears. In one fell swoop, two-thirds of the dragons are gone.

The clap of thunder that explodes over them is enough to send everyone tumbling to the ground and capsizes those boats it did not push back toward the shore they came from.

Morgan's ears fill with a high-pitched ring, drowning out Elaine's screams for retreat. She looks down at Isolder who is cowering against the wall, then turns her gaze back to the shore where now stand three other figures with her tormentor. The raven-haired general is struggling to get her men off the ground. What had looked like such an easy battle to win, now looks like total defeat. Her sisters and daughters scream in fear, begging for the Mother to save them. There is only one way to save them, and she is not sure she has enough power to do so. She turns her back to the massacre as she steps into the stone circle, finding its center. Her gaze lifts to the heavens and her arms raise to the sky. Tears roll down her cheeks as she believes these will be her last moments alive, but she will have saved them all. The words flow from her in a language she barely comprehends, calling upon the water to protect them. The wind howls, and the temperature plummets at a dangerous rate. The waters ripple all around the island at first, but Morgan's heart is in Lloegyr and she would never abandon him to the fate she just witnessed, no matter how much he hates her. She draws in a deep breath and taps into the malicious magic she has had since birth. The violence and malevolence of the earth below her leaps to her beck and call. The wall of mists that have formed between the rulers of Nodd and Avalon begin to billow like a stampede of wild unicorns washing across the waters without care of who they consume. In their wake, dense fog takes hold as an impenetrable wall.

Morgan drops to her knees, the clouds above fading away to the brilliant full moon. She gasps for air, clutching at her chest and unable to draw breath. This is it. She will die alone in the moonlight. It casts its silvery light over her like a comforting blanket. The soft click of hooves draws Morgan's gaze up from the stone to bring her face to face with the gentle eyes of the White Doe. "Mother," she gasps.

The Doe leans her head down and places a gentle kiss on Morgan's forehead. "Rest my darling daughter. You have done enough."

Air fills her lungs and her heartbeat steadies as she slumps down, giving herself over to unconsciousness.

"Morgan!" Isolder screams and runs to her friend. "Elaine, I need you," she calls to the wind.

Elaine appears seconds after, bleeding and wounded from the battle. Tears stain her scaled cheeks from the monumental loss of so many dragons and sisters.

The two women gather Morgan up and take her to her chambers.

"Why is she not waking? Do something Isolder, you are the healer." Elaine growls at her.

"Nothing I do works. Her body is fine, but she will not wake."

Elaine lets out another growl as she throws the chair near her.

Isolder takes care to make sure Morgan is comfortable and checks her over again to insure she is not about to perish. She gazes down at her friend, whose cheeks are still stained red from crying. Her broken heart sings its sorrowful symphony even while she slumbers.

"Arthur," she breathes out.

"I will murder him! He will pay for what he has done!" Elaine snarls.

"No! You cannot murder him. We need him. She needs him! He is her heart."

"He is a man. No man sets foot in Avalon!" Elaine

turns a dark glare onto Isolder.

"Elaine. You saw as much as I what waits on the far shore. Do you genuinely think we are the Avalon of old still? She *needs* him. I do not know how, or why, but I can feel it, just as you can. Her soul cries for him."

Elaine's lip curls, and she huffs in frustration. "Okay, fine. I will get him. It cannot be that hard to find one blow hard in all Lloegyr."

"You cannot hurt him, Elaine."

"What? You said alive, not whole. A few broken limbs might fix what is wrong with him."

"Elaine." Isolder's tone is sharp and reproachful.

Elaine pouts and huffs again. "Fine. I will bring him back, whole, and unharmed." She turns on heel and storms from the room.

Isolder sits on the edge of the bed and gently brushes the ebony curls from Morgan's face. "Fear not, Morgan. We will find him."

Biography

J. R. Froemling was born in Indiana, the second eldest of three. She met her first husband in an online writing community. She met her second husband at a board game convention in 2015. She has a Bachelor of Science in Information Technology from Western Governors University of Indiana. She got her start in an online writing community for Star Wars fan fiction. Over the past twenty years she has transformed that love of fan fiction into works of her own.

Want to find out more about J. R. Froemling?

https://jrfwriting.com

Other Books By J. R. Froemling

The Wolfe Legacy
Mistress Giselle - Book One of Hope-Marie
The Naughty List - Book One of Elijah Joseph

Savannah Nights
The Triple Six

Immortal Love Saga
My Viking Alpha